THOSE
Savage
STARS

A STAR KISSED NOVEL

THOSE
Savage
STARS

A STAR KISSED NOVEL

USA TODAY BESTSELLING AUTHOR
CAMEO RENAE

AUTHOR'S NOTE:

Those Savage Stars is a New Adult Dark Fantasy Romance, which includes some sexual content and language that the author has deemed inappropriate for those under the age of 18. This book also contains subject matter that might be difficult for some readers, including physical and emotional violence, mentions of depression, suicidal thoughts, and murder.

For those who have been in dark places and survived.

ONE

ELARA

I killed him.

Flashes of Cole Valente's lifeless body and vacant eyes chase me as I run barefoot through the darkened streets in nothing but my underwear and his oversized shirt. The stain of his death still clinging to my skin like an invisible tattoo, branding me forever.

Murderer.

My body is trembling, my mind a torrent of questions—too dark and terrifying to even address right now. Questions I'm not sure I even want the answers to.

I don't know how it happened. I'm still unsure if it *was* me. But I felt it. Felt the life drain from Cole's body as I lay in his arms with his mouth ravaging mine.

It wasn't like we hadn't touched before. Tonight, was the fourth time I had been with Cole, but I sensed something was off the moment he touched me. My skin became too hot, the room too suffocating, and Cole's body on mine felt much too heavy.

His bare skin and warm lips caused a sudden burst of searing pain to reverberate through my entire body—through my veins—as if thousands of hot needles were pricking my skin.

I gazed in both awe and terror as the veins in my arms radiated a luminous gold. Then, a shift occurred within me. An indescribable feeling. A rush of power that filled my entire body, almost making me black out, causing me to struggle to stay coherent.

The surge of power was replaced by a chilling dread that gripped my chest as I observed Cole struggle for air, his eyes wide and mouth gaping open. Not a single noise escaped from his lips, which had turned bluish-purple. I watched as his body convulsed like a fish out of water, his grip crushing my wrists until the pain jolted me from my shock.

His eyes, bloodshot and brimming with fear, met mine. "Elara. Why?"

Those whispered words were his last. One I couldn't give an answer to.

Tears poured down my cheeks as I helplessly shook my head. *It's not me,* I wanted to tell him. But I couldn't because I wasn't certain, and if it was... I didn't know how to make it stop.

His hold on my wrists intensified.

"I'm sorry," I sobbed, witnessing him dying right before my eyes.

Then, his entire body went rigid—as stiff as an iron rod—his eyes rolled back into his head until there was nothing left but the whites.

No, no, no.

It happened so fast—too fast. Cole drew his final breath and the hands clutching my wrists slipped away, the marks of his fingers bruising my skin.

I pushed his body off me, but it was too late. Terror gripped me, holding my body in place, showing me what I had done.

I killed him.

My body jolted when I heard a door slam downstairs. Grabbing Cole's shirt off the floor, I flung it over my head before punching out his bedroom window screen and climbing down the side of the house. It's a goddamn miracle I made it down two stories without injury, given the state of my trembling limbs. As soon as my bare feet touched the frigid ground, I ran like hell, moving farther and farther from the scene, tears falling in torrents down my face, blurring my vision.

What the hell happened?

Shadows swirl in the dark corners of the alleyways, beckoning me to run into them. Phantom whispers caressing my ears—whispers carried by the icy fall winds that embrace me, slipping through my long raven hair and wrapping around me in a gentle caress.

"Elara," a familiar voice whispers in my head. *"Elara, they're coming for you."*

I know. I know they will come. My clothes are still on the floor in Cole's bedroom.

If I'm caught, how will I explain what happened when I still don't have a goddam clue?

Somewhere in the recesses of my mind, I know what happened, and that realization scares the hell out of me. Even now, I can feel Cole's life force buzzing inside of me—the essence my body *stole* from his is still coursing through my veins.

What is happening to me?

I duck into a dark alleyway as sirens blare ahead, no doubt speeding toward Cole's house. Whoever came home must have found his body.

My heart is pounding like a violent war drum as I press my body against the icy cement blocks behind me. The overwhelming odors of urine and tobacco linger in the alley, making me want to hurl everything in my gut.

Above me, a full moon is hanging high in the obsidian sky. I can still hear music a few blocks away and know it's the community festival still celebrating Samhain at the park in the center of town. This town loves to party, and festivities carry throughout the night until early the next morning, or until enough participants get piss drunk and the cops force everyone to go home.

I should have been at the festival with Cole, but he insisted on making a stop at his house, saying he had an early birthday present for me. The next thing I know, we're making out, and suddenly... he's dead, and I'm on the run.

I've run from the cops before. For the past year, I've been avoiding them. I'd only committed minor offenses, though. Offenses that are required to stay alive, like procuring food and warm places to sleep.

But this is different. *This* is murder. If they catch me this time, I'll be locked up forever.

I glance at my watch and find it's a few minutes after midnight. It is now November 1st, and I am officially nineteen.

Happy fucking birthday, Elara.

There is no way I can show my face in this town again. A bunch of Cole's friends saw us together tonight on the streets and at the bar. They all know who I am—the vagabond Cole Valente, son of the mayor, recently took an interest in. He was more-or-less a good guy with ulterior motives. He wanted sex, period. I had never been in an actual relationship before, and I wasn't in love with him, but being with Cole allowed me a hot meal, a warm bed and strong arms to sleep in one night a week.

Not anymore.

Now my face will be plastered around town for his murder.

My mind is desperately trying to wrap the hell around what happened. They will search for me. I know Cole's father, Mayor Valente, will demand the police to tear this town apart until they find me and throw me into the deepest, darkest cell for the rest of my shitty existence.

The thought of it sends a rush of adrenaline through my trembling limbs, and when the street is clear, I take off running, hissing as the cold ground bites my bare feet, driving me harder, faster toward the edge of town.

Shadows stir around me as I snake through back alleyways until I finally make it and sprint straight into the forest. The Dark Forest is what they call this haunted woodland. It's known for being inhabited by the dead because of the small cemetery that sits in front of it.

Almost everyone in the town seems to believe the ghost stories and stay away. However, there is always one dumbass who accepts a dare to stay the night, and because of this, I have taken it upon myself to give them a night they will never forget.

I set traps throughout the forest and sneak around stealthily in dark clothing while wearing a *Scream* mask and carrying an ax I found while thrifting. I've gotten the scare tactics down to a T and must say that my voice of death is masterfully horrifying. Especially to those who are already scared shitless.

The shrieks and blood-curdling screams as the dared see their lives flash before their eyes and nearly shit themselves as they sprint out of the woods, brings me the greatest pleasure, and it makes my job of upholding the Dark Forest's reputation, worth it.

The Dark Forest is *my* sanctuary. It has been my home for the past year, and hell if I'll let anyone invade my haven. They might think it's haunted and creepy, but it is the only place I find comfort and solitude.

My exposed limbs are cold and numb as I reach the woods, and my breath is heavy as puffs of white expel from my lips. I zigzag through the thick maze of trees and head for the enormous, hollowed-out redwood near the center of the forest. Pushing forward, I make it to the hidden entrance of my tree home and duck inside. My knees buckle and I collapse on the ground, on a shaggy rug I thrifted.

Seizing my bag—a single duffle containing everything I own—I quickly sift through it. The frigid chill has already settled deep in my bones, so I yank out shirts and sweatpants, anything warm, and throw them all on in layers before curling into a ball and pulling my blanket over the top.

My body is shivering and teeth clattering so hard against themselves I think they might break. Closing my eyes, I try to relax and settle my nerves. If I don't get warm soon, I might die of hypothermia. At least it feels that way.

With my eyes shut and my body curled into a fetal position, I feel the darkness press against me.

Most people are afraid of the dark and what it symbolizes—the unknown, death, and a place where evil dwells.

Me? I crave the darkness. It comforts me and always seems to soothe my anxiety. When I sit alone in its silence, I feel grounded, more connected to the energy of the surrounding forest. The Dark Forest is a place that allows me to detach from the world. It's a place of protection, and even now, as I close my eyes and curl in tighter on myself, I feel the shadows gather around me. I feel warmth enveloping me, and I welcome it.

Letting out a sigh, my shivers slowly recede, and I relax my tense muscles. My mind whirls, cursing the universe for my sick and twisted existence. A life it cursed me with from the very beginning.

Growing up, I was a child of the system. I don't know who my birth parents are. They said I was found as an infant, left on the steps of a church with nothing but a small piece of paper tucked under my blanket with the name Elara and my birthdate—November 1st—scrawled onto it. Whoever left me didn't even bother adding a last name, and after years of pondering, I figured it was because they didn't want to be found.

From the time I could recall anything about my life, it was a living hell. As a foster child, they housed me with people who were abusive, mentally and physically. Well, the wife was. She was a heavyset woman, who had wiry hairs sticking out from her double chin. She also had tattooed eyebrows, and her hair was the color of reddish box-dye. The woman never smiled. She was a pessimist and a narcissist. There was never a kind word that exited her thin lips. Lips that wore a constant scowl.

Her husband was a tall, wiry *'yes dear'* man with thinning chestnut hair who wore thick-rimmed glasses.

One night, when I was ten, he snuck into my room. I don't know what his intentions were, but when I opened my eyes, his tall frame loomed over me. I screamed bloody-murder and his wife rushed in with a bottle of wine, threatening to bash his head in with it. She warned him that if he ever stepped foot in my room again, or touched me, she would kill him.

From that moment on, he stayed far away from me and rarely laid an eye in my direction. She never left him home alone from that moment, and I was grateful for that.

However, they made it painfully obvious they didn't want me. All they wanted was a monthly paycheck, so the lazy bitch didn't have to work.

My room was my world. They never invited me to eat with them. They brought my food into my room on a tray, like a goddamn prisoner. I could attend no sleepovers, and I could never, ever invite anyone over to *their* home.

My foster parents wanted someone invisible, who obeyed and never spoke back. Yet, every Sunday, they would don their finest garb and head to church. I don't know why they went, because every Sunday they left Jesus at the church and brought home the devil instead.

When I was seven, I spoke back. I don't even remember what it was for, but the wife beat me with a wooden stick until my backside bled and denied me food for two days. From that day on, I kept my thoughts to myself, even when I knew I was right.

I never shed a tear, not around them or anyone else. I saved it for when I was alone. And for my entire life, that is how I felt. Alone.

The trees in the Dark Forest are my only friends. They don't speak or judge me, and I crave the peacefulness—the wind rustling through the leaves, the birds chirping, and the occasional critter scurrying around.

However, the nights fall deathly silent—the deafening silence that makes your ears ring. The silence that scares people into believing the ghost stories are true.

As the minutes drag on, my limbs warm, my eyes grow heavy, and the deep silence of the forest lulls me to the verge of sleep.

Cursed. Monster.

My mind is traitorous against me, and I cannot blame it. After what I experienced tonight, after watching Cole die while the veins in my arms illuminated, I swear I'll touch no one again.

My body is still trembling.

What if he's still alive? He couldn't be. I know what I felt. Death was visible in those wide, glassy eyes.

I *am* a monster, cursed to spend the rest of my existence alone. Never again. Never will I allow my heart to open. I will deny myself love. Never wish for it. Starve it until I no longer crave it.

Tomorrow, I'll plan to leave this godforsaken town. I'll disappear and start a new life somewhere else. Somewhere far away where no one knows me.

I never needed anyone, anyway. I know what it's like to fight and survive. I've been doing it for my entire life. Only now, I have a reason to stay away from everyone.

I am poison. I am death. I am untouchable.

TWO

ELARA

Elara, wake up!

The familiar, shadowy voice in my head wakes me from a deep sleep. The voice has been with me since I can remember. It's female and oddly comforting and I have considered it to be my alter ego... the one who actually gives a shit about my life.

They are coming.

It is a warning—a threat that sets off all kinds of bells in my head and gets my adrenaline pumping. The cops must be nearby.

I shoot up and it's challenging with the multiple layers of clothing. I feel like the Stay Puft Marshmallow Man. *Freaking hell.*

My eyes shift to the opening of my home tree. It's pitch-black outside, and I wonder what time it is. With limited mobility, I tug off layers of clothing until I am down to Cole's shirt and a pair of black yoga pants.

I can't wear his shirt, it's incriminating evidence, so I tear it off and throw on a black one with *Aerosmith* scripted on the front, then slip on a pair of thrifted red converse.

11

Crawling forward on hands and knees, I peek outside. There is no sign of anyone around, no crunching of leaves or cracking of branches that would normally alert me to someone's presence. There is only that eerie silence that hangs heavily in the forest.

I slowly sink back onto my heels and let out a shaky breath, trying to steady my frenzied heart from punching out of my chest and running away.

What was the warning for? Why did you wake me from a deep sleep? I huff to the voice in my head.

There is no reply. Figures. It knows not to argue with me.

I thought hearing the voice was normal until I told my foster mom about it. She told me I was mentally unstable and that if I told anyone else, they would throw me into an institution and lock me away forever.

That scared the hell out of me, so I never spoke about it again. To anyone. But the voice is always there, like a friend who gives me warnings or reassurances. I sometimes wonder if anyone else has the same voice in their head. Or maybe... I *am* crazy.

Just before I turn away from the opening, I spot something. My eyes strain to focus on a shimmering iridescent ripple in the air a few yards in front of the tree. I can't help but stare and move a little closer because it looks so pretty—like a pool of water that had a stone dropped into its center. I glue my eyes to this anomaly when I hear a loud *snap* in the air, and suddenly, three large bodies cloaked in black are standing right in front of me.

Gasping, I shove myself back, but the largest figure—the one closest to me—dives forward and grabs my left ankle.

With a loud scream, I heel him in the face with my right foot and hear a snap.

"Fuck!" He growls, releasing me and clasping his nose.

Fear and adrenaline surge through me. With a scream, I catapult out of the space and race through the dark woods, away from them.

Ahead of me, sirens blare, and police lights are flashing.

Shit. Shit. Shit. The cops found me.

I have two choices. Cops or kidnappers, and I don't know which one is worse.

The crunching of leaves behind me kicks my heart into gear, and I sprint away from the kidnappers.

I think I might have a chance when I hear a whirring sound that is followed by pressure around my legs. I stop moving and fall forward onto the ground, the air punching out of my lungs. Thank the gods it is fall because the leaves cushion me.

Glancing at my legs, I see a rope twisted around my ankles and calves just as the three dark figures arrive behind me.

The man I kicked in the nose reaches down for me, but I continue to fight, throwing everything I have into escaping until he clamps something cold over my wrists. Still, I fight, trying to headbutt him, flinging my body away, but he picks me up like I weigh nothing and throws me over his shoulder.

"Let go of me!" I scream.

I see the other man flick a finger at my face, and my voice disappears. *It's gone!*

"Damn, she's tiny but fierce," the one who silenced me chuckles. "She's got more fight than all the rest of them put together."

"No shit," the man holding me growls, still struggling to keep me still. "She's a spitfire, and it looks like we came just in time." His head motions to at least a dozen flashlights now scouring the forest behind them. "Maybe she'll be an asset if the trainers can tame her."

The other two grunt in agreement.

Tame me?

I throw my knees into my captor's gut, making him curse and growl. His arms tighten, pinning my legs against his chest so I can't move.

"Let's go," he barks, and the others obey.

Despite my efforts to get free, the one holding me is too strong. Not only is he about a foot taller than me, but his arms are like steel bands and his body is rock solid.

I can't breathe. My chest is tightening, head spinning, body trembling, while tears of anger and fear stream down my face. I am being kidnapped, and there is nothing I can do or say because they have bound me from moving and killed my voice. I can't call out to the police even if I wanted to.

Another snap in the air reveals five men in crimson robes who surround us. One of them steps forward, his hand grasping a sharp dagger. "Hand her over and you can leave with your lives," he orders.

The man holding me tightens his grip and lowers his voice so only I can hear. "If you value your life, do not fight me. We are here to protect you."

He is truthful. The voice in my head says.

"She is ours. You cannot have her," the man restraining me speaks again with a power I can feel resonating through my bones.

The crimson hooded man nods slowly. "Then you will all die."

The five men in crimson charge forward with swords raised above their heads. I am dropped to the ground with the three men in black surrounding me. One of the men beside me raises his hands and I watch tree roots shoot up from the ground, slamming straight through the chest of one of the crimson cloaked men.

I'm frozen in place, watching the other move his hand, and another root shoots directly through another crimson cloaked man's mouth, punching out the back of his skull, blood and brain matter splattering everywhere.

The man, whose nose I broke, raises his arms in front of him. Black mist coils around his waist and wrists, and then... he throws out his arms. The mist shoots out from him like ropes, wrapping around the necks of two men in crimson. With a flick of his wrists, he thrusts both men against separate trees. The sound of snapping bones fills the air, and both bodies fall to the ground, unmoving.

15

I'm in awe, mouth gaping open, witnessing something that should not be happening. Something I've only read about in my fantasy books.

While the men in black are occupied, the leader of the crimson robes charges at me and grabs my ankle. I scream, but there is no sound as he drags me away toward a dark hole that has magically appeared in the air.

He is the enemy. Fight, Elara, the voice in my head demands.

Dread spreads through my gut as I roll my body sideways, and keep rolling, making him lose his grip on my ankle. He curses and turns, reaching for me again, but as soon as he bends down, I thrust my upper body forward and wrap my bound wrists around his neck. Using my legs, I throw him over me, then quickly twist the restraints around his throat, pushing my feet against his shoulders while yanking back.

His fingers frantically try to release the chain I have tightly secured. He gasps for air, but my adrenaline is holding him in place. If I keep holding, I know he will die.

I hear yelling around me, but it's muffled.

I can't let go.

The police are yelling now, with flashlights aimed directly at us. But I keep pulling back on the restraints until I hear the man gurgling. Adrenaline is giving me the needed strength to hold on.

The man I kicked in the nose seems to gather the shadows of the forest around him and the entire area suddenly falls quiet. Darkness surrounds us until I can no longer see anything, but feel a gentle hand on my shoulder.

"Let go," the one who wields the shadows speaks. "We don't want his blood on your hands."

I'm not a murderer. I want to believe that, so I relax and feel him untangle my restraints. He pulls me to my feet, and his hands rest on my shoulders. "I am going to take you home. Will you come willingly?"

Home? Where is home? It's not here anymore. I would rather be anywhere but here. Besides, the voice told me he was truthful, and it has never let me down.

I can't see a thing with the darkness surrounding us, and still cannot speak, so I nod. As soon as I do, I feel the restraints on my legs fall away.

There is a buzzing in the air, and then I see an iridescent ripple in the darkness, directly in front of me.

"Let's go," the man says softly, his hand gripping my elbow, leading me forward. As soon as we step into the ripple, we fold into more darkness. I feel weightless, as if I am free falling through space. His grip tightens, keeping me on my feet. And then... we stop.

We are no longer in the forest, but in a dimly lit room. All three men are standing around me when my stomach lurches. My weak knees buckle, and I drop to the ground, spilling everything in my guts onto the white-tiled floor.

"We've got another gusher," one man bellows.

Two women hurry into the room with a mop and bucket and quickly clean up the mess, like they have done it countless times before. The man who wielded shadows helps me to my feet and walks me over to a nearby bench. He pulls the large hood down, revealing his face, and I freeze, taking in the most handsome face I have ever seen. Jet black hair, onyx eyes with golden flecks, long lashes, sharp jawline, dark unruly hair, and an almost perfect, bloody nose—compliments of me. He doesn't look much older than I am, maybe mid-twenties.

He stares at me for a moment, then the corners of his lips curl upward as he steps back. "Sorry for scaring you. I am only obeying orders. And for the record, no one here is going to hurt you."

Behind him, the man flicks a finger in my direction. I feel a tingling in my throat, and suddenly my voice is back. I cough, a little dramatically.

"Where am I?"

"Home," he says.

THREE

ELARA

My head is throbbing, but I need answers. "Where is home?" I ask the man.

He pauses, then gives me a curt nod. "How about you get some rest, and tomorrow we'll show you exactly where you are and take you to someone who will answer all the questions you have."

"Who were those men in red who tried to take me?" I ask.

He lets out a loud exhale and rakes his fingers through his thick, dark hair. "I'm sorry. I am not at liberty to speak about that right now, not before I speak to those above me. After a good night's sleep, you will know everything."

"How am I supposed to sleep after being kidnapped and almost killed?"

The handsome man smirks. "We didn't kidnap you."

I sigh and tilt my head to the side. "So, dragging me out of my bed in the middle of the night and bringing me here isn't kidnapping?"

He grins and tips his head forward. "I asked you if you would come willingly and you nodded in agreement. From that point, it was not kidnapping."

I narrow my eyes on him. "You could see me?"

"Yes."

"How? I couldn't see anything."

"It's part of my gift."

I am stunned and impressed, but keep my emotions stable. "Then tell me—"

He holds up a hand. "I'm sorry. I cannot tell you anything. Not because I don't want to, but because it would go against the rules."

I glare at the asshole's beautiful face. He looks sincere, but that does not change the fact they stripped me from my home in the dead of night. I want answers. I want to know where the hell I am and why. "Is there anything you *can* tell me?"

"I *can* tell you that you are here right now for your own safety and that you aren't a prisoner. We need to make sure no one, like those dangerous men who tried to take you tonight, will return. Tomorrow, you will talk to someone who can help answer all your questions." He pulls something from his pocket. It looks like an old timepiece. "I can also tell you that right now it's nearly three in the morning, and I need to leave and get some sleep."

I shoot daggers at him with my eyes and exhale. He chuckles and tucks the timepiece back into his pocket.

The other two men step forward and remove their hoods, and I gasp. Literally gasp. They look alike. Maybe twins, but brothers for sure. They both have sharp features with light-brown hair. But one has forest green eyes, and the other jade. What is going on? *Who are these people and why do they look like they should sell cologne in the pages of magazines?*

They both chuckle at my wide-eyed expression, and I immediately fix a scowl on my face.

"If you don't break my nose," the one with forest green eyes says, "I'll release the binds on your hands." He holds his hands up in surrender, and I shoot him my best evil eye. He looks at his brother and grins. Grins! Like my worst glare is humorous to him.

There is nothing I can do. Not with the three of them here, especially after seeing them wield elemental magic. I exhale and extend my wrists to him.

His head twists back to the one I kicked in the nose. "Like he said, no one here is going to harm you. You are safe here."

I let out a huff. "Like that is supposed to reassure me?"

He shrugs then releases the binds on my wrists and steps back, then all three of them walk toward the exit.

"Wait!" I holler. The one with the bloody nose turns around, but the other two exit the room without so much as a glance back.

"Where am I? Why am I here?" I demand.

His eyes are heavy, and his nose is a little swollen. "Get a good sleep, spitfire," he says, touching his nose with a smirk. "Tomorrow, you will get your answers."

He moves away, but I run after him. "Wait!"

He exits, and the door slides shut in my face, locking me inside. "That wasn't a goddamn answer!" I curse, pounding on the door before pressing my back against it and sliding down to the floor.

I'm alone, taken from my home, and I don't know where I am or why I'm here.

Tears of anger and fear run down my face. My head is spinning as I look around the room, then my heart stops beating as I notice three bodies huddled across the room against the far wall, watching me intently.

Holy shit. I didn't even notice them. They are in the shadows, but they look haggard, like someone has also kidnapped them from a deep sleep and brought them here.

There is one girl who looks younger than me. Twelve or thirteen. She has tanned skin and curly brown hair. The two boys don't look older than fifteen. One has reddish hair and the other blond, and they all look equally shaken.

"Does anyone know why we're here?" I ask, hoping they might know something. Anything.

They don't speak, but the girl shakes her head.

"Do you know where we are?" I ask again.

The older boy, with red hair, clears his throat. "We know nothing. We were all taken from our beds while we were sleeping. I'm Emery, and I'm from California. Lucas is from Pennsylvania, and Lyra is from Colorado."

I nod and stand to my feet. "My name is Elara. I am from a small town in Arizona."

"Do you think they're going to kill us?" Lyra asks, her voice just above a whisper, her glassy, dark eyes wide with fear.

I don't know the answer to that question. They did save me tonight, and said they were trying to protect me, but I still don't know why or who from.

I shake my head and paint on a brave face since I'm the obvious oldest. "Those men said we're safe here and that we'll get answers tomorrow, so maybe we should all try to get some sleep."

I can tell all three of them are exhausted. Their eyes are heavy, red, and swollen.

Next to them, I spot blankets and pillows stacked up, so I walk over and grab one of each, then head back to the bench to lie down. I watch as each of them takes a blanket and pillow and follows until they all end up on the floor right beside me.

I wait until they are all settled before I speak again.

"Look, we'll get through this, okay?" I say, but my heart is pounding inside of my chest, knowing how lost and afraid they look. The two younger ones have tear-stained cheeks and Emery looks like he is about to have a mental breakdown. Maybe if they focus on something else, their minds won't wander to the worst-case scenarios in the suffering silence.

"Tell me about yourselves." I prop my arm up and rest my cheek in my palm, looking down at them. "Tell me about your families."

Emery goes first, and his story makes me a little jealous. He grew up with a loving family and has two sisters. His parents were both teachers. They supported him and attended all his sporting events.

The younger two, Lucas and Lyra, didn't have siblings, but were both raised by parents who loved and cared for them.

My heart feels heavy as I listen to their stories, wondering what it would have been like to have a loving family, people who actually gave a shit about me. People who genuinely cared about my well-being.

One-by-one I watch as their eyes grow heavy, and soon, they all fall fast asleep.

I am happy for them. Happy they were given a chance at a normal life and raised with caring parents and siblings. Happy they did well in school and had friends.

For me, school was an even worse nightmare than my home life. All I ever wanted was to be invisible—the fly on the wall. I tried to make myself as small and as insignificant as I could, but in the sixth grade, I watched a girl get bullied. The mean girls had shoved her to the ground, called her names, and yanked her braids until her face was red and tears streamed down her cheeks. The girl screamed for help, but no one came to her aid. They all just stood and stared.

I may have wanted to be invisible, but something inside of me could not stand there and watch that poor girl get bullied. Stomping up behind the two girls, who were yanking on her braids, I grabbed fistfuls of their hair and yanked them away. Angling myself in front of the girl, I held my head high even though my entire body was trembling and told the bullies to fuck off.

They did, but I had now gained a huge bullseye painted on my back and forehead and made the hit list for the mean girls.

From that day on, the mean girls harassed and tormented me, not only because I stood up for the girl, but because I was a misfit. They teased me because of my wrinkled attire and bedraggled hair. My foster mom didn't give a shit about me, about my hygiene, or what I looked like. I learned basic things from reading and watching television. *Freak. Hobo. Trash. Unwanted bastard.* You name it, I was called it.

The bullying was constant, and because of it, everyone else shunned me. I sat alone for lunch and recess. They never picked me for a team, and I was always the brunt of horrible jokes when the bullies were around.

When the bullying turned physical, my foster parents were called in, which I despised even more. They would pick me up, and I would get verbally abused and then whipped by the wife and sent to my room with no food. It was always my fault, and they punished me for *shaming and inconveniencing* them in front of the teachers. Because that is all I was. For my entire life, I was a punching bag, getting the shit kicked out of me by bullies at school and being a burden to my caregivers.

In middle school, I learned how to tend to my own wounds and bruises. I frequented the nurse's office enough to know her by her first name. I liked Nurse Delores. She was the only person who seemed to care about me. She patched me up and told me I needed to learn how to fight back. The girls were jealous of how pretty I was, according to her. I never believed her though because she was the only one who ever called me pretty.

Her husband was a professional self-defense and combat trainer for the military, so she hooked me up to take classes with him for free. In high school, I joined the classes and learned everything I could. For four years, he taught me how to protect myself in unarmed combat, and how to defend myself against weapons in hand-to-hand combat. I also learned many combinations of martial arts techniques, and he said I was a natural.

For endurance, I started running, and after a few years of persistence and training, I found I could take down even the strongest men and women in the class.

The bullying progressed, and the day I turned eighteen, one girl dumped a carton of rotten milk over the top of my head during lunch in the cafeteria. It was warm and lumpy and smelled like vomit.

Anger grew inside me until I couldn't focus, and everything went blurry.

I marched up to the girl who instigated it and punched her firmly in the nose. There was a loud crack, and I watched blood flow down her lips, chin, and all over her expensive shirt.

She didn't fight back like she usually did. Her eyes were wide with a look of horror and her entire body began trembling. They all had that same horrified look, and I'll never forget it.

"Monster!" they screamed with their fingers aimed at me—at my eyes.

I rushed to the bathroom and looked in the mirror, shocked that my hazel eyes had turned completely gold—whites and all. I looked like a nightmare. Something terrifying.

I stood in the mirror and slowly watched my eyes return to their normal hazel, rimmed with gold, wondering what the hell was wrong with me. Am I a monster?

At that moment, I didn't care. It was the first time I'd stood up for myself and tasted victory, and oh... it was sweet. I didn't care that my hand was sore, or that they suspended me for three days afterward. Didn't care that my foster parents locked me in my room for the entire three days without food. That victory was well worth it.

After that day, the physical attacks at school stopped, but the harassment did not. I was now the monster that *everyone* shunned, and I had to admit, I liked it that way. Words were nothing to me. I could manage words and didn't care what anyone had to say. *Sticks and stones.*

All the abuse that was meant to break me... didn't. What it did was mold me, bend me, drive me forward even harder. It pushed me and forced me to strive to get out of this cursed town. I trained in combat extra hard and kept my grades up, until last year, I graduated at the top of my class. I celebrated that night alone in the woods, with a bottle of whisky I had heisted from my foster dad. It was glorious, except for the damn hangover I had the next morning.

After graduation, I ditched the system and left the foster home. They had no say, because I was eighteen. No one even bothered to check on me because they knew they wouldn't be able to keep track of where I was. I got a part-time job at the local library, to pay for food and necessities, but I find most of my treasures rummaging through bags dropped off after hours at the thrift stores and found a home in a hollowed-out redwood in the Dark Forest.

Now I'm here. Wherever here is.

My mind is restless, and even though I know I'll be crushed with exhaustion in the morning, I stay up. I can't help but wonder why they've taken us. Why is Emery here and not his sisters? Why Lucas and Lyra?

Glancing down, something in my chest tightens and makes me protective over these kids. Makes me want to make sure no one else comes in and steals them away. This alone is an unfamiliar feeling. I've never had to worry about anyone else besides myself.

I think back to how I arrived here. The ripple in the air must have been a portal. I mean, I'm not ignorant. I've read my fair share of fantasy and sci-fi books to know what a portal is. It must be the government or a secret branch of it, targeting us, but I cannot, for the life of me, figure out what we have in common.

FOUR

ELARA

During the night, I fall asleep, because I am suddenly awakened by the sound of the door sliding open. Jolting upright, I see two men stride in, fitted in military attire. They are dressed in black pants, long-sleeved shirts, and vests, with blades strapped to their waists and chests.

The man nearest me, with raven hair and eyes, gives me a grin. "Everybody up! You have ten minutes to get dressed and follow us," he says in a deep voice.

The other dark-haired man behind him has a stack of clothes in his hands, which he sets down on the floor in front of us. A woman, one of the two that cleaned up my vomit last night, steps in behind him with four pairs of boots and sets them next to the pile of clothes. Each set has a name attached to it.

I glare at them, even though my stomach is twisting with fear and anxiety. "Where are you taking us?"

He gives me a lopsided grin. "To someone who will answer your questions." His tone is light, not harsh like I would expect. "Time is ticking."

Emery, Lucas, and Lyra, who look equally exhausted with red-eyes and bedraggled hair, glance at me with looks of concern, so I give them a reassuring nod.

"Where do we change?" I ask, slipping out of bed and grabbing the clothing and boots with my name attached to them. *Wait.* How did they get my name? I then realize I had told the other kids' last night, so they must have overheard us.

"The doors at the back are washrooms," one says. I nod and proceed to one of them, while the others gather their clothes.

Inside, the washroom is huge, almost luxurious, and much nicer than any washroom I have ever used. It has two stalls with toilets, a large shower, and two sinks. There are towels and toiletries in baskets. What kind of holding place is this?

I immediately open the door and peek out. "Lyra, come with me. We can get ready together." Her eyes light up and she hurries toward me. I glance at the boys, who still look lost. "You two get ready in the other one." They nod and head toward the other door.

The two men glance at me curiously, but I duck back into the washroom.

They said ten minutes, but hell if I won't shower. I strip out of my clothes on the way and when I turn on the water, it is immediately hot. On a small ledge are bottles with soaps, so I quickly scrub my hair and body and then rinse off. The soaps smell wonderful, like sweet florals.

Lyra has already changed and is ready when I step out.

"I showered last night," she says in a soft voice.

I nod and smile at her, then quickly dry off, throw on my underwear, and change into the clothes which comprise of black pants, a plain black t-shirt, white socks, and then slip on the black combat-like boots and instantly feel like I'm on my way to military training.

There's a bang on the door. "Time is up. We have to go."

I quickly braid my damp hair and head out of the room with my old clothes and converse shoes wrapped in my arms. "What do I do with these?"

"Leave them. You won't need them anymore," the man with the dark hair answers.

As much as I love the red converse, I nod and place them on the ground before following them out.

The light-haired man stops and gestures to a tray set on the bench. "Grab something if you like."

There are warm rolls and cups filled with juice and coffee. I grab a roll and a coffee, and motion for Lyra to do the same, except she grabs a juice, as do the two boys.

We follow the men as they lead us out of the room and down a long, brightly lit, stark-white hallway. Before we make it to the end, I devour my roll and drain my cup of coffee. My stomach is still twisting in knots with all the unknown questions.

"Those under the age of eighteen follow me," one guard says.

Lyra turns to me with wide, tear-filled eyes. She is trembling, so I speak up. "Where are you taking them?"

"I will take them to the assessment with others in their age group and from there, we will house them accordingly."

What does that even mean?

"Will they be safe?"

"Yes." The man exhales, and his hard face and eyes soften. "I give you my word. They will be safe and well taken care of. You don't have to worry about them."

I look directly into Lyra's eyes. "Just stick with Emery and Lucas. They will take care of you."

I glance up at the boys and they nod in agreement. Lyra sniffles, then wipes away a stray tear, and I watch them leave with a slight ache in my chest.

"This way," the other man says to me.

I follow him down another hallway that leads toward a red door at the end. I can only hope that the red door doesn't mean danger.

As soon as we exit, my eyes widen, and my legs stop moving as I soak in the breathtaking scenery. It's like nothing I've ever seen before.

The man has paused and is looking back at me. "What's wrong?"

"Where are we?" My words come out in a whisper.

"Celestria," he answers.

My heart is hammering against my chest and my breath is heavy. "Oh, Toto. We aren't in Kansas anymore."

His expression twists, and eyes narrow. "What?"

"It's a quote from a movie." I shake my head. "Never mind. I'm not on Earth anymore, right?"

"No."

Of course, I'm not. There are two moons, or large planets, above us, hanging in a bright sky. But the sky is colored differently than on Earth. Hues of violet and azure with clouds that look like they've been painted with watercolor.

He walks away, and I have no recourse but to follow.

The smell of this place is heavenly. It's floral and sweet and makes me lightheaded. The air is neither hot nor cold, the breeze gentle, and there is a light buzz that tickles my skin.

Welcome home, Elara. The shadowy voice in my head finally speaks.

Home? Celestria, or whatever this place is, is not my home.

I would run, but where would I go? I don't know where I am, or if I'm still in the same galaxy as Earth. My head is spinning. I can barely catch my breath when...

I open my eyes to find I am on the ground, looking up at a handsome, familiar face with onyx eyes flecked in gold.

"Hey, spitfire," he says with a lopsided grin. "You fainted."

I groan and close my eyes, pressing my fingers against the bridge of my nose.

"Come on. Let's get you up." He securely grabs my elbows and helps me to my feet. When he lets go, I wobble, so he places a hand on my back to steady me.

"Where's the other guy?" I ask because he is nowhere around.

He shrugs. "I just happened to pass by and told him I would take you to your assessment. He eagerly left."

I sigh and stare at his handsome face, at his firm jaw and now perfect nose, trying to figure out who this man is.

"Your nose—" I point out. There is no swelling or bruising.

He gives me a sinful grin. "As good as new."

"How?"

He wiggles his fingers in front of me. "Magic."

Shaking my head, I feel a little nauseous.

"Come on, you need to get to your assessment."

As he leads the way, I figure I'd try to get a few more questions answered, so I ask, "What is Celestria?"

"Our home."

"How did I get here?"

"Through a Celestrial portal." He pauses for a moment. "There isn't enough time to explain everything to you right now, but I promise, someone will after you're done."

He wants me to shut up, but I want to know, "What's your name?"

He gives me a dimpled smile, and for a moment I am lost in the depths of his eyes. I blink when he clears his throat. Then blink again, trying to compose myself.

"I'm Remington," he says. "But my friends call me Rem."

I nod. "Well, Remington," I say, and he offers me a dubious grin. "Can you please explain why I'm here? I'm okay with a condensed version."

He stares at me for a moment, then moves forward, my arm still in his grip. "Soon. You're going to be late for your assessment."

"Assessment for what?"

I notice we are heading across a large lawn toward another building that looks like a circular villa. It is two levels and on the ground floor, the windows are floor to ceiling with marble columns precisely spaced around it. There is a small circular area just outside, with trimmed hedges and a small wading pool reflecting the water-colored sky. Around the wading pool are five statues.

I look at how detailed each statue is when Remington steps beside me.

"They represent the five kingdoms of Celestria," he says, "and the assessment today will tell us which one of these kingdoms you originate from."

When I raise my wide eyes at him, he continues. "The Dragon represents the northern realm known for night and winter. The Pegasus represents the eastern realm, known for spring. The Winged Lion represents the western realm known for fall. The Phoenix represents the southern realm known for summer, and the Leviathan is the central realm, which claims all seasons."

Five kingdoms in Celestria I know nothing about.

"Am I really from this place?"

He gives me a slight nod. "You're a Changeling, Elara, and for whatever reason, your parents decided you were better off in the mortal realm." I feel an ache inside my chest when he speaks my name. His dark eyes find mine and they are softer, kinder.

"Changeling? Isn't a Changeling supposed to be an immortal child who is exchanged with a human child without the human parents knowing?" I had read many books on the subject and even though they were fairy tales, I never understood how they could do such a thing. Either their immortal child was sick, or they never wanted a child to begin with, so instead of killing it, they would take it to the mortal realm and exchange it for a human child, who had a brief life span.

Remington nods, the crease in his brow deepening.

"They left me on the steps of a church. I wasn't exchanged at birth or given to loving parents. They handed me over to a shitty system and placed me with the literal scum of the earth."

His eyes widen. "That cannot be. They place all Changelings with parents the birth parents have researched and approved of."

I laugh, scoffing at his reply. "Yeah, well, I guess my parents *really* didn't give a shit about me."

The look he gives me makes me turn away. He looks empathetic.

"I'm sorry, Elara. We will find out why this happened to you."

I don't respond. How can I? My entire life has been a lie.

"Growing up in the mortal realm, did you ever feel you didn't fit in?"

The impact of that question slams me. I fight the tears that immediately want to fill my eyes. It hits me directly in the heart, so I quickly swipe the stray tear that trails down my cheek before I respond.

"I have never fit in. Ever. I was always an outcast, beaten and ridiculed, and had to fend for myself most of my life."

He places a gentle hand on my shoulder. "Well, you are home now. Hopefully, you can find some answers, and in a few hours, you will discover where you originate from and what magic you possess."

I gape at him. "Magic?"

He nods, and I shake my head.

"I don't have magic."

"Then what happened last night? Why were the authorities after you?"

Flashes of what happened to Cole pulse through my mind, but that was not magic. It was my body sucking the life out of his. I could never explain what happened or tell them what I did. I am a murderer, and now the reality of that fact is sinking in. If I told them, they would probably lock me away, or execute me. The thought makes my mouth dry and my pulse race.

"I survive, and sometimes, the cops get involved."

His eyes narrow on me. "All of them?"

I sigh, knowing there's no way in hell I'm going to tell him. Instead, I dodge his question by asking another.

"Why now? Why, after nineteen years, have you brought me here?"

"Come," he says, moving toward the large glass doors, but before we reach it, he pauses. "They sent my team to collect you because there is a threat to our world. A dark and dangerous threat that intends to take over Celestria. They have been kidnapping Celestrian Changelings in the mortal world and using them to fight against us." He turns to me, brow furrowing, just as I was about to jam more questions down his throat.

"Why? What's so special about... us?"

"Celestrian children left in the mortal world have no real identity and can be easily manipulated and trained. Since they come from Celestria, those taken and trained have become deadly and efficient weapons for our enemy. They are virtually undetectable."

"That's terrifying," I said. "How long has this been going on?"

"We found out they took the first Changeling about six months ago."

"How did you find out?"

He shakes his head and gives me a pointed look. "You're full of questions."

"My life at this moment is precisely that. One big question I have yet to crack." I sigh. "What happened to the Changelings who were taken?"

"One I know of became a servant, who swiftly climbed in ranks, gaining trust and an excellent reputation until he had access to the palace. He seemed trustworthy, and everyone who worked with him admired him. But one day, while he was serving the prince lunch in his private quarters, the servant snapped and attempted to kill my prince. The prince stopped him, and upon questioning, we realized the Changeling had been deeply brainwashed. What method the enemy used, we do not know." He gives me a side-eyed glance. "You're lucky we got to you first."

I was indeed lucky, but one thing he said stood out to me. "*Your prince?* Which kingdom are you from?"

There is a faint glimmer in those dark eyes. "I'm from the northern realm, the Kingdom of Terr," he says, placing a reverent hand to his chest.

"Where do you think I'm from?"

He tilts his head and gives me a sinful grin. "I have my suspicions, but there is not enough time to explain everything to you now. After your assessment, whatever kingdom they assign you to will help you."

"Fine," I exhale, relenting.

He's told me a lot already, and those answered questions have my nerves wracked. Just the fact I've learned that after nineteen years, I am not who I thought I was, is giving me acute anxiety. I feel like there is a vise grip over my chest that keeps tightening and tightening the longer I have to wait to find out more answers. I just want to get the assessment over with.

Inside the building there are four guards posted at a stairwell at the back of the circular room that spirals upward toward the second floor.

When the guards see Remington, they bow their heads and slap a fist to their chests. "Captain."

Captain?

Remington grunts at them and when I look at him, he gives me a smirk and shrugs, making his way up the stairs. He leads me up to the second floor and down the hallway to the right. Then he opens the first door on the left. My heart is hammering, but I follow.

He stops at a desk, where a beautiful woman with fair skin and blonde hair tied into a bun is sitting at a desk.

"Rem," she says, smiling up at him, batting her long lashes. She is easy to read, lust swirling in her sea-green eyes.

Remington steps toward her and bows his head. "Aurora, I've brought Elara for her assessment."

The woman glances at me, her eyes sweeping me from head to toe with a look I'm accustomed to. It's disapproval, but I'm not sure what for. I just met her. It could be several things, but I really don't care.

She nods at me, without a smile and hands Remington a piece of paper, which he signs. After he pushes it back to her, he turns to me.

"Follow me, Elara." He walks through another door, so I smile at Aurora before following him. She ignores me and fumbles with her paperwork.

It's nothing new. I've dealt with people much worse.

Remington is standing at the door, and I notice the look of distaste in his expression, his eyes glaring at Aurora. Once I pass him, he follows me and closes the door.

"I apologize for her rudeness."

I shake my head at him. "Don't apologize. It's not your fault. I'm used to it."

"Well, you shouldn't be. And for that, I am even more sorry."

His words and the sad look he is giving me are making my heart thrum and stomach twist. Good god, he is even more gorgeous than I would care to admit, and I have to turn away, because I can feel my cheeks heat.

"This way," he says, leading me toward another door, which he holds open.

Inside is a waiting room where four boys are sitting, who all look just as lost as I am. They must be here for the assessment, and I suddenly feel uncomfortable being the only girl.

"Have a seat, Elara," Remington says, pointing to a chair nearest the door. "They will call you when they're ready." He looks at the boys and then back at me. "Will you be okay?"

I nod, knowing I'm trained to handle myself against any threat. And after assessing the four boys in the room, I know I could take on any of them. I've taken bigger and stronger men down.

He gives me another lopsided grin that makes my heart beat a little faster. "I'll see you around, spitfire."

I give him a sly grin as he exits the room, leaving me in a room of strangers.

FIVE

ELARA

"What's your name?"

I look up to see all four sets of male eyes on me. They are all handsome in their own way and each one of them is at least six feet tall.

I hate the attention, but I don't want to be rude, so I answer. "Elara."

Does everyone on this planet have extraordinarily good looks? Maybe they are elves, or Fae. I don't know, and I shouldn't even be guessing. It's just another question added to the ever-growing pile.

The boys look exhausted and just as anxious as I am. The boy who asked me the question has blond hair and green eyes and looks close to my age. "I'm Thomas. Where are you from?"

"Arizona," I reply, keeping my answers as short as possible. I just want to get through this assessment and move on.

"I'm from Phoenix," Thomas says with a wide smile. "They took me from a dead sleep last night. Do *you* know what's going on?"

They all wait, eyes narrowed on me for my answer.

I shake my head. "I know just as much as you do." I might know a little more thanks to Remington, but I keep that thought to myself.

He nods with a look of disappointment on his face.

A door opens and a girl exits. She has short, sandy hair and jade green eyes. When she looks at me, she gives me a tight smile, then quickly exits the room. I notice a small paper clutched in her hand and wonder if it's her assessment and if it tells her where she is from.

In the doorway, a tall, spindly man appears with chestnut hair and freckles. He holds a clipboard, his eyes fastened to it. "Jason," he calls out. "Please follow me."

One boy gets up and walks toward him, and when he enters the door, it closes again. The room is quiet, and I force myself to remain calm even though my anxiety is nearly punching through the roof.

Thomas's green eyes meet mine. He leans over and whispers, "I don't know if it's true or not, but Jason said he overheard someone say that we are going to be assessed and taken to whatever kingdom we originated from. Whatever power we have will determine what we will do next." He looks at me expectantly. "What power do you have?"

I swallow and shake my head. "I don't have any power."

The room falls into a dead silence as they share confused glances. Glances that bring my already damaged insecurity right to the forefront.

"You didn't get your power?" Thomas asks.

Again, I shake my head. "Did you?"

Thomas holds out his hand, palm up, and above it a vine shoots out. It stops about twelve inches above his palm, then sprouts leaves and then... a bright red rose blooms right in front of my eyes. I am in awe, watching him wield his magic. "My gift came when I turned eighteen, and it scared the shit out of me. I knew it wasn't normal, so I didn't tell anyone."

The other two boys nod in agreement, also confirming they received their magic at eighteen.

Was I defective? My gut tightens at the thought of me remaining an outcast.

The boy with silver hair and grey eyes raises his hand and a ball of water appears above it. Using his fingers, he shapes it into a fish that swims in the space above his palm. I can't help but watch in wonder. It's incredible.

The third boy, with red hair and amber eyes, holds his palm up and a ball of flame dances within it. He raises his hand and the flames thread through his fingers. He looks up at me. "How old are you?"

"Nineteen," I murmur, embarrassed that I seem to be the only one who doesn't have a magical gift. Maybe I'm broken. Maybe I am worthless.

I clearly remember my eighteenth birthday. I spent it alone in the Dark Forest. When I turned eighteen, I felt nothing out of the ordinary, nor could I wield an incredible gift like growing flowers or conjuring water or fire in the palm of my hand.

The voice inside my head has been with me my entire life, so it couldn't be my gift. The only significant thing that happened was last night with Cole, when I witnessed the veins in my arms turn gold. Is that my gift? Sucking the life out of someone?

It couldn't be. That isn't a gift. It's a curse.

Thomas leans toward me and holds out his hand, offering me the rose he magically conjured. "Maybe girls get their powers later."

I give him a tightened smile, wondering if that could be true, then reach over and take the rose.

"Thank you."

He then turns his attention to the other boys. "If what Jason overheard is true, it means our distinctive gifts won't allow us to be placed in a kingdom together."

They nod in agreement but remain silent.

The door opens again, and Jason exits with a paper in his hand. "Give the paper to the woman at the desk out front," the spindly man with red hair says behind him. He nods, then walks past us with a bow of his head and heads out the door.

"Elara," the man calls.

My heart surges and knots tighten in my belly. I slowly stand and straighten my back.

"Knock 'em dead," Thomas whispers with a wide grin.

"I'd rather not," I murmur, walking toward the man.

He steps to the side as I enter, and as soon as I do, he follows and shuts the door behind us, making my heart kick up a beat.

"Please have a seat," he says, gesturing to a white, cushioned armchair seated in front of a huge wooden desk. "My name is Finnick Dunn, Director of Assessments."

I walk over and slide into the chair while he takes the seat behind the desk, looking over notes on a clipboard. Letting out a breathy exhale, he gives me a pointed look.

"Elara Bard?"

I cringe at the surname the state gave me. I hate it. "No. It's just Elara," I say with a little too much bite. "Bard is the name of my foster parents. It's not mine."

He pauses, then slowly nods, his eyes narrowing, assessing.

"All right," he says. "It will be Elara until we find your true surname."

I nod in agreement, thankful he is amiable.

"You're nineteen." He glances back at his clipboard. "Today?" His eyes widen as he glances at me.

I slowly nod.

"Well, happy birthday, Elara," he says with a smile.

"Thank you."

"I am going to do a quick assessment, so I need you to lay your hands on the desk, palms up, and just relax."

My pulse kicks up. He cannot touch my skin. So far, I have not been in direct contact with anyone's skin. Remington and his guards completely covered themselves and were wearing gloves when they took me. After what happened with Cole, I am terrified of what could happen if I touch someone else.

It's hard to breathe. My heart feels like it is going to beat out of my chest, and the air is stifling. Sweat is thick on my palms, it's dotting my brow and dripping down the sides of my face, down my back, between my breasts.

"This won't take long. I promise," he says with a nod and a reassuring smile. A smile that tells me to relax and that everything will be okay. But I know it won't. I know that if he touches me, I might kill him.

Elara. Why? Cole's voice seared itself in my mind.

Should I tell him? I need to. I cannot have the death of this man on my hands. Not while I'm in a foreign place, I know nothing about. Who knows what they would do to me?

Director Dunn gives me another gentle nod, so I place the rose Thomas gave me on the desk, then put my shaking, sweaty hands on the table and carefully slide them toward him, palms facing upward.

The director leans forward and places his hands, palms down, an inch directly above mine.

No! I gasp and quickly yank my hands back, curling them in my lap. My breath is hard and quick, my fingers trembling.

"What's wrong?" The concern in the deep furrow of his brow makes the tension in the room grow to almost suffocating.

I cannot do this.

"I—I can't. I don't want to—" I can scarcely speak.

His eyes soften, gazing at me as if he can read my thoughts. "You are safe here, Elara. I won't hurt you. I promise."

His promise means nothing if he ends up dead. I glance up at him with tears brimming in my eyes. "I'm not worried about *you* hurting *me*."

"Then what is it?" The crease between his eyes deepens.

I don't know how to answer him, and when I don't, he speaks again. "You were sent to a world without your knowledge and raised by people who did not understand you. Whatever happened there is not your fault."

Tears fall from my eyes and trail down my cheeks. My heart is aching, and I don't know what to do, or how much to say.

"You don't know what I've done."

He lets out a deep sigh that coils around me. "I know you had to do whatever you needed to survive. Nothing that happened in the mortal realm is your fault."

I shake my head, knowing that what happened to Cole was not out of survival. "You don't understand." I bury my face in my shaking hands. "I don't even understand what happened to me."

Trust him. The voice in my head says. It has been mostly quiet since we've arrived, only welcoming me home. But I don't trust just anyone. You must earn trust. I've been burned too many times by people who betrayed my trust, who left me with emotional wounds and scars that will last a lifetime.

Six

ELARA

The director inhales a deep breath, then slowly exhales. "I can imagine whatever happened to you was scary. Humans are vulnerable to your gifts because you are not from their realm. You are not mortal, Elara. They left you alone and never knew about the power flowing through you, or how to wield it." He shakes his head slowly. "Whatever happened there, no matter what it is, is not your fault."

His words tighten my chest, making tears brew in my eyes and flow down my face.

I *was* helpless. Whatever happened, I couldn't stop it. I didn't know how.

"Come, child. It will not hurt, and just know that you cannot harm me." His eyes hold sincerity, like he understands my inner turmoil.

"Just place your hands on the table and relax."

The voice told me to trust him. It's never led me astray, so I slowly lay my hands on the table again, palms up. Director Dunn places his hands an inch above mine and closes his eyes. A bright golden light emanates from his palms, and I instantly feel the heat in mine. I watch his eyes cinch shut

49

and his brows pinch tight. Beads of perspiration form on his forehead, and after a few minutes, he opens his eyes and stares at me with a bewildered look.

The look tells me something bad happened and sets off all kinds of internal alarms.

"What's wrong?"

He leans back in his chair and runs his fingers through his bright red hair. "Something has blocked your Celestrial channel, and I cannot seem to pinpoint it. Whoever did it used potent magic and was thorough."

I shake my head. "I don't understand."

He leans forward on his elbows, tenting his fingers. "Someone has bound your magic, Elara. Someone powerful."

Bound my magic? "Who?"

"I don't know." His eyes go distant, like he's looking straight through me. "There are only a few Celestrians who know the spell, a spell which is forbidden here. There is a similar spell cast only on prisoners who have committed unforgivable crimes."

Gods. More unanswered questions claw at the back of my mind. I attempt but cannot suppress the quivering in my bones or dampen the growing anxiety attempting to suffocate me.

Maybe he can answer one question. "Do you know which kingdom I'm from?"

He leans back, and his eyes soften. "I can safely say you are from the Kingdom of Terr, but there are... *inconsistencies* with this assessment."

"Inconsistencies?"

He nods. "You are the first Changeling I have run into that has truly confounded me. Could you give me a moment? I think I need to contact my superior."

"Sure," I say, dropping my head to avoid his gaze, to avoid him reading my emotions. Nothing has ever come easy for me. Nothing. So, I'm not surprised to hear his words, although they don't make me feel any less devastated.

I am here, in a foreign land and at their mercy. They have magic, and I have nothing except a sense of dread for what is coming.

Director Dunn excuses himself and exits the room. I sink back into my chair. My head is spinning, my stomach is one huge bundle of nerves.

He said I am from the Kingdom of Terr, the same kingdom as Remington. That thought releases a bit of tension. Would I ever see him again?

Time moves too slowly, and just when I think I'm forgotten, the door swings open and Director Dunn strides in. A tall, pale elderly gentleman wearing a black robe, who has grayish eyes and dark gray hair, follows after him. Behind the man, Remington steps into the room. When his eyes catch mine, he gives me a bemused grin, and I cannot help but wonder what the hell is going on.

"This is Elara, sir," Director Dunn says, informing the elderly gentleman.

The man steps forward and tips his head toward me. "Hello, Elara," he says with a warm smile. "My name is Cyrus." He then steps forward and holds out his hands to me.

The voice in my head has gone silent, and I internally curse at it for not being of any help.

I hesitate and glance at Remington. He offers me a slight nod, his eyes sliding to Cyrus's hands. My eyes then move to Director Dunn, who also gives me a reassuring nod. "You cannot harm him, Elara," he says.

I hope he's right. The last thing I need is for this old guy to keel over because of me.

With my heart thundering in my chest, I gently place my hands in his.

Cyrus grips his fingers around my hands, pressing his palms flat against mine. I flinch, then immediately feel heat. This time, the heat travels entirely through me, and a heavy pressure builds in my chest and in my head. My body, from scalp to toes, is tingling. I cannot explain it, but I can feel his power coursing through me.

My heart lurches, wondering if he will know what happened to Cole last night. It's too late to do anything about it. I'm helpless at this point.

After several long minutes pass, Cyrus gasps and releases my hands. He stumbles backwards, but Remington catches his arms and steadies him on his feet.

Director Dunn pins his attention to his superior with an expression I cannot read. Cyrus blinks a few times and runs his hands down his robe before straightening his back and taking in a few deep breaths.

"You're right, Dunn," he finally exhales. "They bound her gift with powerful magic. More powerful than I have encountered before. I tried but couldn't break the spell. However, I feel her magic seeping through the barrier, which tells me her gift is powerful."

Remington's dark eyes shoot to me, but he addresses Cyrus. "If you can't break the spell, who can?"

"At the moment, I can't think of anyone," Director Dunn adds. They all share a look of concern.

Remington runs a hand through his thick, dark hair and mumbles, "Why would anyone block the channel of an infant Changeling?"

"I don't know," Cyrus replies. "But to do so means her birth carries a secret. My only assumption is that whoever cast the spell did it to protect her identity. We will have to dig further. We must find out if there were any missing royals around nineteen years ago from any of the five kingdoms. I feel a trace of ether in her, but also—" he pauses.

Wait. Did he say missing royals? And what is... "Ether? What does that mean?" I question. This conversation is making my head spin, but I pin my attention on Cyrus and wait for his answer.

Director Dunn steps toward the man. "What is it, Cyrus? What else?"

The man's gray eyes find mine, his lips tightening into a thin line. "I believe Elara is a Death Dealer."

I stop breathing. My worst nightmare has stepped into the light. He knows. Cyrus knows I killed Cole.

What will happen to me now? Will they imprison me? Execute me?

The walls press in around me, forcing my shaking legs to give, dropping me into the armchair.

"Death Dealer?" Remington all but yells in response. "There is only one other Death Dealer in the entirety of Celestria. There hasn't been another one—"

"In a long time," Cyrus cuts in. "She must be trained. She must learn how to manage this power, even if it is a remnant." His eyes show worry and concern. "I also felt something else."

"What? What else did you feel?" Director Dunn asks, but Cyrus shakes his head.

"I cannot say yet. An inaccurate assessment is not only dangerous, but illegal. We must carefully assess and note each person in the system. Without it accomplished correctly, things are bound to go wrong. Especially during these dark and desperate days we have fallen into."

Director Dunn nods and places a hand on Remington's shoulder. "Until we find the truth, she will need to be protected. For now, we must keep this secret. If she is important, she will become a target. The enemy will come for her."

Cyrus nods. "Especially if they find out she is a Death Dealer. This must remain between us until we release the binding on her power. Until then, I cannot give a truthful assessment."

Remington steps to my side. "She will be under my supervision, but I will need to place her somewhere. I cannot cover the fact her assessment is inconclusive or that she cannot wield a gift."

My gut is in knots and my head is in a tailspin. "Wait," I speak, almost breathless. "You say I am a Death Dealer. Does that mean my gift is killing people?"

Cyrus shakes his head. "No, Elara. It is one of your gifts, but it is rare. A Death Dealer is someone who holds the power of life-or-death in their hands. They can strip a soul from a person with ease. Right now, whatever I feel is a trace of your power—whatever is seeping through the barrier."

Director Dunn looks at me as if I am an enigma. "Through the years, Death Dealers have been both feared and revered in Celestria. It's best not to tell anyone. Especially after the horrifying news we just received about our rulers."

"Yes, yes," Cyrus agrees. "I'll have to leave directly after this to meet with the counsel regarding this matter."

Fear. It's bubbling inside of me. "What happened?"

Cyrus runs a hand down his gray beard. "The rulers of each kingdom are missing, and we all believe the enemy has taken them." He pauses and all three of them share a look of distress. "The kingdoms are being thrown into chaos. The five princes will gather at the Central Court in three hours' time. I suspect you will be there, Captain?"

Remington nods. "If the prince is attending, I will be there."

What will happen to me? "Will others be in danger because of me?" That is all I need to know. I have to make sure that if I come into direct contact with someone, they won't die.

"Not right now," Cyrus replies. "Not with most of your power sealed. But there is enough that you could take a life. However, you cannot hurt another Celestrian unless it is intentional. Unless you desire to hurt them and direct your power to do so." He gives me a tight-lipped smile. "Once your power releases, you cannot take your gift lightly. You will need someone to guide you." Cyrus then turns to Remington and gives him a look... a look that has Remington nodding. But I also see concern embedded in his eyes. A concern that makes the knots in my gut tighten even more.

"What should I do with her since her assessment is inconclusive?" Remington's eyes shift over to me. "I cannot accurately place her without knowing her gifts."

"There is one thing I'm good at," I interject. "I am proficient in military combat. Maybe I can be a guard?" I shrug my shoulders. Five years of training should account for something.

Three sets of eyes widen. I clear my throat and straighten my back. "They bullied me in school and the nurse's husband was one of the top military combat trainers in the nation. I have learned from the best. Well, the best on Earth."

Remington chuckles, his fingers graze his healed and very straight nose. "Now I understand why you were so hard to catch. I will find a suitable position for you." He then turns his attention to Director Dunn and Cyrus. "I must return to Terr and keep an appointment with the prince but will make sure she remains close and supervised and will place her in a suitable post that should *hopefully* avoid scrutiny. I will also search the records for information regarding her birth in the Kingdom of Terr's archives."

"Good. Good," Director Dunn says, nodding. "I'll also request access to the other kingdom's archives as well."

Cyrus takes a step forward, toward Remington. "Captain, I will contact you directly if we find anything." Remington bows his head, then Cyrus swings his attention to me, and I notice a softness in his eyes. "I will find a way to release the magic binding your power, Elara. Hopefully, we can find out who did this to you and why. When we do, that information should lead us directly to your birth parents."

I nod because there is nothing else I can do. "Thank you."

I quickly compartmentalize all the bits of information. My entire life has been a mystery, and the huge stress is knowing the biggest answers will not come soon. I should be used to it by now, but I'm not. I have never felt more like an outsider or more alone than I do at this very moment, knowing that my powers are bound in a world where everyone has magic.

Did my birth parents really do this to me?

They really must not have wanted me, especially to seal my gifts and leave me with nothing but a first name on a planet that was not mine. The life they forced on me was hell.

In my heart, I don't desire to know who my parents are. They're cruel for what they did to me, and I don't care to find them. In my heart, the moment they left me alone on the steps of the church, they were dead to me. They no longer exist.

"Take care of her, Captain," Cyrus says, then gives me a reassuring smile. "I have a feeling there is a lot more to this one than meets the eye."

I don't feel like anything other than a broken vessel. A vessel with fissures caused from years of being used and abused. Fissures so deep, I am nearly torn in two. My heart holds the greatest of this damage. A damage I slowly tried to mend, carefully constructing a solid callous around.

Remington bows his head to both men before turning his attention to me and gestures to the door with his hand. "Shall we?"

"Where are we going?"

"To our kingdom."

Our kingdom.

He gives me a lopsided grin that makes my heart flutter.

Another wave of anxiety builds in my belly, not knowing what waits for me there. There is so much about this world I know nothing about, and it scares the hell out of me. All I can do is keep breathing and hope for the best.

Remington opens the door and leaves, so I turn back and wave to Director Dunn and Cyrus. They smile and incline their heads before I also leave the room.

SEVEN

ELARA

As soon as I enter the waiting room, the three boys who remain are staring at me. After seeing Cyrus and Remington enter the room, they must know something happened.

"Is everything okay?" Thomas asks, leaning toward me. I can see the questions stirring in his eyes—their eyes—but I cannot tell them anything.

"Her assessment went as expected," Remington replies for me, holding the door open. "Sorry, guys. We are on a time restriction." I gratefully nod in agreement, glad I didn't have to answer, and wave goodbye to Thomas as I head out of the door.

As we exit, Aurora stands to her feet, her eyes visually molesting Remington.

"Rem, why are you back?" She bats her eyelashes at him before turning to me and thrusting out her hand. "Paperwork?"

Remington faces her, his back straightening. "Her paperwork is with the Director. I have orders to return to Terr immediately, so I must be on my way."

She crosses her arms over her chest with lips turned down into a pout. "What will I do with her until then?"

"She is returning to Terr with me."

Aurora shoots me a savage glare, and if looks could kill, I would already be dead.

Instead of lowering myself and being a snide bitch, I smile at her and head for the door that Remington is already holding open. He offers me his arm and I sidle up to him, linking my elbow around his. I don't have to look back to know Aurora's daggered stare is on us.

As soon as we step outside and the door snaps shut, I exhale, grabbing the sides of my head.

"Are you okay?" Remington asks, pausing.

"I'm fine," I say, although I am anything but. "It's just a lot to take in right now. Everything that happened in that room just added to the surmounting questions I already have. I'm tired and I'm hungry."

"I'm sorry." He lays a gentle hand on my shoulder. "As soon as we get back to Terr, I'll get you something to eat."

I nod. "How long will it take us to get there?"

"Seconds." He grins, then waves a hand in the air. I hear a snap and watch an iridescent ripple form in the space directly in front of us.

Oh no.

"What is that?" I swallow hard, pointing to the ripple. I don't think my stomach can manage another trip like last night.

"It's a Celestrial portal."

"Is that how everyone travels here?"

"No. Only those from the Kingdom of Terr can open Celestrial portals. Our gift is that of ether—the place where sound and energy travel without resistance. Ether is the element that makes life possible. It is both nothing and everything, the essence of emptiness and the awareness of space. It is how we can teleport, amongst other things." I see pride in his eyes and in the upward curve of his lips as he holds out his hand to me. "You will also be a Portal Jumper once they release your gifts."

I point to my chest. "Me?"

He nods, his grin expanding. "That is only a small part of it. The citizens of Terr can do much more than that."

I cannot deny the desire to conjure magic and open portals to travel through. But right now, I feel paralyzed, inadequate, knowing everyone in Celestria has received their gifts... except me. All I can do is accept my fate—for the time being—and trust that Cyrus will unlock the block placed on my power.

Remington notices my hesitation, his eyes sliding down to my hands and my tightly knit fingers. "You can't hurt me, spitfire."

Spitfire. The pet name gives me all sorts of feelings. It's awkward, and I can't tell if I like it or hate it. To be honest, I think I like it, but I would let no one know, especially him.

Remington seems to be trying to gain my friendship. All I've ever wanted was to be accepted. To have someone I can trust wholeheartedly, to have a strong, genuine relationship with. I've been burned by so many people. Wounded too many times by wolves in sheep's clothing. Countless individuals who left my heart raw, exposed, and vulnerable. I trust no one, and although my heart may appear hardened, it's made of glass. It is fragile, and I will let no one close enough to shatter it.

"Things work differently here in Celestria," Remington continues. "Like Cyrus explained earlier, you cannot harm anyone unless you direct your power to do so—unless you purposefully intend to harm them."

I soak that information in. It sounds reasonable, and Remington is slowly earning my trust. I will never wholeheartedly trust anyone until I have put their loyalty to the test. But I am in his care, so I have to give a little.

He stretches his hand a little farther and I grasp it before we both step toward the ripple and fold into darkness.

As soon as the darkness dissipates, I am thrown off-kilter and immediately drop to my knees, my palms hitting the ground in front of me. My stomach feels as if it's turned inside out, so I suck in a deep breath, trying to ease the nausea.

Remington grasps me by the elbow and helps me to my feet. "In the beginning, it's like this. It takes a little getting used to."

I give him a side-eyed glare. "Even for you? That's hard to believe."

"My father served the king and taught me how to Portal Jump when I turned five. At that age, I didn't have any reservations, and loved the thrill of it."

"Wait, so you could portal jump when you were five? I thought gifts didn't come until you're eighteen?"

He shakes his head. "In Celestria, you are born with your gifts, and the realm nurtures it. When they take Changelings to the mortal realm, their powers become dormant. It takes years for them to awaken and manifest. Eighteen years, to be precise."

I nod, then offer him a smirk. "Learning to portal jump at five? I bet you've never been sick."

That devious grin is back. "I can't say that I have."

"Well, if you don't want me to vomit all over this pristine floor, you'd better get me to a bathroom."

I glance up and notice we are in a grand hallway. The floor is black marble with veins of gold running through it, the walls are rock in a dark ebony. Rich tapestries hang along the walls, along with golden, gilded sconces.

There are guards everywhere, wearing their black guard attire with weapons strapped to their waists. A crest with a black dragon is on the center of their chests.

When they see Remington, every single guard slaps a fist to their chest, bows, and then greets him. "Captain," they say with reverence.

I raise a brow at him as we walk away. "You must be a big whip here."

He crosses his arms over his broad chest. "Big whip?"

I tilt my head and raise my brow. "High rank."

"Oh." He casually shrugs. "I guess you could say that."

He has aroused my curiosity. "How highly ranked?"

He stops and gives me a sinful, dimpled grin. "I am the prince's personal guard and captain of his army."

Holy shit. My eyes widen. He *is* a big whip, a huge deal in the kingdom and to the prince.

"How are you supposed to guard the prince and lead his army when the director put you on babysitting duty?" I point at myself.

He gives me another sly grin. "Don't worry, spitfire. I excel at multitasking."

I shake my head and notice that at the end of the hall are two more guards.

"What is this place?" I breathe.

Remington places a hand to his chest and tips his head toward me. "Welcome to the Ebony Palace, Elara."

My eyes widen, and my mouth is gaping. I am in complete awe. It looks like a dark palace taken right out of one of my fantasy books. It's even grander than I could have imagined... and this is only a hallway? I can't wait to see what the rest of the palace looks like.

"The restroom is just around the corner," he says, leading me forward, his hand still on my elbow.

As we make it to the end of the hallway, the guards slap their fists over their chests and bow their heads at Remington. He acknowledges them with a nod and pulls me around the corner. Stopping at a door, he inclines his head. "The ladies' washroom."

"Thank you," I utter, bolting for the door, but stop and turn back to him. "You're going to wait for me, right?"

His chuckle sends heat to my cheeks. "I will wait right here. Just don't take too long. I have an important meeting with the prince."

I pivot and enter the washroom. If I thought the holding room's washroom was grand, it does not hold a candle to this room. It looks like a goddamn spa. There is a large mirror over a dark stone sink. Behind me are two stalls made of rich wood. I use the bathroom and wash my hands. The soap smells amazing and there are real hand towels that are extremely soft, and a basket to throw the used ones in.

I rinse my face with cold water and glance at myself in the mirror. *Good god.* I'm looking rough. The dark circles under my eyes tell me I need a decent night's sleep, and the rumbling in my stomach demands I find food soon. At least the nausea is gone.

I tuck in my shirt and head back out to find Remington casually leaning against the wall, arms crossed over his chest. Christ, he is so damn gorgeous. I swallow as his dark eyes meet mine and his signature grin rises on full lips.

"Ready?" he asks, pushing off the wall.

I nod and follow him, but he slows until we are walking side-by-side.

"I'll have to leave you for a moment to meet the prince, but I will have one of the guards take you to get some food. Will that be okay?"

"Do what you need to. If there is food, I'll be a happy girl."

His lips turn upward, his dimples deepening. "Good then. I'll find you when I'm done."

We make it to the end of a hallway where there are two large doors made of rich wood that have two dragons exquisitely carved into them. Remington pauses and speaks quietly to one of the two guards standing at the door, then turns back to me.

"Elara, this is Gale, a friend of mine. He will take you to the dining room to get something to eat."

I nod and smile at Gale. He is also tall and handsome with dark hair and eyes, but not as handsome or as built as Remington. It seems everyone I've met from the Kingdom of Terr has dark hair and dark eyes. Maybe that is how to distinguish the kingdoms.

Gale moves from his post and bows his head at me. "Please, follow me."

I glance back at Remington, who gives me another smile before he opens one of the large doors and walks inside. The prince must be in that room, and the thought of it, a *real* prince, makes my heart beat a little faster.

"You're a Changeling?" Gale asks, snapping my attention back to him.

I nod. "I guess I am. They brought me here last night."

His face and eyes brighten. "How was it... living on Earth?"

What do I tell him? Earth sucks and so do most of its inhabitants. Well, the ones I have come across. It's true, but I don't think that's a suitable answer.

"It's nothing great. Just a place people exist," I finally answer.

"Oh," he exhales, his expression deflates.

I realize I've made things awkward. He was probably looking for an exceptional tale about my upbringing. Some wonderful and exciting adventure with beautiful descriptions of Earth, but what he got was a boring answer that said *I don't want to talk about it.*

Story of my life. I am an expert at deflection and an introvert by force. I haven't had many friends to talk to, so I am lacking in the way of having any deep conversations. I can turn it on if I have to, but I keep people at a distance for good reason. Books have been my constant friend and my escape.

We walk the rest of the way in silence and when we round a corner, the scent of food wafts in the air. Something is baking, and it smells divine. A mixture of sweet and spice, and it makes my mouth water.

We enter another room at the end of the hallway. It's not that big but has four round tables with four chairs around each. "This is where we come on break," Gale says. "Have a seat. I'll be right back." He bows his head and heads out of the room.

The room is simple, four walls with two arched windows against one side. I'm curious what view the windows overlook, so I head over to one of them.

My eyes swallow a large, hedged labyrinth with manicured areas inside it filled with a stunning array of blooming and colorful flowers. At the center of the labyrinth is a large water feature with an enormous statue of a dragon curled around an elongated stone with wings outspread. There are only two words I can think of to describe this setting.

Magical. Majestic.

Inside of me, I feel a sense of calm that coats my bones and tempers my fear. It is a feeling I'm not used to, but this place feels familiar. Even though I have never been here before, it feels like I somehow belong. It feels like... *home.*

EIGHT

ELARA

Soaking it all in, I don't hear Gale as he enters the room. He clears his throat and I jump and spin to find the table set with pastries and an assortment of cheese and fruit.

There is a girl, around my age, placing a mug down and pouring coffee into it. She also has onyx eyes and dark hair tied up in a bun.

"You must be hungry," Gale says.

I nod and my stomach growls in response as I make my way over and take a seat.

He sits on the opposite side of the table while the girl steps over to the wall and stands there with her hands folded in front of her.

Gale notices my gaze. "She is here to provide you with whatever you need. If you wish for something else to eat, let her know and she will get it."

The girl smiles and bows her head at me, but she looks nervous, and I suddenly feel bad that she not only has to serve but wait against the wall.

"You aren't going to eat?" Gale shakes his head when I ask him.

"I had a big breakfast. Besides, Rem ordered me to keep you company while he meets with the prince."

I nod again, grab a muffin, that has crumble over the top, and sink my teeth into it. It's warm and soft and my taste buds burst with flavor. It's sweet with sugar and cinnamon and softened chunks of apples swirled throughout it. The topping adds the perfect crunch. I let out a moan, closing my eyes, savoring the taste when I hear a giggle.

Sliding my eyes open, I see Gale grinning and the girl covering her mouth, so I straighten my back and swallow, then take a sip of coffee to wash it down.

Gale leans forward on his elbows. "It sounds like you're enjoying that."

"Immensely." I nod then glance at the girl who is now straight faced. "Please, come and sit," I say, patting the chair next to me. "There is too much food for me to eat, and I feel uncomfortable eating alone."

"Oh, no. I couldn't." Her expression is one of pure shock, her eyes darting to Gale.

"Why not?" I ask.

Gale speaks up. "It's improper for servants to dine during work hours."

Crossing my arms over my chest, I tilt my head toward him. "What if I don't want her to serve me? I would feel more comfortable if she sat at the table with me than standing in the corner." I glance back at the girl, her eyes shifting from Gale to me.

"What's your name?" I ask her.

She pauses, then bows her head. "My name is Gemma, miss."

Unfolding my arms, I rest my elbows on the table. "You can call me Elara. Please, come and sit with me."

Her eyes dart back to Gale, who gives her a shrug, his head gesturing to the chair. "She requested it," he sighs. "I see nothing wrong with you doing as your guest requests."

She hesitates again, her eyes slipping to the door before she slowly walks over and takes the seat next to me.

"Have you tasted these, Gemma?" I ask, picking up one of the warm muffins.

Her eyes drop to the table, and she shakes her head.

"*Never?*"

"The servants consume whatever is provided for them," Gale explains as he points to the muffin in my grasp. "These are luxuries."

I take Gemma's hand and place the pastry into it. "Please, take a bite and tell me if it's as good as I believe it is."

She glues her eyes to the muffin but doesn't move or speak.

"If I'm wrong and you don't like it, you don't have to eat it."

She slowly clasps it in her hands, raises it to her mouth, and takes a bite. I feel bad because she looks scared, like she's disobeying the rules, so I turn away and take another bite of mine, moaning as I get a soft piece of apple.

Glancing over at her, I raise my brows. "It's good, right?"

She nods, but still looks uncomfortable, so I pour her a cup of coffee and slide it over. Again, she pauses. The last thing I want to do is make her feel awkward.

"Look, I get that you're supposed to be serving me, but I'm no more important than you are."

She quickly places the muffin on the table. "I shouldn't. I could get into trouble."

"Where I come from, I have done everything on my own. I don't need to be served." My eyes shift to Gale. "Are you sure you don't want anything?" I widen my eyes at him and look down at the food, hoping he can see my indirect intention.

He does. "I'll take an apple," he declares, leaning over and plucking a bright red one from the platter. He takes a bite and juice runs down his lip. He nods, letting us know it's a good one. "So, Elara, are you going to tell us anything about where you grew up?" He leans over to Gemma. "She is a Changeling from the mortal realm. She arrived this morning."

Gemma gasps, her eyes widen as they shoot toward me. "Are you really?"

I nod, knowing they want me to share something about my life with them. Grasping the coffee cup, I bring it to my lips, gulping the hot drink and washing down the muffin, as I decide to tell them about my time in the Dark Forest.

I share how it was my home for the past year, and how I scared the kids who entered the forest on a dare to spend the night. They both roll with laughter at my stories, and Gemma relaxes, finishing the entire muffin and cup of coffee while I devour everything else on the platter.

"Well, I think we should get back." Gale stretches his arms over his head. "Rem will be finished soon."

I nod, and Gemma hops out of her seat, promptly gathering the dishes.

Standing, I place a hand on her shoulder. "Thank you for the company, Gemma. I hope to see you around sometime."

She smiles and bows her head. "It was my pleasure, and if you ever want a tour around the city, I'll be more than happy to be your guide."

"I just might take you up on that offer."

"Good," she returns. "I'll look forward to it."

I follow Gale back out and down the luxurious hallway until we reach the large wooden double doors we left Remington at. The single guard acknowledges Gale and quickly dips his head to me.

Leaning over, I whisper to Gale. "So, what is your prince like?"

He clears his throat. "I am not at liberty to speak about the prince."

"Oh," I breathe. "He must be an asshole."

Gabe's eyes grow wide. "I didn't say that."

"No. But if there was anything good to say, I'm sure you would have no problem speaking freely."

The other guard leans forward, biting back a grin.

"He's not an asshole," Gale whispers loudly, in defense.

I cross my arms over my chest and tilt my head to the side. "Then what is he?"

He pauses, weighing his next word. "Complicated."

One of the double doors abruptly swings open and Remington steps out. As soon as his eyes land on me, he gives me a smile that makes my heart flutter. "Hey, spitfire, did you get something to eat?"

I roll my eyes at the nickname he's no doubt keeping. "I did."

"Good. I'll take you to the training center where you can stay until we get a proper place set up for you."

I nod and sigh, wondering how we'll get to this training center. "We aren't going through any portals, are we?" I can't afford to lose the food I just ate.

"No, we'll walk," he says with a grin. "The center is next to the palace."

"Thank the gods. I can't afford to be sick for the third time on my birthday."

Remington points at me with a surprised look. "Your birthday is today?"

"It is." I give him a grin. "Are you going to treat me to dinner and drinks?"

He was about to answer me when —

"Captain," a rich, husky voice behind Remington interrupts.

The air suddenly feels heavy, nearly suffocating, as a tall figure emerges from the double doors and pauses at Remington's side. I try to tamper the rush of adrenaline that surges through me as his dark eyes meet mine.

He is the most gorgeous man I've ever laid eyes on. Remington is beautiful, but this man is on another level. He looks like a god. A breathtakingly gorgeous god.

He looms a few inches higher than Remington, with onyx hair and eyes that resemble the night sky—pitch-black and ringed in gold. Everything about him screams regal and wealth. He is perfect, from his flawless skin, straight nose, sharp, angled jaw, lush lips, and broad shoulders.

Atop his head is a crown of onyx and gold that matches his eyes. Eyes that meet mine and widen for a split second with an expression I cannot read. But it's gone just as fast, nostrils flaring, eyes like fire, burning straight through me before he turns that heated gaze to Remington.

"Who is this?" he addresses the captain, his voice as sharp as a double-edged sword.

Remington turns to me. "My Prince, this is Elara. She is a Changeling I recovered from the mortal realm this morning, newly assessed, and found to originate from Terr. I was about to take her to the training center."

I am frozen, my feet rooted to the floor, not knowing what to do with myself. My hands. My head. My eyes. This man is royalty. What the hell do I do?

"Elara, this is Prince Kage Dargan," Remington says.

My eyes widen, and my jaw slacks with the confirmation. Should I bow? Curtsey? Hold out my hand? Say something? Or stay silent?

"Bow," Remington whispers from my side.

I dip my head and when I look up, the prince's eyes are glacial as they survey me from head to toe. I feel disoriented, like there is an electricity buzzing in the air between us and I feel my traitorous body sway forward, toward him, like a flower seeking the sun. *What the hell is wrong with me?*

"A Changeling?" The prince spits the words with disdain, making me step back. "You know we forbid Changelings from roaming the palace, Captain. Especially after what happened with the last one. We cannot afford any more attempts on my life."

Remington mentioned a Changeling attacked him, so I understand his concern. But I am not a threat, and his words feel like a dagger sliding across my skin.

I don't know the rules here or if I am allowed to speak, but I do anyway because I feel I need to say something. Especially if I am going to be a part of his guard.

I train my eyes to the floor. "Your Highness, I am not brainwashed, nor am I a threat to you or your kingdom. I just want to find out the truth about my life and who I am."

The prince scoffs. "That's what the last Changeling said before he tried to take my life."

Shaking my head, I keep my eyes focused downward. "I never had a choice. They abandoned me in the mortal realm, left to rot in a world that shunned and abused me, raised by people who didn't want me." My voice is shaking, along with my limbs. I hate being in this position. I hate that I feel like I have to plead for mercy for a life I was never given a say in. And until now, no one on this planet knew I existed or gave a shit about me.

I tuck in my emotions and play my role, not knowing if I'll be next to be thrown into the dungeon, or prison, whatever the hell they call it here. "I did not have the luxury of choosing where I was placed. Like I said before, I am not a threat. I'm just a girl who discovered my entire life was a lie. Who was abandoned and forgotten on a planet that did not accept me. A girl who wants to find her place here and fit in. That's all."

I raise my head and my eyes meet his, and for the briefest moment, they are soft. With a blink, his emotions shift, and a scowl tightens on his lips. His face turns rigid, stoic, and those dark eyes pinned on me are like fire, torching my insides.

The air is stifling between us, and I can't seem to breathe in enough of it.

He detests me because I'm a Changeling, but it's something I can't change. I had no choice. Swallowing hard, I turn my attention to Remington, hoping he will say something to get me out of this uncomfortable situation. And he does.

"My prince," he says, bowing his head. "The enemy came for her last night, but we retrieved her first. I was there at the assessment and can confirm she is not a threat."

When I glance back up, the prince's dark eyes are still fixed on me. I turn to Remington and grab his wrist.

The prince's gaze snaps down at the movement, his eyes darkening, the muscles in his jaw tightening. Maybe it's improper for me to touch his captain, so I quickly release my hand.

Remington shifts and straightens his back. "I will take my leave and will see you at the meeting at Central Court," he says, slapping a fist to his chest and bowing at the prince. He then turns and offers me his arm. "Come on, spitfire. Let's go."

Pausing, I see Remington's warm smile, so I grasp his arm and let him lead me away. I feel the prince's heated gaze on my back, and as we round a corner, I glance backward to confirm he is still watching.

Those deep obsidian eyes are going to give me nightmares, or perhaps wonderful dreams. Either way, I'm glad we are moving away from him, because the farther we get, the easier it is to breathe.

NINE

PRINCE KAGE

I exit the throne room to see a girl with Rem. When I glimpse her face, it's as if time suspends. The girl is familiar to me, but I have never met her in person.

That exquisitely shaped face, captivating gold-rimmed hazel eyes, long, dark hair and full lips...

This girl has been in my dreams since I was a boy.

Rem is my most trusted friend and personal guard who I've also made captain of the army. Although he is two years younger, we grew up together. His father served my father, and now, Rem is serving me. He has been with me most of my life since the dreams first started, and I've shared them with him countless times. He knows her too, but he would never recognize her. He's never seen her face like I have.

"Who is this?" I ask Rem, my emotions unhinged.

"My Prince, this is Elara. She is a Changeling I recovered from the mortal realm this morning, newly assessed, and found to originate from Terr. I was about to take her to the training center."

Rem then addresses her. "Elara, this is Prince Kage Dargan."

Elara. I now possess a name to the face that has frequented my dreams. But she is a Changeling.

Why would a Changeling be in my dreams?

She gasps softly, and the look she gives pleases me.

"Bow," Rem whispers to her.

They are friendly and comfortable speaking to each other, and I don't know how the hell I feel about that. I shouldn't give a shit about it, or her.

Elara lowers her head, but I keep my expression rigid. I cannot and will not lower my defenses, especially with a newly placed Changeling. Besides, keeping her at a distance is not only proper, it's necessary. I am engaged—an arranged marriage set by my father almost two years ago. I don't have time to figure out why the girl from my dreams has materialized, and is standing in front of me. Is fate fucking with me?

"A Changeling should not be roaming the palace, Captain. You know what happened to the last one. We cannot afford any more attempts on my life," I say with a little too much bite.

Rem is about to say something, but the girl speaks first. In my dreams, over all those years, she has remained silent. I'm struck, hearing her voice for the very first time.

"Your Highness," she says, addressing me. Her voice is soft and sweet and promptly fills my cold, dark chest with warmth. "I am not brainwashed, nor am I a threat to you or your kingdom. I just want to find out the truth about my life and who I am."

She's brave and has the guts to speak up despite knowing who I am. I will credit her for that, but I still cannot trust her. "That's what the last Changeling said before he tried to take my life."

She shakes her head, avoiding my gaze. "I did not have the luxury of choosing where I was placed. Like I said before, I am not a threat. I'm just a girl who discovered my entire life was a lie. Who was abandoned and forgotten on a planet that did not accept me. A girl who wants to find her place here and fit in. That's all."

"My prince," Rem says, bowing his head. "The enemy came for her last night, but we retrieved her first. I was there at the assessment and can confirm she is not a threat."

I feel my anger rise, knowing she could have been a victim, but I let out a breath, calming myself.

Elara reaches down and grabs Rem's wrist and my heart clenches at the act. When her eyes meet mine, she abruptly releases her hand, and unbeknownst to me, I feel gratified... no matter what the reason.

"I will take my leave and will see you at the meeting at Central Court," Rem says, then offers her his arm. "Come on, spitfire. Let's go."

He brought her in this morning and has already given her a pet name. I also overheard her say it was her birthday today, and she asked Rem to take her out for dinner and drinks.

My mind is spiraling and for the first time in my life, I feel like I'm losing control of my emotions. The girl in my dreams is real, and she is here in Terr with my best friend. It is her birthday, and I treated her with contempt and called her a threat.

What the fuck is happening?

TEN

ELARA

Remington nudges me with his elbow as we make our way out of the palace. I take in all the luxurious and elegant decorations. Everything in the Ebony Palace is dark—black marble and onyx, but it also feels warm and inviting with the warm flickering sconces along the walls, the tear-drop crystal chandeliers, and everything gilded in gold.

"I know the prince came off harsh, but he is under tremendous pressure," Remington says. He stops and glances around, like what he is about to say he doesn't want anyone else to hear. "His father disappeared last night, and he's left to deal with the repercussions. These are dark times in Terr, and I suspect they will only grow darker."

Gods. Maybe life on Earth wasn't so bad.

I hear him chuckle. "You did well, meeting the prince. Most women throw themselves at his feet and would do anything for him to even glance at them."

I laugh and shrug my shoulders. "It was easy. He detests me."

A deep, pitiful sigh expires from his lips. "He doesn't detest you."

I throw him a pointed gaze, which makes him chuckle.

"Okay, okay. He is not fond of Changelings, but you can't fault him for that. The last one did rise in rank to become a trusted servant and then tried to kill him."

"No, I cannot fault him for that. He has a valid reason to keep his guard up, especially being prince of the kingdom. But why would the Changeling try to kill him? Wasn't the Changeling kidnapped by the enemy?"

"He was."

"So, *you* didn't kidnap him from Earth?"

"We do not kidnap. We extract," he exasperates, throwing me a pointed look. "And yes, another one of our teams brought him here from Earth."

"But I thought the enemy took him?"

"They did but returned him. I guess it's a new tactic of theirs—returning newly brainwashed Changelings to Earth, only to be extracted by us. We extracted them, processed them, and sent them to their rightful kingdoms. We never questioned if they were planted."

Heavens. "Did he realize he had been brainwashed?"

He gives me a nod. "He knew, and whatever lies and hatred they planted in his mind only grew while he was in Celestria. Whatever methods they used to turn them against their own race is effective and terrifying."

"Well, I don't think brainwashing Changelings would be difficult. Their birth parents and people rejected them and abandoned them on a planet that isn't theirs."

Remington nods. "I see your point and can't argue that it makes it easier for the enemy to infiltrate their minds."

"So—those men cloaked in red who came the same night you did... they were the enemy?"

Remington stops walking and turns his gaze toward me. "They were. If we hadn't gotten there when we did, they would have taken you. You would have been a victim."

Holy shit. It was literally minutes after Remington and his team came for me.

"Fate is on our side, it seems, along with your skills. You avoided getting taken into their portal. That choke hold you had on their leader would have killed him. They underestimated you."

The thought of it sets an uneasiness in my gut. "If I were alone, I wouldn't have been so lucky. So, thank you... for *extracting* me when you did. I owe you one."

"I'll take it, but tonight I'm treating you since it's your birthday *and* you have no money." He shoots me a wink, and a dimpled grin.

"Sounds great." I can't help but smile. Dinner and drinks with the handsome captain sound like an exceptional way to spend my birthday and my first night in Celestria.

Remington leads me forward, toward a large reception room. "How many other Changelings have you collected from Earth?"

"Around twenty-five."

My eyes widen. "How many of them are from the Kingdom of Terr?"

"As of now, two, but the other is in a cell awaiting judgment."

"He tried to kill the prince, so I'm assuming it won't end well for him."

He shakes his head. "Attempted murder of a royal is execution. Besides, whatever methods they used on him drove him to the point of insanity. He is no longer in his right mind."

Fate must be on my side, and I count myself blessed by the stars that they spared me. "Who is this enemy that is brainwashing Changelings and kidnapping royalty?"

"They are savages from the planet Avka. Mysteriously, the Emperor and Empress of Avka recently fell sick and died, and their son, Prince Adhan Merak, took over rulership. From what we know, he is ruthless. A tyrant, in charge of the Avkan military, that has had his eyes set on Celestria for years."

"Did he kill his parents?"

Remington rakes his fingers through his thick, dark hair. "There is no reason to believe otherwise. As soon as the king and queen were buried, he assumed the throne and immediately began his attacks. We believe he has been planning this for some time."

"Why Celestria?"

"Because Celestria is rich with an abundance of resources and wealth. Prince Adhan has an extraordinarily strong and well-trained army, and he believes he can rule our planet better than we can."

"Do the Avkan people have gifts like the Celestrians?"

He shakes his head. "No. They rely on weapons and brute force, which is why it's difficult to know how they made it past the guards of all five kingdoms to kidnap the rulers."

"Could it have been a Changeling? One who could portal jump?"

His broad shoulders shrug. "That is a possibility, but highly unlikely for a Changeling, recently recovered from the mortal realm, to be so precise with their gifts. Especially with no training. Few Celestrians can accurately portal jump to a pinpointed location... like directly into the royal chambers."

I tilt my head to the side and raise my brows. "Can you do it?"

He smirks.

"You can." I shake my head, in awe of his gifts. "When Cyrus releases my power, you'll have to teach me that. Okay?"

He holds out his hand to me with a single nod. "Deal." I take his hand and we shake on it.

"All right, spitfire. We need to get you set up at the training center before I leave."

"To your meeting with the prince at Central Court?"

"Yes."

I nod as we exit the Ebony Palace. An icy breeze wraps around me, and the sky looming above us is an angry shade of gray. The sound of thunder rumbles across the heavens and I catch glimpses of light pulsing through the monotonous clouds. The scent of rain hangs heavy in the air, and I have a feeling we are going to get dumped on. Soon.

My eyes sweep the area and notice the palace is built on a large hill that overlooks a massive city that rests in a valley. Between the city and the palace, a large swollen river cleaves the land in two. The riverbanks on each side are filled with thick and lush woodlands.

I understand why they built the palace here. The scenery is breathtaking, even with the dreary weather. Also, it's easy to spot anyone attempting to travel up the slopes to reach the palace.

They impeccably manicured the grounds with cobbled pathways, trimmed hedges, and an array of multicolored flowers precisely placed around trees, statues and small stone benches. I can only imagine what it must look like on a sunny day, or if there are many of those days up here in the northern realm.

Remington leads me to the right, and we stroll down one of the cobbled paths that lead through the gardens.

"It's going to rain," I note.

Remington's head tilts back, his eyes scan the sky. "Yes, I suppose it will."

A stray water-drop kisses my cheek, and then another. Another falls and drips down my arm, and before I can say a word, the heavens open, drenching everything under it.

Everything... except us.

Next to me, Remington's hand raises, his fingers splayed open. I follow a shadowy mist that is coiled around his wrist, through his fingers, and shooting up above us. It's the same mist I saw the night they took me. The same he used to kill the two men in crimson cloaks. He flattened it into a circular dome above us, protecting us from the rain. *A shadow umbrella,* and I can't help but gape in awe, even if it is a simplistic use of his gift. I can't wait to do impressive shit like that myself.

The training center is impressive, a massive building off the side of the palace where they spared no expense. It is a place that would draw the guards and soldiers of Terr. Inside, the entire center of the building is for training. It is the size of two football fields, with everything they need to train a soldier—weapons, weights, an obstacle course, dummies. They equipped it with so many things, my eyes cannot soak it all in.

Around the arena are clusters of men pummeling each other with wooden swords and fists. Some are on the mats, grappling, going head-to-head through rigorous training, which oddly makes me feel right at home.

I am no stranger to training like this, but as my eyes scan the area, I quickly realize that I am the only female.

"Rem, you dog. What did you drag in?" a man closest to us says. His chocolate eyes slide down my body, making me feel uncomfortable. He is handsome and shirtless, like all the others training. Sweat glistens on his muscular frame. His dark hair is shoulder length and tied back at the nape of his neck.

I straighten my back, narrowing my gaze on him.

"I suggest you keep your eyes in your head, Talon, before I remove them," Remington says in a low, cautious voice.

Talon's eyes don't leave mine, a Cheshire cat smile rising on his full lips. "Come on, Rem. It is not a sin to admire beauty," he says, wiping his brow with the back of his hand. "Is she yours, or is she free game?"

Bastard.

Remington takes a step closer, his shoulder rubbing against mine. "If any of you so much as lays a finger on her, I will deal with you personally."

Talon steps forward, and I see it, a challenge in his eyes as he offers me his hand. "It's nice to meet you."

Yeah, right. I know this scenario all too well. He's testing me. Testing my grit.

Pure instinct and years of training kick in. Stepping forward, in one fluid motion, I sweep my leg around and behind his ankles while pushing his shoulders backward. Talon goes down like a sack of potatoes. Before he can make a move, I slam my elbow down at his face. He winces, but I stop short, just above his straight nose. I see it in his wide, blinking eyes. I've proven my point.

I quickly stand, looking down at him. "Nice to meet you, too."

The shit faced grin that grows on his face makes my stomach turn. *What have I done?* Reality and regret sink heavily in my gut, but I can't let them see it. I've proven my point, but now, I've also put a goddam target on my back.

"Don't underestimate this spitfire," Remington says to the men, stepping to my side. He then takes my hand and pulls me away from them. "Get back to training," he snaps over his shoulder.

"Yes, Captain," Talon says, sitting up with a smirk that tells me to *watch my back*.

"Ignore those assholes," Remington exhales, obviously pissed. "They aren't accustomed to seeing women in this building, nor has a woman ever challenged them."

"There are no female guards?" I question.

Remington shrugs his broad shoulders. "There were a few, but they never lasted."

I let out a sigh. "With men like them around, I can understand why."

"Most women in Celestria would never choose the life of a guard or soldier, knowing they would have to live here for six months to train alongside these men. Training hours are long and rigorous, and after that, we send them to remote areas for weeks, or even months at a time, having to leave loved ones and endure some of the harshest elements to keep our realm safe. Few women have tried, but none made it past the six-month training period."

I don't blame them, especially after watching the men train. Most of them were over six-foot tall with corded, muscular frames, and lean, athletic limbs. They look like world-class athletes, and even now, I doubt myself, unsure if I would fit in. Especially given the reputation of the last

Changeling. But it's all I know and something I'm good at, and I refuse to let a few assholes make me quit.

We stop at a door at the end of the hall when Remington extracts a key from his pocket and slides it into the lock. When it clicks, he turns the knob and pushes the door open, sliding to the side and ushering me in. "This will be yours until we can find you something more suitable."

I step into the room and take it all in. It's small, but better than anything I've ever had.

Everything is white, but it's quadruple the size of my old bedroom, complete with a small kitchen, bathroom, living area, and a small room with a twin bed. After living in a tiny bedroom for most of my life and sleeping in the hollow of a tree for a year, this is luxury.

"Will this suffice?" he asks, his brow furrowing when I don't answer.

"It's perfect. Thank you." I can't help but smile and could happily stay here for as long as they would have me.

"Good then. If you need anything, I am in the room just across the hall."

My smile grows, knowing he's close. Plopping down on a small armchair, I cross my arms over my chest. "Am I across the hall from you because of your vow to protect me?"

He pins his dark eyes on me. "I have never taken a vow I have not kept."

His words heat my cheeks and warm my core. He is handsome, loyal, and honest. Too perfect of a man.

Remington clears his throat and leans against the wall. "You've been *informally* introduced to the men, and after careful consideration, I think you should accompany me to the meeting."

My eyes narrow on him. "You think I can't handle myself?"

"I'm sure you can handle yourself just fine," he says with a chuckle. "It's the men I don't trust."

I won't fight him on that. He promised to be responsible for me. Besides, I don't know anyone else here, and I'd like to see more of this new place I call home.

"It would be the chance of a lifetime," he adds, brows raised. "It's rare for all five princes to gather in one place."

"Are you sure I'm allowed to attend?"

"No one will say anything if you're with me. After it's over, I will take you out for your birthday dinner in the city. How does that sound?"

"Wonderful." The thought of having dinner in the city with the handsome captain makes my smile grow. "What will I have to do at the meeting?"

"We'll just stand and wait until they're done. A word of warning. It will be boring as hell and will probably end in a pissing match with all the testosterone, tension and the need to prove which kingdom is more powerful."

A giggle slips from my lips at the thought, and I dare to ask, "Which kingdom *is* more powerful?"

His arms cross over his chest, head tilting to the side. "Terr of course."

"Of course, you would say that. You're biased."

"I am, but there is a reason they fear our prince within the five kingdoms."

"Hmm. Sounds like... fun." I feign a smile as Remington lets out a chuckle, then pulls out the antique timepiece from his pocket and glances at it.

"I have to check on the men but will be back soon." He places the key on a small dining table and turns to leave.

"Remington," I say, making him pause. Pivoting, his dark, golden flecked eyes meet mine.

"Thank you. For everything."

"It's my pleasure, spitfire," he says with a devilish grin as he exits the room. "Stay out of trouble. I'll be back soon."

Eleven

ELARA

After acquainting myself with my new living space, I quickly realize I need to make some money for basic living necessities. I've never had to rely on anyone before, and I don't want to start now.

I still haven't fully come to grips that I'm not on Earth anymore. Hell, I'm not even sure where the hell Celestria is. Is it in the same galaxy? The thought turns my gut.

A knock at the door has my stomach twisting. When I open it, Remington steps inside, then shuts the door behind him and locks it. He is wearing his black captain uniform, his weapons strapped to his sides. He grins and ambles to the center of the room.

I let out a moan. "Portal jumping?"

He nods and makes a motion with his hand. With a snap, another portal opens right in the middle of my new living room.

"The more you do it, the quicker you'll adjust."

I shake my head, my stomach tightening, already feeling nauseous. "I don't know if I'll ever get used to the weightless feeling. I've always had a weak stomach."

He chuckles, shaking his head. "For a spitfire like you, that's hard to believe."

"I trained constantly for four years, and I still have a lot to learn."

He holds out his hand. "You ready?"

"As ready as I'll ever be."

Sucking in a deep breath, I take his hand before we step forward, folding into darkness.

With a jolt, we reappear in a small office, and I immediately slap my palms against a large wooden desk in front of me, focusing on my breath, trying not to puke. From my peripheral, I see Remington's frame slide next to mine.

"Are you alright?"

I nod, breathing deeply—in and out.

Shifting my eyes to the side, I meet a dagger sheathed on his belt. "Why don't you carry a gun?"

"Gun? Why carry a weapon like that when we have magic?"

"That *is* a weapon." My eyes shift to his waist and the dagger hanging below it.

A devilish grin climbs on his full lips. "Where exactly are you looking, spitfire?"

I glance up, cheeks warming, as I narrow my gaze on his handsome, snide face. "I meant the dagger."

"Mmm," he hums, crossing muscular arms over his chest. "The dagger is there as a last resort. And for the record..." he gestures below his belt, to his weapon and the large bulge in his pants. I swallow hard, noticing it for the first time. "I brandish *both* weapons with no reservation and no regret."

Good gods.

My face heats and I swallow hard, which makes him chuckle.

He is going to be trouble. So much trouble.

Remington leads me into a large meeting room that is buzzing with people. In the center of that room is a wooden circular table with about twenty seats around it. It reminds me of King Arthur's round table. Not that I've ever seen it, but if I had, I envisioned it would look much like this.

"Captain." A tall, dashing man with blond hair and turquoise eyes, addresses Remington.

"Prince Archer," Remington says, placing a fist to his chest and bowing at the waist.

When the prince's eyes slide to me, I bow my head.

"Who, pray tell, is this fine creature?" The prince asks with a hint of playfulness in his voice. His eyes roam freely up and down my body, making me uneasy.

Remington steps to my side. "This is Elara, a guard in training and under my supervision."

The prince raises a brow at Remington, his lips curling into a sinister grin. "Yes, I suppose you would want to keep this one close." He reaches down and takes my hand in his, pressing his lips to the back of my fingers. "It's a pleasure to meet you, Elara."

Remington clears his throat. "Elara, this is Prince Archer Eros from the Kingdom of Asteri in the western realm. The people in his kingdom are known for their *wild* natures and wield the gift of wind."

Prince Archer winks at me, then finally releases my hand. "We may be wild, Captain, but we are wild in the best ways," he says, those turquoise eyes and devilish grin assaulting me.

The room is stifling, and my uniform suddenly feels too tight.

There is a sudden charge in the air that makes it hard to breathe and causes my skin to prickle. Prince Kage suddenly appears out of nowhere, slapping a large hand down on Archer's shoulder from behind. "Archer," he laughs, and the sound alone hums to my bones. Those gold-rimmed obsidian eyes fix on mine and it's as if his presence alone siphons the air from the room.

Why does my body react to him this way?

It's the second time my entire being wants to gravitate toward him, but I fight it with every damn thing I have, taking two small steps back.

"Kage," Archer sighs.

"Archer, this is not the time nor the place to pick up riffraff. It's our *world* that needs saving. Not your dick," Prince Kage says, loud enough for those standing around us to hear.

My face heats with the obvious insult, and I ignore the stares of the surrounding men.

Who the hell does he think he is calling me riffraff? Arrogant bastard. I don't give a shit if he is the prince of the universe. He doesn't even know me but has treated me with contempt since we met. He's an asshole. A gorgeous asshole, but an asshole, nonetheless. And fuck him.

Prince Kage's eyes snap back to mine, a wicked grin rising on his lips. There is a look in his eyes, a knowing. And then it hits me. *Can he read my thoughts?* This place is not like Earth. The people here have magic that I know little about. I'll have to talk to Remington, because if any of them can read my thoughts, that's a goddamn invasion of my privacy.

Gold-rimmed, obsidian eyes behind long dark lashes are still pinned on me, burning, suffocating, looking a lot like he *did* just read my mind. He sneers at me before he all but pushes Prince Archer away. The prince of wind glances back. Those turquoise eyes wink at me before walking over to the round table and taking a seat.

Cyrus enters the room next, along with three men dressed in finery with crowns atop their heads. With their arrival, everyone quiets and takes their seats. Cyrus's gray eyes scan the room, spotting me. He gives me a bright smile and raises his hand. I smile and wave back at him, then notice that all eyes in the room have shifted to me.

Wallflower. Be a damn wallflower.

Dropping my head, I aim my eyes to the ground, knowing I shouldn't have come. Staying back would have been fine. I couldn't care less if I'd met any of the princes.

I lean over to Remington. "Should I wait outside?"

"No," Remington says, taking my wrist, leading me around the room to a far wall where he has a total view of the Prince of Terr and his surroundings. A personal guard thing, I'm sure. "You're new and beautiful," he whispers. His glimmering eyes heat my insides. "They're assessing you. Just ignore them, and they'll get over it as soon as the meeting starts."

New and beautiful. Two words that have never been used to describe me. I sink back, wishing, hoping that for the rest of this meeting, I could be a fly on the wall.

As I scan the men sitting at the table, it's obvious that every single prince is handsome in his own way. But the Prince of Terr stands out amongst them. He's in a class of his own. Too incredibly gorgeous for his own good.

Just as the thought enters my mind, gold-rimmed onyx eyes pin me down, a devilish grin curling on his lush lips.

Shit. I drop my gaze. *Clear your damned mind.*

Cyrus stands from his seat and begins speaking. "We are all deeply burdened by the disappearance of our rulers and have received confirmation that they are being held in Avka."

The room erupts with voices. Cyrus raises his hands, and they all quiet down. It's obvious he's an authority figure here, one that even the princes obey.

Cyrus speaks of their enemy, the Avkan prince named Adhan Merak. He's killed hundreds in calculated attacks throughout the five realms, targeting leadership and their armies. There is no doubt this is just the beginning of his invasion. The wicked ruler has clarified that his goal is to conquer Celestria. Taking out their rulers was one of his boldest and biggest moves.

I've only just arrived but can see how heavy and vital it is to save their rulers, the glue holding the kingdoms together.

"We should dispatch our armies and defeat them once and for all," a younger looking prince with red hair interjects.

Remington leans over to me and whispers, "That is Prince Drake Centauri from the Kingdom of Sol in the southern realm."

I nod.

"We can't send our armies and leave our lands unguarded," another prince interjects. "That's what the bastard wants. He wants to separate us and conquer." This prince looks older than the others, maybe in his early thirties, with silvery hair and storm gray eyes.

"Prince Kano Oberon of the Kingdom of Nahla. Central realm," Remington supplies.

I nod again, filing away the information.

Cyrus raises a hand, silencing the room. "We cannot afford to send our armies, especially without weighing the repercussions. This needs to be planned carefully. We currently have a few spies planted in Merak's guard. Spies that can help take a team to our rulers."

"A rescue mission? How?" Prince Archer questions. "They have devices that can detect Celestrian power. No one will get past them."

They continue talking, but I am interrupted by the voice in my head.

Elara, you can go. You can bring their rulers back.

Ummm. Hell no! I reply in my head. *You're mad to think I would even consider something like that.*

The enemy cannot detect you, Elara. They blocked your power.

Nope. Celestria is a planet filled with people, and I'm sure there is someone much more qualified than I am. I just got here and will NOT stick my neck out for people who left and forgot me.

I know you will do what is right. This is your calling. You are destined for greatness.

I huff, shaking my head in frustration. *You're crazy. I won't do it.*

You must.

"No!" I growl, fisting my hands at my sides, but quickly realize I said it out loud. The room falls silent, and all eyes are now on me. I freeze and slink back to the wall behind me. Heat of embarrassment burns my neck and face. They must think I've gone mad.

Remington nudges me from the side. "Are you okay?"

My wide eyes meet his and I nod, not able to answer.

"Elara, do you have a suggestion?" Cyrus asks.

"Who is she?" the silver-haired prince asks, his eyes narrowing on me.

Gods. This is not good. The fly on the wall has been seen.

"She is Elara, a Changeling we brought in this morning," Remington says, saving me again.

"Elara?" Cyrus asks.

There is a light in his eyes, and I don't like what I'm reading in them.

Against my own wishes, I straighten my posture and take a step forward. "I would like to help."

No, I don't. Not really. But everyone who matters in this world is here, looking at me.

"Help?" Prince Kage scoffs, his dark eyes meeting mine, sending a shiver down my spine. "How can you help? What can you do? You are—" his hand addresses me with an up and down motion, "fragile."

My chest heaves, my hands fist at my sides. "Don't you dare stereotype me because of my sex," I snap, glaring at him.

His nose flares and jaw feathers. The tension in the room is palpable, but I won't back down. I will allow no one to disrespect me here. They don't have the right.

"Whoever sent her to Earth bound her powers," Cyrus says, stepping in. Eyes widen on me, knowing this is not normal protocol for a Changeling. "Because of this, the Avkan devices cannot detect her." He gives me a slight nod and my eyes widen because this was supposed to be kept a secret. "I trust everyone in this room, Elara. Whatever is shared will not leave here."

"She is not as fragile as you think," Remington adds, stepping to my side. "While retrieving her, she broke my nose and nearly killed the Avkan who tried to kidnap her. And right before we came here, she took down one of my best guards because he challenged her." He looks at me and gives me a well-pleased smile. "She's had years of military training on Earth, and I can vouch that she knows her stuff. Right now, she's an asset. The best we have."

"She's new to Celestria. She has not proven her loyalty or character," Prince Kage growls.

"Time is of the essence, Prince Dargan," Cyrus sighs. "We don't have time to vet anyone else."

"I trust her," Remington says. I smile at him, hoping he can read how thankful I am for that trust.

"As do I," Cyrus adds with a glimmer in his eyes.

I keep my face calm, but my emotions are battering me from the inside out. Remington and Cyrus have outwardly expressed their faith and trust in me, along with the damn voice in my head. Why? I've done nothing to prove it.

Fate seems to have thrown this task in my lap. Maybe all the years of training *were* meant for this purpose. I've always wanted to go on a mission, and my trainer always said, '*go big or go home.*' Maybe this is my chance to prove my worth.

I suck in another deep breath and steady my trembling knees as best I can. "I honestly don't know if I'm the right person for the job, but I'd like to try."

Prince Archer gives me a wide smile. The rest nod, showing me a bit of respect. Except *him*—the Prince of Terr, who stares at me with contempt. He hates me for no good reason, and because of it, I hate him, too.

"It's settled then," Cyrus finally says. "We will need to prepare her."

TWELVE

ELARA

"Are you serious?" Prince Kage barks, slapping his hands against the table. "We're putting the fate of our world in the hands of a *Changeling*? You know what happened to the last one who served me. This mission will be *worthless*. How do we know she won't turn on us?"

I've had enough of his bullshit and take a step forward, straightening my back, my anger reaching the boiling point. Remington grabs my wrist, but I shake his grip off and standoff with the bastard, despite the shaking in my limbs.

"First, I have a goddamn name. It's Elara, not *Changeling*." I grit my teeth. "Second, I just arrived this morning, *against my will*. They took me from a dead sleep and brought me to a world that never knew I existed. A world that *left* me as an infant on a cruel planet and *forgot* about me. While you lived here in luxury, I was used and abused, fending for myself, learning to fight and survive.

"Now, I'm here, and your world is in the middle of a war, and *I* will risk *my worthless* life to help. I don't care who you are or what position you have. You don't know the first thing about me, and you have *no* fucking right to judge me."

Prince Kage stands and slams his fists on the table, his predatory glare slicing through me. "Do you know who I am?"

Crossing my arms over my chest, I give him a smirk. His eyes become molten with rage. "No, not really. I'm a newly gathered *Changeling*, remember?"

The entire room is dead silent, thick with whatever the hell is happening between us.

"I think I've just fallen in love," one prince speaks up, breaking the deafening silence. He's got ash brown hair, the greenest eyes, and the largest dimpled smile. "The tension rolling between you two is... *fuck*." He fans himself. "But if she can stand up to Kage Dargan like that, I say she's more than worthy of the job."

"Fuck you, Sebastian," Prince Kage growls, pinning those molten eyes on him.

Prince Sebastian tsks him, turning to meet his gaze. "If you're so worried that she is brainwashed, why don't you see for yourself? Your gift can take you inside her mind to find the truth. You can vet her right here. Right now."

I snap my attention to Remington, shaking my head, and whisper-shout at him. "No way. There is *no* goddamn way he is getting inside my head."

Remington gives me a sad smile and takes my hand. "If you want their trust and backing, I suggest you let him. It's your choice, spitfire, but it will prove to everyone you aren't brainwashed."

I shake my head. This is bullshit. He'll know. He'll see what happened to Cole.

It wasn't your fault. The voice in my head tries to reassure me, but I know the bastard will look for anything to turn against me.

Cyrus makes his way around the table until he stands in front of me. Taking both of my hands, his eyes fill with sincerity and warmth. "I know what you're afraid of, Elara. I saw *everything and* believe me when I say it means nothing. Whatever happened was *not* your fault."

I fight to hold back the tears swelling in my eyes, but I can't, and they fall. There is too much emotion raging inside me to hold it back. I haven't had time to process what happened that night, let alone allow myself to mourn Cole. I know he died because of me, and although I've been trying to block it out... the guilt, I carry so much guilt for it. I took a life. An innocent life and then disappeared with no repercussion. I believe in Karma. I believe it will come for me, and that one day, I will have to pay for that life.

"Elara, it's our fault," Cyrus breathes. "We failed you. We should have found you sooner and should have rescued you." There is no condemnation in his eyes, only kindness. "If you can agree to this, and put everyone's mind at ease, we are one step closer to saving our world."

I shake my head, hastily wiping the tears from my eyes as uncertainty churns in my gut. "Do you truly believe I am the best choice for this mission?"

He gives me a reassuring smile. "You won't be alone. There will be a small team going with you. Because of your training and the fact that your powers are bound, I strongly believe you are our best hope."

I nod, the reality of this entire meeting sinking in. The Avkans kidnapped their rulers, putting their entire world in danger of being taken over. And as fate has it, I am not here by chance. I am here, right now, at this meeting because fate wants me to play my part. A part I have agreed to and will play, although I'm not happy about the idea of prince asshole rummaging through my brain.

Cyrus turns and signals Prince Kage, who gets up and strides toward us. I hate myself for admiring his muscular frame and devastatingly handsome face. His eyes are lethal, intimidating, and somewhere in my sick mind, I find it all alluring.

The closer he gets, the heavier the air is between us. I breathe in the most heavenly scent. A scent I cannot describe. It's both appealing and seductive. It's woody with hints of citrus, leather, and spice.

He stops a foot away, and there is an unmistakable charge in the air that causes my knees to go weak.

Why? Why does he have such an effect on me?

His expression remains stoic as those onyx eyes penetrate mine. The energy between us is palpable and undeniable. He hides it well, but I notice the twitch in his jaw, the slight clench and unclenching of his hands at his sides, and the small furrow in his brow. He feels it too.

I force my eyes to break away from his hold and focus on Cyrus. Crossing my arms over my chest, I try to hide the shaking in my hands. "So, how does this work? He just gets a free ride in my mind?"

Cyrus gives me a sad smile, which is confirmation. "It will be like what happened between us," he says, which tells me Prince Asshole will have to touch me.

"This is not my first ride," Prince Kage says, and I turn to him to see a smirk on those full lips.

My eyes slide back to Cyrus. "Is this really necessary?"

"If you want to prove the enemy has not infiltrated your mind, then yes," Prince Kage adds, his voice cold as ice. "Unless you have something to hide?"

I turn to his infuriatingly beautiful face. "Cyrus already assessed me. He can vouch for me."

"He can, but this is our world and every life in it is at stake. We must ensure that you are not compromised, and I don't think anyone here will oppose a second opinion."

I glance around the room, and no one is rebutting him. They all want to know, to make sure I'm not a brainwashed mole.

I concede with a deep sigh, taking a step toward Prince Kage, holding up my hands, palms up, like I did with Cyrus.

A mischievous grin creeps on the edges of the prince's full lips as I watch his arms rise until his hands clasp the sides of my head. There is a snap of electricity between us, followed by a wave of energy that tears through my entire frame. My back involuntarily arches, mouth goes slack, and eyes snap wide. Prince Kage's hold tightens as his own eyes turn fully black, unreadable emotions twisting in his expression.

Instantly weakened, I grasp onto his wrists to keep me up.

"What the hell?" Remington calls out, his tone peppered with confusion.

But there is nothing I can do. I'm now at the prince's mercy.

The world goes silent as he encases us in darkness.

My life plays out before me like a video on a screen, showing bits and pieces of my memories. Memories that have stuck with me from the time I could remember. Memories that have not only haunted me, but have molded me into who I am.

In the first flash, I see a tiny room with a tattered bed. It's the room I spent most of my life in... alone. Torn mismatched curtains hang on the window. There is a small, sagging dresser, but only the top drawer contains clothes. Against the wall is a bookshelf, filled with thrifted books.

The scene shifts to a young girl's dirty, tear-stained face. She's lying on a lumpy, stained pillow, with a threadbare throw blanket that barely keeps her warm. Her eyes are filled with emotion as she stares out her window at the moon and stars while hugging a one-eyed raggedy doll.

The next scenes, in succession, seem like duplicates, but they aren't. The girl is growing, and the scenes are the same mundane life she's lived, day in and day out. Alone. A slave to seclusion.

My heart cracks as I watch the girl's hardened and vacant expression from years of isolation, and the verbal and physical abuse from the caregivers who were supposed to love and care for her. They treat her like she's invisible, with no regard for her heart that begs for any kind of love and affection.

Her caregivers supply her with thrifted books to keep her occupied, and those books become her escape, her haven. They've taught her many things and have taken her on wild adventures. Through them, she's made the most wonderful friends.

Next, she is in school, staying invisible until she sees another girl being bullied. As much as she wants to remain invisible, her heart won't allow her, so she confronts the bullies and sticks up for the girl. The next scenes show the hate, rejection, and segregation she received the following years because of her act. But her will is strong, and her heart is guarded.

The next set of memories shows the nights she sneaks out into the forest and slumps against a tree, hugging her knees to her chest. She's so young—middle school—and all alone, gazing up at the moon and stars. This is the only time she becomes vulnerable, releasing the weight of the burdens she's been carrying inside.

I feel her sobs reverberating through my chest as tears stream down her face. She's utterly broken inside, but she'll never let it show. She'll let no one see what she's been hiding. Before she leaves, she pieces herself together again and secures her mask back on.

Next, she is in high school, and the bullies are relentless. She keeps her head down and focuses on studying. Her face is hard, resolute, but I know this girl intimately. If you look close enough, you can see through the tiny cracks, see the hurt and pain hidden behind the mask she wears.

She's sitting in a cafeteria, eating by herself when she gets rotten milk dumped on her head. The room erupts with laughter, but she stands, fists at her sides, seething while her classmates point accusing fingers, calling her monster.

She stares at her reflection in a bathroom mirror. Visibly trembling, there is fear in those wide eyes that are glowing *bright gold*. I can see the questions brimming in those eyes. Is she a monster?

She's taking military training classes and immerses herself completely into learning. Her trainer pushes her above and beyond, seeing her potential. After years of dedication, it pays off. She excels, taking down men twice her size and using weapons with incredible accuracy.

She's graduating high school at the top of her class, and that is the first time I see a genuine smile on her face. A look of relief and triumph. She's made it, and not long after, leaves the shitty home she grew up in and seeks refuge in a large tree in the middle of a forest.

The next scene has my heart hammering against my chest.

I try to pull away from Prince Kage's hold, knowing what is coming, but he's too deep inside my mind and not letting go. The memory of Cole is still fresh, and like a knife to the gut, it shreds me to pieces. I fight to release his hold, but the asshole is making me relive that night, moment by horrifying moment.

I see Cole, alive. We're walking the streets, then at a bar where he's smiling at me.

Next, we are at his house, in his room, and on his bed. Cole is kissing me, his hands roaming my bare body. His eyes suddenly go wide, and then he convulses. I watch, helpless, as the veins in my arms illuminate gold.

I relive the absolute fear, confusion, and terror.

In seconds, Cole is gone.

Deep sobs tear from my chest, as I am haunted once again with those wide eyes, void of life.

I killed him. I know I did, but I don't know how.

Next, I'm curled up in my house tree in the middle of the forest when Remington and his men show up. The following scenes show everything. My fighting and running from them, the police scouring the forest, then our run in with the Avkan men. It reveals the red cloaked man dragging me toward a portal, but I fight him, putting him in a chokehold that will kill him, until Remington stops me.

We enter a portal and I'm in the holding cell. Next, it flashes to my assessment with Director Finn, Cyrus, and Remington. The scenes continue until Remington, and I arrive here.

Then it stops.

I gasp, my entire body and mind spent. My legs give and I fall forward, but powerful arms encompass me, keeping me on my feet. I'm immediately wrapped in that heavenly scent. I want to speak. I want to push out of his grasp, but I can't. My limbs are worthless, and I'm near the point of passing out.

I hear Prince Kage speak, his voice clipped and quiet. "Cyrus, she's—"

"She is," Cyrus replies, so only we can hear, "and she will need to be trained once we release her power."

"So, Kage, what did you see?" Prince Archer asks from behind him.

"Everything I needed to," he replies solemnly.

"Well, what's your assessment?"

"She's clean."

"Hey, what happened between you?" Remington whispers.

There is no response, none that I hear, my eyes still heavy and closed.

"What the fuck, Kage?" a harsh female voice snaps.

I am suddenly handed off into another set of arms. Remington. I know from his scent. Leather with hints of vanilla.

"Rem, she doesn't leave Celestria until she can put up an *impenetrable* mental shield. That's an order," Kage orders, urgency in his tone.

"Yes, my prince," he responds.

Forcing my eyes to open, I see a gorgeous woman, tall, curvy, with long blonde hair and ice-blue eyes heading our way. She clenches her jaw, eyes narrowed and molten. I can feel the burn from where we stand.

"Don't be jealous, Vera," Prince Archer chuckles behind us. "He was only assessing her for an upcoming mission."

She shoots a wicked glare at him.

"Come on, sis. Give my future brother-in-law at least half his balls."

Archer is her *brother*. I compartmentalize that information for later.

The beautiful woman stops in front of Prince Kage and her floral scent fills me. Long, slender arms cross over her more than ample chest. "Who is this?" Those molten eyes are on Kage, but a manicured finger lazily drops to me.

"I will not do this now, Vera. I told you I had a meeting."

"Meeting? If this is a meeting, why am I walking in and finding another woman in your arms?"

I can see his jaw tense. "You shouldn't be here. We'll talk afterward."

"*I* shouldn't be here? *I* am a *princess* and can be wherever the hell I choose. The question is... why is *she* here?" Her finger thrusts at me. "Who the hell is she?"

"She's a Changeling who needed to be vetted before we send her to Avka," Remington answers. She gives him a death stare, then steps forward to the prince with lust in her eyes.

"It's inappropriate to have another woman in your arms, fiancé," she purrs, running a finger along his lips. He grabs her wrist, stopping the movement.

"It's not what you think. We can discuss this later," he clips.

I turn my gaze to Remington. "Can we leave? Please?"

His eyes shift to Prince Kage, but I don't look. I'm spent and can't keep my eyes open any longer.

Remington shifts, and I'm soon cradled in his arms. Wrapping my arms around his neck, I sink my head onto his shoulder.

"Let's go, spitfire," he whispers in my ear, and then he moves, my body relaxing the further we get away from *him*.

Thirteen

ELARA

I rouse, my eyes heavy with sleep.

"You're finally awake," a familiar voice says from across the room.

Slowly pushing myself to a seated position, I realize we're back in my room in the training center.

I press a palm to my throbbing temple. "How—"

"Portal jumped," Remington interjects, appearing in front of me with a glass of water and a wide smile. "I was glad you were out." He pushed the glass into my hand. "Drink. You're still weak."

I take it and sigh. "Weak is an understatement. I feel like I've been slammed by a mac truck."

His brow crumples. "A what?"

"Never mind." I shake my head and gulp the water until the glass is empty, instantly making a face. "Ugh, this is bitter."

"They're herbs that will help you recover faster."

"You could have warned me." He shrugs, taking the glass back. "How long have I been out? Is it still my birthday?" I shoot him a toothy grin.

He takes a seat on the armchair across from me and pulls out the antique watch tucked in his pocket. "You've been out for a little over two hours, and yes, it is still your birthday. With all the madness, I forgot the city has a huge celebration tonight. A party I think you'll enjoy if you're up for it."

"What's the celebration for?"

He tilts his head. "Your birthday."

"Yeah, right." I give him a smirk and shake my head. "No one ever celebrates me or my birthday. What's it really for?"

I see a hint of sadness cross his eyes, but it's quickly gone. "It is a huge festival called Messis, which is a celebration of the harvest. Everyone gathers around huge bonfires and there is dancing and drinking, tons of food, and well... everyone wears masks."

He's piqued my interest. "Why masks?"

"It's believed that on this day, the gods become visible in our world and play tricks on people. The masks are a way, I suppose, of confusing the gods. But it is also a way for royalty to come down and mingle with the people without being recognized."

"It sounds a lot like Halloween we celebrate back on Earth."

"I suppose it is." His eyes narrow and I see questions in them.

"What?"

"What happened earlier when the prince touched you?"

I shake my head, thinking back to the moment.

Something happened. I'm just not aware of what it was. I cannot deny that electric buzz in the air that pricks at my skin whenever the prince is

118

nearby. But when he touched me... I felt a detonation that sent a shockwave between us—straight through us. It almost consumed me.

Still, everything in and about this world is new to me. I don't understand how their magic works, especially with mine strongly locked away.

"I don't know," I finally answer because I truly don't. "Wasn't everything that happened normal *protocol* for invading a mind?"

"No," he responds, his staid expression making my gut churn. "The prince *rarely* touches anyone. He doesn't have to with his gift."

His words have my hands fisting and heat coursing through my body. "You mean to tell me he could have seen into my mind without touching me?"

He nods.

"Son of a—"

"Something happened between you two." It's not a question. His eyes are distant, voice low and guarded.

"What do you think happened?" He seems to know, so I ask.

"I'm not sure," he replies.

I know he's hiding something. I can see it in his expression and in those dark eyes.

"Nothing happened," I add, sinking back into the couch. "The asshole scoured through my mind and had a front-row seat to everything that mattered in my entire existence, and there was no way of stopping him."

"I'm sorry if he invaded your privacy." His voice is quiet.

"Don't apologize on his behalf. He knew what he was doing."

"He's never—" He doesn't finish.

"He's never what?" I press.

"He's just been under a lot of pressure, and with his father gone..."

"I understand the pressure, but that doesn't give him the right to be an asshole."

"No, it doesn't. But he's a good man. He's loyal to his people."

"And what about the woman who barged into the meeting? Is she really his fiancé?"

His lip twitches. "She is, and as you can tell, she seethes with jealousy of anyone who comes near him or garners his attention." Remington sighs and shakes his head. "Vera is beautiful, but she's not someone you want to share an entire lifetime with. I pity him because I know he only tolerates her."

I shake my head, confused. "Why are they engaged if he has to tolerate her?"

"She is a Princess of the Kingdom of Asteri of the western realm, and it is an arranged marriage. One to help strengthen Terr."

"You're kidding, right?" I scoff. "They arrange marriages here?"

"It's not typical. They set this one up almost two years ago."

"They shouldn't force people into marrying someone they don't love. It's barbaric."

"I agree with you," he says, sitting back in his chair, crossing one leg over the other. I can't help but admire him and the muscles that stretch his uniform. "At birth, the prince was promised to another, but the child and her mother were murdered while she was still in the womb. I remember that day, even though I was just a child. Everyone in Celestria was mourning, and I didn't understand why. It was a dark time for our world, and it seemed as if everyone attended the funeral."

"She must have been important."

He nods. "She was the Celestrian Empress—the ruler of our world."

"I don't understand. Aren't there rulers in every realm?"

"Yes, but the Empress governed over them all. She kept every ruler in line, making sure they didn't use their powers arbitrarily, and against the good and will of their people. She was the most powerful being in all Celestria and was loved and revered by everyone in it."

"And now?"

"Since her death, there is no one, past or present, worthy of taking her place. Her only heir died with her, and they were buried together in a mausoleum near the Central Court. It's a beautiful place, surrounded by an enchanted garden that blooms year-round and is protected by magic."

"She was that powerful?"

"She was, but she never displayed her full power. My father said she could draw and command all power within Celestria—terra, air, fire, water, and ether. She was an unmatched force, but never abused her power. She only used it for the betterment of the people. There was none that rivaled her and none who witnessed the full extent of her gifts."

"What about her husband?"

"She never married, and no one knows who the child's father was."

The plot thickens.

"Do they know who killed her?"

He shakes his head. "It is said that a very dark and forbidden magic was used to cover all tracks of the person or people who murdered her and her child."

"So, the murderers are still walking around?"

He nods, a glint in his eyes. "You are mighty inquisitive, spitfire."

"I need to be. I want to know everything I can about this place, especially if I'm going to help save it." I give him a smirk. "So, is the evil Avkan prince the head suspect? It's obvious he had a motive for killing her."

"No," he says with a straight face. "Prince Adhan Merak is an imbecile, using our misfortune to his advantage. Our head analysts suspect the murderer was someone close to the Empress. Someone she knew and trusted, because there was no sign of a struggle and there was no magic used. They found a powerful drug in her blood that causes neuromuscular paralysis, which led them to believe the Empress was conscious but incapacitated. She was helpless to do anything to save her and her child while she was being murdered."

"Gods." The image he painted made me sick inside.

He shakes his head, his eyes sad. "They ruthlessly stabbed her repeatedly in the chest and stomach. My father was there when they cut the child from her belly in hopes she would still be alive or there was some way to resuscitate her. But she was dead—also stabbed multiple times. She didn't stand a chance. My father came home and said to never ask him about what he saw. He was sick that night and the day after."

"How did you find out... if your father never wanted to talk about it?"

"Kage told me. *Prince* Kage," he corrects with a smirk. "He was sneaking around the palace when he overheard his father and mine discussing the murder. He didn't tell me until years later, though."

I let out a deep sigh. It's a tragic tale, one that is now costing them their world.

"So, how long did the Empress rule?"

"Nearly five hundred years."

My eyes bulge as I swallow hard. "She was five hundred years old when she was pregnant?" I squeak. My mind is about to burst just thinking about it.

His snarky grin is back. "Actually, she was closer to six hundred."

My slack jaw and wide eyes have him throwing his head back with laughter. "Celestria differs vastly from the world you lived in. We are immortal. *You* are immortal, Elara. You now have a long, long life ahead of you."

I love the sound of my *real* name coming from his lips, but I keep that to myself. "I hope you're right. I hope it's different from the life I lived on Earth, and that's *if* I survive the upcoming mission."

"They will select a team and give you a full briefing on everything you need to know. You will undergo strict training—the ins and outs of the entire mission—before you leave. Should the mission fail, and the team cannot reach our rulers, they will promptly transport you back. We won't put more lives in danger."

"How long before they leave?"

"Five days, and the training starts tomorrow."

My heart is hammering in my chest. I'm going in blind and putting my trust in a team I know nothing about, and that's terrifying.

"Let's not think about the mission right now," he says, breaking my growing anxiety. "Tonight, we'll drink and dance and celebrate your life."

I give him a wide smile. "That sounds good, *but...*" I swipe a hand down my frame, "I have nothing to wear."

His eyes narrow like he's deep in thought before he slaps his hands together. "I have someone who can help. She owes me a favor."

"Are you *dating* this someone?" I say carefully.

His brows rise and dimples deepen. "Are you jealous, spitfire?"

I shake my head. "Just curious."

He lets out another laugh. "No, I am not dating anyone, and she is my cousin, who owns more gowns than the shops who sell them. And for your information, my job won't allow me to settle. Not while I'm in service. It's the price I must pay for being the prince's head guard."

My insides twist at his confession. I've been friend-listed.

He is like one of those gorgeous guys you fall for that have the greatest personality, only to find your heart crushed because they will *never* love you. Never, because they love another man. Untouchables is what I call them. Forbidden candy that you crave but can never indulge in.

Against my better judgment, my unfiltered, unruly mouth opens. "You aren't a priest. They can't forbid you from *playing*, right?"

He pauses, then I see a hint of a smile as he realizes what I'm saying. "No, spitfire, they cannot forbid me any pleasures." His grin turns devilish, and I instantly feel warmth flush my face and spread to my core. "You are full of questions today."

"Like I said... just curious." He does not know how many questions I have, and right now, knowledge is my power. "What about your father? He obviously settled and had you."

"He did, after serving the king for two hundred and fifty years. That is the term of being a personal guard to a royal."

I can't help but gape at him. The lifespan of a Celestrian is doing a number on my mind. "How long have you served?"

"Three years."

"Holy shit. That means you have—"

"Two hundred and forty-seven years left."

I let out a loud, exasperated breath. "I never thought I'd make it to fifty, and here you all are living multiple lifetimes."

"You'll get used to it."

I roll my eyes. "Doubt it."

He lets out another boisterous laugh.

"What?"

The smile on his face doesn't fade. "I haven't met anyone like you."

"I'm probably the furthest thing from a cultured Celestrian woman you can get."

"They are boring. Never change, spitfire." The look he gives me makes my insides melt, and for the first time, true happiness coats my bones. I don't know what the future holds, but I know I want more, *crave more*, of that feeling.

Remington is handsome, and a gentleman, despite being a personal guard and captain of the army. Everyone respects him. That much I've pieced together in the brief time we'd been together, and I know any woman would be lucky to have a man like him.

Through the years, I've been a people watcher, and can read most like a book. Call it a sixth sense, but I sense Remington is one of the good ones. However, for the next few hundred years, he is a slave to the system. I'm happy to be his friend, but secretly hope that, just maybe, in the future, our friendship could mature into a friends-with-benefits relationship. I wouldn't be against that.

An honest smile upturns my lips.

"I don't plan on it."

FOURTEEN

ELARA

I thank Remington as he leaves with his promise to contact his cousin.
I've never been excited to meet anyone, but because she is his cousin,
I'm elated to meet her.

Pacing my new living space, I'm nervous. My belly is fluttering with
the thrill of attending a festival in the city, getting dressed up, wearing
a mask, and experiencing all of it with the dashing captain. It's hours
away, so I must bide my time.

Whatever was in the drink he offered me was magic. I no longer feel
like my body is boneless... exhausted and aching.

With nothing better to do, and the lingering tenseness in my muscles,
I decide to take a shower. Stepping into the bathroom, I look into the
large mirror above the sink, and holy mother of God, for the first time,
I notice how different I look.

The girl who lived on Earth was lackluster. Despite the years of
training, she still appeared malnourished, her skin pale, hair dull, and
she had dark circles embedded under her eyes.

Leaning toward the mirror, I run my fingers across my skin which seems to glow. The dark circles have almost completely vanished, and even my hair seems shinier. I'm the same girl, but this place *is* magical. I've felt a little different ever since I arrived. Maybe because I'm finally where I belong. I'm home and transforming into my true self.

Whoever left me on Earth denied me of a life here for nineteen years. The life they thought wasn't good enough for me would have been far superior to what I experienced. Anything would have been better. I was dying on Earth, and now that I'm back where I belong, the stain of that slow and painful death is fading. This is *my* world, and I know I can create a new and wonderful life here.

The heated spray of the shower cascading over my head and down my shoulders feels amazing and I can feel the tension melting away.

Somehow, I lose track of time and jolt when I hear a knock at the door.

"Shit, shit, shit." It must be Remington's cousin.

Another knock has me jumping out of the shower, wrapping a towel around my naked, soaked body, and tiptoe dashing through the living room.

The next knock has me yelling, "I'm here!" while I throw the door open.

A beautiful girl, around my age, with chin-length chestnut brown hair and light-brown eyes, gives me a once over before her lips curl into a wide, blinding smile. Tossed over one shoulder are a bunch of dresses, and over her other is a duffle.

"Elara?" she asks. I nod. "I'm Rem's cousin, Maeve."

She shoves a hand toward me, and I shake it. My hair and body are dripping wet, leaving a puddle at my feet. My brain finally catches up as I move back and open the door wider.

"I'm sorry. I was taking a shower and lost track of time. Please come inside and watch out for the puddle."

Maeve laughs and hops over it like a pro before heading toward the couch. I was about to close the door when I hear someone clear their throat. Glancing up, I see Remington leaning against his door, arms crossed. His heated gaze rakes over me from head to toe.

Embarrassment floods my face with heat, and I clutch the towel around me like it's a lifeline. "I—I." I don't even know what to tell him. I know I look like a drowning dog, my long black hair is plastered to the sides of my face and shoulders, and there is definitely a second puddle under my feet.

I grab hold of the door as words tumble from my lips. "Well, now you can say you've seen the worst of me."

Those dark eyes find mine. "Gods, spitfire. If this is your worst, I'm afraid to see what you look like at your best."

I roll my eyes, which makes him laugh. If this is flirting, I don't know how to respond.

"Rem, ease off and let the poor girl go dry off. We'll see you in a few hours," Maeve hollers while emptying the contents of her bag. She turns and twiddles her fingers at him. "Bye."

"I guess I'll see you later," I say, my face and neck burning.

"I can't wait," he says, before sliding into his room.

Closing the door, I make a beeline for the bathroom. "I'm sorry, Maeve. It's nice to meet you, but I would have preferred it with clothes on."

"Me too," she giggles, "but my cousin didn't seem to mind."

Gods. "I—I'll be out soon," I stammer, closing the door behind me.

"Take your time," she hollers.

With clothes finally on and hair towel dried and brushed, I finally step out of the bathroom.

"There she is." Maeve stands and heads toward me. She wraps me in a hug when I was about to hold out a hand.

I'm not a hugger. As a child, I was never hugged. People never just walk up to me and wrap their arms around me. It's uncomfortable, but me standing as stiff as a board is making the situation completely awkward.

Winging it, I place my hands on her back and tap, tap, tap.

Satisfied with my attempt, she steps back. "You are just as beautiful as Rem said you were."

I swallow hard, my eyes widening. "He told you I was beautiful?"

"Of course. His exact words were," she clears her throat and deepens her voice, "I'm calling in a favor, Maeve, so grab some gowns and masks and whatever the hell else you need and come with me...now. There is a beautiful damsel who needs your help." She leans in. "He never mentions girls to me and never calls them beautiful, so I had to come and see for myself. Even soaking wet with a towel wrapped around you, you are still dazzling."

I laugh so hard that I snort. "I'm nothing special but thank you for coming. I'm sorry he put you in a position. I would have been just fine wearing the uniform."

Her face twists. "Gods no. This festival comes once a year, and no woman should ever be caught wearing a guard's uniform." She grabs my wrist and tugs me to the couch. "Rem also might have mentioned it's your birthday... and that you're a Changeling. That's so freaking awesome. And by the way—Happy Birthday! Pick a dress and a mask. They're on me."

"Really?" I ask and she nods. "Thank you," I breathe. No one has ever given me a present on my birthday, so I don't know what to think.

Gods, what else did he tell her?

Maeve watches me carefully as I eye the five gowns laid out on the couch. There is gold, one in forest green, navy blue, red... but I choose a gorgeous fitted black dress. It's floor length, backless, and there is also a little V in the front.

"Great choice," Maeve says with a clap of her hands. "Now choose a mask."

There is one that stands out and I immediately pick it up. It's black and outlined in gold and cut in a way that looks elegant, with swirls that look like feathers. "Another great choice," she says with a smile in her voice. "It's called the phoenix."

She heads over to the table where she's set out an abundance of makeup and pats the chair. "Have a seat."

For the next hour, I sit while Maeve works her magic, talking non-stop about her life. I found out that I'm a year older than her and she has a younger brother named Henley. Both of her parents work at the Central Court, where they met and fell madly in love. Her father is from the eastern realm, the Kingdom of Doone. Her mother is from Terr and is the sister of Remington's mother. They live in Terr but take yearly vacations in Doone. I also found out Remington is an only child and was hand-chosen to take care of Prince Kage because his father was the king's personal guard. He practically grew up in the palace, where he and the prince became best friends.

At twenty, he entered the palace as the prince's full-time guard. They gave him the title of captain a year later, and he assumed a leadership role in Terr's army. So, Remington is not hundreds of years old, like I suspected. He's twenty-three, and the prince is twenty-five.

As it seems, there is no biological time clock ticking for Celestrial women. They can have children whenever they want. One hundred, sure. Five hundred, you're in your prime. A thousand, I'd say that's pushing it, but *you go, girl*! Just do you.

That's one privilege of being immortal.

Maeve stands back and studies my face, then leans over and dabs a few spots.

"Done," she says, stepping back, her face beaming. She touches my hair, which she did in between the makeup. "This is my best work yet. You are *gorgeous*, Elara."

I give her a sincere smile because she deserves it. "Can I look?"

"Of course, you can," she says, pulling me to my feet. "And while you're in there, put on the dress. I want to see you all put together."

I head to the couch and retrieve the dress before heading into the bathroom. Maeve has become one of my favorite people. The girl can talk a mile a minute, but she's the closest thing I've ever had to a friend. No one has ever extended kindness to me like she did. Of course, it was Remington's idea, but she didn't have to come, and she made me feel like I was already part of her world. Like I belonged.

Avoiding the mirror, I strip out of my uniform, slip on the dress, and zip up the back that falls right above my tailbone. It's risqué, showing more skin than I'm used to, but it fits like a glove. And tonight, I don't care. It's my birthday and I feel like celebrating my new life. The new me. I take a breath and finally turn to the mirror... and gasp.

The girl in the reflection is radiant. Her skin is flawless, makeup perfect, hazel eyes glittering behind long lashes. Her dark hair has a silky shine to it, and... she's beautiful. I never thought I could look *beautiful*.

I take a slow spin and can't believe the transformation. Maeve is a makeup goddess. Everything is perfect, from the foundation to the long lashes, the smoky eye, rosy cheeks, and last, the full red lips. My hair is straight, but she curled the edges, which fall halfway down my back. The V cut makes my breasts look amazing. It's classy, not trampy.

"Elara, come out. I want to see!" Maeve bellows.

My emotions are bubbling inside, and I fight them. I never went to prom or to any parties. Tonight, is the first of many things I haven't done. It's the first time I've ever *really* dressed up, my first time wearing heels, first time I've worn real makeup, and the first time I'll be going to a festival, eating, drinking, and celebrating with a handsome guy I feel comfortable with.

I'm so excited but refuse to let my emotions ruin my makeup. Maeve will never forgive me.

Opening the door, I step out and watch Maeve's hands fly to her mouth.

"Gods above. You look like a dream."

I give her a spin.

"Elara, if I loved women, I would snatch you up and lock you away."

I let out a loud laugh. "I don't think there is any greater compliment. Thank you, Maeve."

She heads over to me and wraps me in another one of her hugs. I take it that's her love language, so I wrap my arms around her and squeeze. She pulls away, her face lit up with a bright smile.

"Now that was a hug," she says. "The first one you gave me was pretty pathetic."

I love her directness. It's refreshing, and it makes me feel like I've known her for a lifetime.

"I have to go get ready," she sighs. "The festival starts in an hour."

"Oh, no! I'm sorry I've kept you. Why don't you get ready here? I won't be much help, but you're welcome to use anything."

She shakes her head. "Thanks, but my dress is at home, and I can put myself together in no time."

She picks up the mask and places it in my hand. "Have Rem tie it on for you before you leave. I wish I was here to see the look on his face when he sees you. I'll bring a bunch of napkins to the festival."

"Napkins?"

"To wipe the drool from his mouth."

We both laugh before she gathers her things and heads for the door. "Don't let Rem see you yet. Let him suffer a bit." She gives me a wink. "See you at the festival. I'll be wearing a red dress with a matching red mask."

"I can't wait."

She gives me another wide smile. "Lock the door behind me."

I follow behind her and do just that. Pressing my ear to the door, I listen as she knocks on Remington's door. He opens it immediately and then I hear muffled voices before...

"Do you have a burial plot picked out, Rem?"

"Why?"

"Because you are going to DIE when you see her."

Remington laughs, and the sound is just as beautiful as he is.

"Thanks, Maeve. I owe you one," he says before the voices disappear.

They must have portal jumped.

A knock at the door has every butterfly in my belly flitting around. It has to be Remington.

A quick re-check and spin in the bathroom mirror tells me I'm ready, so I grab my mask and open the door, only to have my breath stolen from me.

Remington is standing there, looking like a dream. He's wearing his black uniform, which hugs every muscle on his tall frame. His hair is slicked back, and he is wearing a black mask that covers the right side of his face. It screams Phantom of the Opera, which is one of my favorite movies, but it's the look in his eyes that has me melting.

He shakes his head while biting his lip. "Fuck, spitfire. You are breathtaking."

Heat rushes to my face and straight to my core. No one has ever cursed a compliment at me, but I take it as a win. A big one.

"You look... dashing," I say, but he knows I'm downplaying. I'm equally good at giving compliments as I am taking them. He saw the same look in my eyes, and it's confirmed with his broad, dimpled smile.

"Can you help me put this on?" I ask, holding out the mask.

"It would be my pleasure." He takes it as I turn around, showing him my bare back. Twisting my head slightly, I catch his eyes delving, and from the looks of it, he likes what he sees.

He hands me the mask while holding onto the ribbon, and I hold it in place as he gently ties it behind my head.

"All done," he says, and I feel the brush of his fingers on my shoulders as he turns me around. He gives me another dashing smile before offering me his arm. "Shall we?"

"We shall." I take his arm and breathe in his wonderful scent of leather and spice.

"Stay close to me tonight, spitfire. I have a feeling your night in the city is going to be unforgettable." He then summons a portal in front of us and I groan.

Gods, I hate portal jumping.

Fifteen

ELARA

Our portal lands us in front of a couple. The man casually dips his head and says, "Happy Messis," like we didn't just appear right in front of him.

"Happy Messis," Remington replies.

Sucking in a heavy breath, my knees buckle, but Remington grasps my arms and steadies me on my feet. The nausea isn't nearly as bad as it was before, and after a few deep breaths, the feeling is fading. Maybe it's the wonderful scents of the blooms surrounding us.

I still find it odd that portal jumping is a common means of travel here in Terr, but it's a fantastic way to get somewhere quick.

"How do you all not portal jump right into each other?" I ask.

"Our portals open where no one else is. It's magic I guess. It just knows." He shrugs and grins. "Wait here for a second."

Remington heads to the front of the shop where a woman greets him by name.

The shop smells of wonderful, like sweet florals and has the most beautiful arrangements on display. Flowers I've never seen before in stunning, vibrant colors.

Remington and the shop lady are quiet with their exchange before he heads back to me with a box in his hand. Then, he holds it out to me.

"What's this?" I ask, tilting my head.

"Just a little something for your birthday."

My brow crumples as I take the box and open it. Inside is the most beautiful wrist corsage. It's the first time I've seen flowers like these. They are small and delicate, black with a shimmering, gold center. He carefully takes the corsage from the box and slips it onto my wrist.

"You are now set for the evening."

"It's beautiful," I breathe. "What kind of flowers are they?"

"They are called starlight asters. They only grow in Terr and represent good luck and great fortune. I thought you might need some of that while you're here."

I hold my wrist out in front of me and admire the shimmering flowers. "Thank you. I love it."

"I'm glad." His grin blooms as he offers me his arm. "How about we get the hell out of here and find you something to eat?"

I can't help but smile. It's been too long since I felt like someone truly cared for me, and I wonder if maybe, just maybe, Remington is someone I could share my damaged heart with.

"That sounds wonderful."

Crowds fill the cobbled streets of the city. It has an old town feel, and I love that. Everyone is wearing masks and are dressed finely for the Messis celebration. Gowns, dresses, suits, some elegant, some simple, but it doesn't matter. The mood is lively.

Thousands of twinkle lights are draped through the streets, and down a ways, we watch them light a huge bon fire in the center. Cheers immediately erupt, and people dance and twirl around it. My chest feels light, watching them celebrate without care.

As we make our way down the street, masked people passing us dip their heads and say, "Happy Messis." We've walked twenty yards and I've said the damn words about fifty times.

"So all of this is to celebrate the harvest?" I ask Remington.

"Yes, that and the abundance of Terr. Our royals want to show their appreciation to the people, so on this night, everything is free."

No wonder everyone is in a good mood.

At the end of the street, there are lines of people facing a large cul-de-sac where vendors are serving food and drinks. The wonderful aromas of spices and meats make my mouth water.

Remington leans in and whispers, "Whatever you do, drink anything that is bubbly and sparkles."

I tilt my head toward him. "Why?"

"For a newcomer, Celestrian wine will knock you on your ass."

Hmmm. I glance at the colorful, bubbly and sparkly drinks in the hands of a cluster of girls, laughing and twirling ahead of us. The women have huge smiles on their masked faces and are dancing like they don't have a care in the world. That makes me want to drink one, just for the hell of it.

"Rem!" a woman hollers, recognizing him even with his mask on. She's tall and thin, with long raven hair and huge boobs that look like they're straining to stay in her tight golden dress. I see the same fetid lust in her large blue eyes as Aurora—the desk girl at the assessment—did. My insides cringe as she sashays toward us. The other masked girls are right on her heels.

She's gorgeous. They're all gorgeous. Everyone in Celestria has an unearthly beauty, and I guess that's the difference between Celestria and Earth.

Remington exhales loudly, then turns to me, and I see silent desperation in his eyes as he leans down and whispers in my ear. "Spitfire, I'll get you anything your heart desires tonight *if* you keep her away from me."

Her? He must be referring to the raven-haired girl.

I raise my brows. "I thought everything tonight was free?"

He lets out an exasperated breath. "Okay, I'll treat next time."

The poor guy looks desperate. "*Who* is she?"

"An acquaintance," he says easily.

I narrow my eyes. "Ex-lover?"

"No. Yes. But it was only once, and she's been obsessed with me ever since. Help. I beg of you."

I laugh at the fact that he is begging, his eyes wide and pleading.

"Fine," I say, "but how many more of your ex's will I be fending off tonight?"

A smirk curls on the corners of his full lips. "Hopefully, none."

I groan as the busty, raven-haired girl makes it to us, a little wobbly in her heels.

"Rem, I knew it was you," she slurs, running a finger down the unmasked side of his cheek. "My, you look handsome and positively edible." Her screechy voice makes my skin crawl.

I clear my throat and her annoyed, dark eyes shift to me, aggravatingly sweeping me over from head to toe before shifting back to Remington. She's ignoring me, and obviously doesn't care that I'm here.

"Come dance with us, Rem," she begs, tugging his arm, leaning forward so her boobs are practically bouncing right under his chin. "We'll make sure you're well taken care of. Even better than last year's Messis." Her tongue sweeps across her bright red lips, and it makes me want to gag.

Grabbing Remington's wrist, I step to his side. "I'm sorry. The captain is with me tonight."

Her attention shifts down to my hand grasping his, and her lip curls into a festering sneer. Evil eyes snap to Remington. "Did you give that to her?"

She must be referring to the wrist corsage.

"I did," he says.

I watch her blue eyes dilate, becoming darker, chest heavily rising and falling.

The ladies behind her are murmuring. Their brutal glares attempting to batter me, but I'm used to this and casually brush it off.

She glances at the girls behind her, but her finger is pointing to me. "Who is this bitch?"

I take a step forward because I won't let anyone step on me again. I have been ridiculed and beaten all my life for just existing. Not anymore. I'm not weak. I'm not a punching bag. Especially tonight, on my goddamn birthday.

I take another step forward, inches from the woman, and notice a small crowd has gathered around us.

Clearing my throat, I point to myself. "Excuse me. Are you talking about me?" She turns with venom dripping in her stare. "If you are, this *bitch* is Remington's date for the evening, so you can twirl your bitch ass self away and find some other needy soul to entice." I back away, yanking Remington's hand, and he follows me from the seething woman, whose eyes are now wide and mouth agape.

Gasps and whispers erupt around us, and I hear her say, "Find out who she is. That bitch doesn't know what's coming to her."

Mean girls. Been there, done that, and tonight, I don't give a shit about any of them.

I hear quick footsteps behind us, clattering on the cobbled street before a hand grasps my free one. I abruptly turn to find Maeve standing next to me, and she is stunning. Her dress is a shimmering, dark red and fitted on her lithe body. Her silky, chestnut hair is delicately curled under her chin, and the red mask and red lips make her look like a runway model.

"Girl, the celebration is just starting, and you are already my favorite person here," Maeve states. "Pissing off Zarah in front of a crowd will be a treasured Messis memory of mine for all time. You know she's the Chancellor's daughter, right?"

I freeze in place, my heart stopping as I gawk at her. "Chancellor's daughter?"

She nods, excitement riddling her radiant face.

"What is a Chancellor?"

Maeve laughs and waves her hand in the air. "They're like the heads of the government."

"Gods, my royal enemy list is growing by the hour. First Princess Vera, and now her?"

Maeve lets out a boisterous laugh. "Holy shit! You pissed off the princess too? I don't know if I should stay the hell away from you or become your best friend."

I glance at her and grin. "I'm not against either."

"Best friends, it is," she replies, squeezing my arm. "I hope you know I will need every scandalous detail. And for the record, I utterly despise Zarah and her whorettes."

I raise my brow at her and laugh. "For the record, nothing scandalous happened. And... Whorettes?"

Laughter bursts from her again.

"I owe you one, spitfire," Remington finally says beside me, his fingers now laced in mine. "You saved me tonight and I will repay that brave act with whatever your heart desires in the coming week. Food, drink... it's all on me."

Maeve leans past me. "Doesn't she look like a goddess, Rem?"

His smiling eyes sweep over me from head to toe, making the butterflies take flight in my belly. "She does."

"Captain." A man in a uniform, with a black mask covering his entire face, steps in front of us, fisting a hand on his chest. "Can I have a word?"

Remington immediately releases my hand and dips his head, then leans over to us.

"Stay with Maeve. I'll be right back." I nod, watching him walk away with the guard.

Maeve elbows me in the side. "You will make a lot of women jealous tonight. Not only because you're gorgeous and stand out in the crowd, but because you're with my cousin." She glances down at the wrist corsage. "It looks like he's already staked his claim."

I raise my wrist and twist it. "Staked his claim?" I shake my head. "No, he said this was a gift for my birthday. A sign of luck and good fortune."

Maeve laughs at me and shakes her head. "During Messis, when a guy gives a girl a wristlet, he's saying she's taken for the night." She looks at my face and probably sees confusion. "You see that couple over there?" She points to a guy and girl standing in front of another flower shop, facing each other. The girl is squealing with happiness, her face is beaming like the sun as he slips a similar band of flowers, in pinks and purples, on her wrist. She throws her arms around his neck, and he hugs her back. "See, he's claimed her for the celebration by placing the wristlet on her."

I glance down at my wristlet and my heart constricts. Has Remington really claimed me for the evening? Why didn't he tell me? Why did he say it was a gift? I'm not sure what he meant by it or how it makes me feel.

I know Maeve's words are true because the Chancellor's daughter was pretty pissed when she saw it.

Remington returns from the crowded street and stands beside me. I raise my flowered wrist in front of him and he tilts his head in curiosity.

"What did you truly mean by giving me this?" I ask.

He lets out a slow breath. "Did Maeve tell you?"

I nod while Maeve stays silent beside me.

Remington clears his throat. "It was a gift, spitfire. I presented you with a flower wristlet during Messis to show that you are taken, but with good intentions."

"Which are?" Maeve pushes, brows raised.

Remington gives her a pointed look before his eyes shift back to mine. "I did it, spitfire, so riffraff won't bother you tonight. It's your birthday, and I know you'll draw unwanted attention. Believe me. I gave this to you as a gift."

"That's it? Nothing more?"

He holds up his hands. "No strings attached. Unless you want strings?"

Nope. No strings are fine with me. "What I want is a drink."

"Hell, yes," Maeve chimes in. "Drinks for the birthday girl... and for me!" She grabs my arm and drags me toward the crowd of people lined up in the vendor's cul-de-sac.

Maeve stops at the back of a line that seems like it's the longest, at least a hundred people, and I gape at her. "It will take an hour to get a drink."

"Cousin," Maeve pleads to Remington with praying hands. "Our throats are dry, and lips parched. Please get us some Celestrian wine."

"Hell, no," he reprimands. "You are not letting her drink that shit. Remember, she's new here."

Maeve lets out a deep and pitiful sigh. "Fine. Two black lotuses will do then."

"That, I can do," he says. We watch him march past the line, right up to the table on the side of the vendor. The man taking the orders stops when he spots Remington and immediately takes his order, then prepares the drinks. I glance at the faces in the line, and no one looks angry.

"Everyone in Terr knows Rem. As captain and the prince's personal guard, he will always have priority, just like royalty," Maeve says, as if reading my mind.

In a few minutes, Remington is back with two long glasses filled with an ombre drink, graduating from purple to black.

"Two black lotuses," he says, handing them to us.

Uneasiness settles in my gut when I glance at the surrounding crowd and see that many of the eyes are watching us. Taking in a full breath, I focus on Remington.

"Where's your drink?" I question him.

"I can't drink tonight. I'm on duty."

"What?" I hiss. "The asshole won't give you the night off?"

Remington gives me a look of admonishment and shakes his head. "He'll be here tonight, and I am his personal guard. With the impending danger, we must always be on high alert."

"If it's so dangerous, why have the celebration?"

"Because we need to make our people feel safe. That despite what the enemy has done, nothing can bring down our spirits."

I nod because I agree with that reasoning.

"Happy Messis," Maeve says, raising her glass to me.

"Happy Messis," I return, clinking my glass against hers.

I take a long pull and, goddess above, the drink is sweet and tastes like the most exotic, delicious fruit I have ever tasted. I don't even taste alcohol in it, and if there is, I'm screwed because I am definitely having another.

Sixteen

ELARA

After three black lotuses, which is my new favorite drink, and one sip of Maeve's glass of Celestrian wine, I'm feeling tipsy and oddly happy. Glancing over, I can tell Maeve is too.

I need food, but she insisted on having our drinks first.

"I'm hungry," I plead to Remington. My stomach is grumbling, pissed that I've only filled it with alcohol.

"What do you want?"

"Something savory and extra yummy."

"I know just the thing!" Maeve chimes in, raising a finger in the air. Grabbing me by the wrist, she pushes her way through the steadily growing crowd, practically dragging me behind her. There are too many people. Too many jostling bodies, too many eyes and masked faces. With every step, I feel heated. The communal air is thick, causing sweat to bead on my forehead and drip down my back.

A large body slams into me, breaking Maeve's grip on my wrist. Thrown to the ground, I land hard on my ass, and it freaking hurts.

Stunned, I look up to see a muscular brute with a half buttoned-down shirt, exposing his broad chest. He has raven hair hanging just above his shoulders, and a full silvery mask. "Oops, sorry," he slurs, shoving a hand toward me, his other gripping a large sparkling, bubbly drink.

Before I can blink, Remington slaps his hand away and grabs my arms, helping me to my feet. "Are you okay?" he asks.

Heat of embarrassment crawls up my neck, burning my cheeks. I nod, but I know there is going to be a bruise where he hit me on my side and one on my ass.

Remington swings around to face the man. "If you can't handle your fucking drink, go home."

The man lowers his head, as if he is a child being punished. "Yes, Captain."

It's obvious they all know who he is.

I hear chuckles and turn to see the Chancellor's daughter standing a few yards away, arms crossed, and a wicked smile curving on her full lips before she and her groupies disappear into the abyss of bodies.

I know she had something to do with it, and I let out a sigh, knowing I'll have to watch my back for the rest of the evening.

Maeve finally pushes through the tangle of bodies, her wide eyes landing on me. "What the hell happened?"

"Nothing," I lie. "Some guy bumped into me."

Remington is still holding onto my arm, and with him next to me, the people give us a wide berth. I'm thankful for the slight relief.

"I need to get out of this crowd," I exhale.

He gives me a knowing nod, then pulls Maeve close.

"Get some food and meet us at the Evergreen," he tells her.

"Will do!" she chimes and disappears into the crowd.

Remington leads me back toward the still busy but less populated street. I don't know if it's the drink, or that I'm inebriated, but I feel dozens of heavy eyes pinned on us. On me.

"What's wrong, spitfire?" Remington's brow knots.

"I'll be fine. I just need to get some food in me."

He brings my arm to wrap around his, linking us at the elbows. "I'm sorry. Are you truly okay?"

He's asking about the fall.

"Yes," I say, letting out a breathy laugh. "I think it bruised my ego more than anything."

"I should have been a little more attentive." Glancing up, I see the sadness in his unmasked eye. "I know she doesn't seem the type, but Maeve can drink most guys under the table." He shakes his head. "I wasn't thinking."

"Don't worry about me. It's fine."

"No, it's not, and I shouldn't have involved you with Zarah. I'm sorry."

I glance around at all the people laughing, dancing, partying, and wish I could be as jovial. Tonight, I'm supposed to be celebrating. Supposed to be eating and drinking and having fun in this brand-new city.

"I would have run into her, eventually." It's obvious she has an unhealthy obsession with him, and befriending him, especially being female, I'm an automatic threat. The target on my forehead and back has grown larger, and I realize I can't drop my guard. I also need to figure out a way to stay out of more trouble and stop pissing the mean girls off, which happens to be a gift of mine.

"Almost there," Remington says, leading me up the street toward a small restaurant with big letters engraved on a wooden plaque on the front that says Evergreen.

"How long does this celebration last?" I ask.

"For me, once the prince leaves."

"Is he here? The prince?"

He nods, and knowing he's out there, knots my gut. "Aren't you supposed to be guarding him?"

He turns and tilts his head with a grin. "He is the most feared man in all Celestria, even over his father. No one can rival his power or his gifts. And if you're asking why he would need me as his personal guard... it's because I was born and trained to be at his side. The first king of Terr chose my ancestor to protect him, and from then on, each direct descendant has served the king. It helps that the prince and I grew up together and are best friends."

Best friends.

Ahead of us, jutting out from the roof, is a green canopy that has lights zigzagging across the bottom, casting the half dozen tables and chairs below it in a warm glow. All of them are occupied, but the restaurant is closed.

A single, dark-masked man, sitting on a chair at one table, stands as we arrive. "Captain, I was about to leave. This table is free," he says, bowing his head before scurrying off into the crowd.

Shooting Remington an incredulous look. He smirks and leads me over to the empty table, pulling out a chair for me.

"Thank you," I say, as he helps push it in after I'm seated, then walks over and takes the seat across from me. "You're well respected here. Everyone recognizes you, even half masked."

He shrugs. "They're all here tonight celebrating because I and the other soldiers in Terr afford them this safety. It's not free. Respect is earned here, it's not given, and everyone in Terr knows it."

The golden ambiance of the string of lights hanging above make the flecks of gold in his dark eyes seem to shimmer. Again, I don't know if it's the three drinks in my empty belly, but the way he's looking at me makes my stomach twist and my heart thump faster.

"Tell me something about your life, spitfire."

My eyes break away from his and drop to my twisting hands on my lap. "There isn't much to tell."

"Oh, I think there's a lot to tell."

Shaking my head, I cross my arms over my chest. "I'm sure your story is a lot more colorful than mine."

"I'll tell you anything you want, but you'll have to tell me something in return."

I nod my head. "Fine."

His smile widens as he leans forward on his elbows. "What do you want to know?"

"Who exactly is Zarah?" He groans and shakes his head. But she's clearly an enemy as long as I'm with him, so I want to know more about her.

"She's a pain in my ass, and like you already know, she's the Chancellor's daughter. Her father is from Terr, and mother from Asteri."

"Which is why she has blue eyes," I add, and he nods.

"We met in the palace when I was around sixteen. I was there to see the prince, and she had accompanied her father to speak to the king. From the moment I greeted them, she had a look in her eyes."

"Lust?"

He nods again. "At a palace celebration, we hooked up. I was shit drunk and made the mistake of having sex with her." His eyes close, his thumb and pointer finger pressing against the ridge of his nose. "Ever since, she won't leave me the hell alone. And she's threatened anyone I have an interest in."

"That's pretty pathetic."

"You have no idea. It's an unhealthy obsession, one I despise her for. She's a manipulative bitch who can do whatever she wants and gets away with it because her father is Chancellor of Terr and friends with the king."

"I'm sorry," I sigh. "I know her kind too well. Earth. Celestria. They're all the same."

He leans in. "Now, it's your turn to tell me something about your life."

Shaking my head, I let out a deep sigh. "There was nothing significant about my life. It was one of isolation, sadness, and pain. I don't like to look back or dwell on it because that's how I survived. I never looked back. When I was younger, there were countless mornings when I woke up and watched the sun rise over the horizon, casting its warmth into my dark and dismal room. I would plead with the universe, on my knees with palms and fingers pressed together, praying, wishing, begging that it would be a better day than the last. That's all I wanted. One good day and one good friend."

There's a stinging in my eyes, and the water gathering there betrays me, sending a tear to trail down my cheek, which I quickly swipe away.

"You never had a friend?" he asks, in a low, quiet voice.

I shake my head, eyes still aimed down at my hands. "I wanted a friend, desperately, but no one dared to come near me for fear they would become the next target of the bullies."

"They were that bad?"

He has no idea. No one knows, except me and... my predators.

"You can talk to me, spitfire. I'm your friend."

My friend. My eyes snap up to his, and I see nothing but sincerity and concern.

"You really want to know?"

He nods. "Unless it's something you don't want to talk about."

I shake my head. I've never really told anyone the details of my abuse. My classmates knew I was getting bullied, but they never knew the extent, because my abusers always did it out of sight. Usually in an empty bathroom where they'd lock the door.

"There were five of them," I exhale, my chest aching and stomach twisting.

Bringing back the memories I've tried hard to tamper down is like tearing off a fresh scab, reviving the original wound. But I continue.

"One girl, their leader, hated me because I stuck up for a poor girl they were bullying. From that day on, I became their target." I let out another exhale, feeling nauseous as the memories flood back. "On good days, they verbally abused me or dumped something on me. Sour milk, mustard, ketchup, hot drinks that blistered my skin." I don't dare look up at him. I don't want his pity.

"On bad days, they would drag me to the girl's bathroom and lock the door. On those days, they beat me until I had bruises all over my stomach, ribs, and back. Never anywhere visible. They made sure they did most of the damage under my clothes."

"Spitfire." I hear the pain in his voice, but I shake my head.

"They would hold me down and make me kiss their feet or stick my head in a toilet someone used. They stole my lunch daily, no matter where I hid it. Several times, they replaced my lunch with dog shit. The other students would do nothing, say nothing. Some would even laugh for fear they'd be the next victim.

"One day, they recruited a boy who dumped a bottle of liquid over my head right before school started. It was urine. I did my best to wash it out in the bathroom, then hid the rest of the day in a janitor's closet. Right before school ended, I snuck out and ran home, only to have my foster mom waiting for me with her beating stick in hand. The principal had called her and said I'd missed school. She beat me that day and sent me to my room without dinner. I tried to explain, many times, but they never listened. No one ever listened."

I look up, tears streaming down my face.

"You know how many times I contemplated suicide?" I didn't mean to say that out loud, but it's out. Telling him is like a release, unfettering a river of pain and emotion that's been dammed up inside me for too long. "Too many times," I breathe, my damaged heart splintering a bit more. "But a voice in my head kept telling me things would get better. To hold on, because although these trials were breaking me down, they were creating something stronger, something sharper, and building me up to be something greater."

Remington reaches across the table and wipes the tears from my cheek, and that slight gesture makes me flinch. I'm not used to kindness or gentle touches.

"I'm so sorry, spitfire," he says, with a pained look in his eyes. "What you went through is something no one should ever endure. I wish I could go back and right the wrongs, but I'm glad you survived. I'm glad I found you."

I give him a tight-lipped grin. "I am, too."

Suddenly, there is an explosion a street over. People are screaming, and some are cheering, probably thinking it's part of the celebration. But by the look on Remington's face, I know it's not.

A guard rushes toward him, chest huffing, and gives him a nod.

"Stay here," he says to me, already on his feet. "I'm going to check it out and will be right back. Wait for Maeve. She'll be here soon."

"Go. I'll be fine."

He nods, indecision in his eyes as he turns and runs down the street toward the explosion.

I can't believe I just dumped my pathetic life on him. And that's not all of it. I'd had years of abuse from my caregivers and bullies. But I feel lighter. The weight of some of those well-kept secrets floating away on the cool night breeze.

The sound of chairs scraping has me turning to see everyone seated at the Evergreen get up and move. I turn back toward the street to see a group of people moving toward us.

My skin pricks, and a coldness sweeps down my spine. Something is off.

Then I see her behind the group. The black hair, blue-eyed temptress, and I have a feeling they're coming for me. The explosion was probably a setup to separate me from Remington. Who the hell knows what they've done to keep Maeve from coming? It seems everyone on the street has moved down, away from the area.

Another explosion on the opposite side of the city has the crowd below cheering. They think it's part of the celebration, but it's a decoy. A setup just for me.

Right now, I wish I didn't have those three black lotuses. But I'll deal with it. I'm not one hundred percent, but even at seventy percent, I can still kick some ass. And believe me, I will not go down without a fight.

Quickly assessing the group with her, I notice the guy who pushed me down is there, along with four other males. They aren't as tall or muscular as the pusher, but they look like dregs—easily manipulated and eager to serve the main manipulative bitch.

The voice in my head hasn't spoken to me since the meeting at the Central Court, which is unnerving. She usually gives me advice, but now... she's quiet.

I stand and face the assholes, knowing that if I run, it'll make matters worse. There is a wall about a hundred yards behind me, but it looks like there are alleyways before it that connect to adjoining streets.

The area around the Evergreen is now empty.

"Hey, lovely. What are you doing up here all alone?" The pusher says. "I'd like to apologize for what happened earlier."

"There's no need to. I'm fine."

I spot Zarah and her band of shrews and immediately see it. That deadly fire churning in her icy blue eyes. I know that look. It's a look I've become all too familiar with. A look of hatred and calculated cunningness. I can feel it pressing heavily on my chest, making it hard to breathe.

"Listen," I say, taking a step forward, hands up. "I'm not here to cause any problems."

"Too late," Zarah says, twirling one of her long black locks in her fingers. "You're with my Rem, and dared to call me a bitch in front of a crowd?"

"Look, Remington is just a friend," I say.

Her eyes go deadly, a wicked smile growing on her face.

While I'm trying to keep the situation calm, I notice the guys are encircling me. This is a terrible situation to be in. I need to leave.

I move toward the crowd down the street, but the pusher comes and stands in front of me, tilting his head. "Don't leave, lovely. We just got here."

I plow forward, but before I push past him, he brings his hand up in front of my face, palm open and blows. A fine dust hits my face. My eyes sting and lungs burn as I inhale whatever the hell it is.

SEVENTEEN

ELARA

I gasp and cough, trying to expel whatever he blew in my face. My heart hammers as panic coils tightly around my chest. My vision blurs, and a wave of nausea hits me.

The pusher tries to grab me, but on instinct, I thrust my leg up with all my might, my foot connecting with his crotch. He wails in pain, cupping his balls and dropping to his knees. But I don't stop. I turn and slam my elbow into his nose. It cracks, his head snaps back and blood flows. Grabbing his wrist, I twist it behind his back, bending his thumb at a painful angle.

The pusher wails, making the other guys step back.

I lower my mouth to his ear. "*Leave me* the *fuck* alone," I say through gritted teeth, twisting his thumb harder, yanking his wrist higher.

"I will! I will," he whimpers.

Pushing him forward, I take a few steps backward, but the street is tilting and turning on an invisible axis. No, no, no.

They drugged me.

I have to keep my wits. I have to stay coherent.

A few more steps and my weakening limbs almost give. My heart is palpitating, my body now covered in a sheen of sweat, while dots of darkness stain my vision. My skin is burning, and the dress suddenly feels too tight.

I've been here one gods-damned day, and have already been shoved, drugged, and surrounded by degenerate assholes with no way of escape. I should have stayed in my room. I have no magic, no money, and no way of contacting Remington or Maeve.

Zarah and her bitches are blocking the way for me to go down the street. With arms crossed over her busty chest, a feral smile rises on her lips.

The edges of my eyes are darkening, but I fight, my consciousness clawing against the force trying to drag me into darkness.

"What did you do to me?" I snap at Zarah, my words slurred.

"Oh, don't be mad," she says with a pouty face—a face I'd like to sink my fist into. "The drug he gave you is awfully expensive, and extremely hard to get. It won't be long before it completely kicks in, and when it does, you'll want to have sex with anyone and everyone at the celebration... except for my Rem."

No. I shake my head, body trembling. But the ground beneath me is unsteady, and my limbs are growing heavy. So incredibly heavy.

She murmurs something to the guys, and they all move toward me, evil intentions etched on their smug faces and stained in their dark eyes.

"Let's see if Rem will want you after they've had their way with you." The look on her twisted face is one of pure evil. "I'd stay and watch, but that's not my thing."

"You can't do this!" I snap, trying to stay steady on my feet.

"You'll learn quickly who rules here," she hisses, then turns and walks away.

The girls behind her laugh and follow, but the guys are stalking closer.

A wave of panic surges through my body. Kicking off my heels, I bend down and pick one up before I turn and run. It's the only damn weapon I have, but my unsteady legs give, and I hit the ground, scraping my palms and knees.

The drug hits hard, making my mind a hazy, muddled mess—a puzzle that is scattered, and I'm struggling to place the pieces back together.

This place is too hot. The dress too suffocating. So suffocating, I want to rip it off.

I claw to find the zipper but can't reach it. A desperate sound chokes from my throat.

My head is heavy, my limbs feel weighted, like I'm wading neck deep in thick sludge.

Shadows are circling me like predators after prey. Voices are muffled. Figures are bleeding and reappearing out of the darkness. Heat courses beneath my hypersensitive skin, blooming in my core and throbbing between my legs.

"Help me," I wail, dragging my ladened body across the cobbled street.

From behind, strong arms clamp around my chest like a vise grip, constricting my breathing. I can't fight. I can't move in his grasp.

"Bitch," he hisses in my ear. "I'll tame you tonight." *It's the pusher.* "You like it rough, little minx? Well, so do I."

I punch and kick, struggling to shove out of his clutches, but the drug has oozed into my blood, dulling my limbs, inhibiting their movement.

There is a strand of consciousness keeping my mind and eyes from being entirely immersed in darkness, and I'm grasping at it, holding on as tight as I can, because I know my life depends on it.

My body jerks as I'm flung over the pusher's shoulder, head and arms dangling at his back.

"Stop!" I shout repeatedly, but my voice is weak, and my struggle to free myself is worthless.

"Somebody. Anybody. Help me. Please." I send the plea out to the universe. To the stars hanging in the sky. The same stars that have observed me from the moment I was born. Stars, I've spoken to, begged, and pleaded with, but never answered. Cold stars. Indifferent and savage for watching me suffer and doing nothing to help.

With the fight draining out of me, there's a sudden shift in the air.

A bitter darkness sweeps over the street, coated in power. Incredible power that hums against my bones. Power that feels like delicate fingers brushing across my heated, sensitive skin.

The shadows spread, leeching all color and light from the world around me.

I'm suddenly dumped on the ground. Curses resound as a furious roar rattles everything around us.

Suddenly, a thundering voice erupts. "Who the fuck did this to her?"

It's not Remington. It's a deep and euphonious voice saturated with power and control.

Screams of pain echo around me, then dead silence. But I can't focus. My eyes won't focus.

A firm arm wraps around my back and another under my knees, lifting and pressing me against a solid chest.

"Leave me alone," I sob, using my fists trying to beat my way free, but my punches are landing with zero damage.

Heavy. Everything feels so heavy.

Those powerful arms tighten around me. "You're safe now, Elara."

Safe.

I let my exhausted arms drop and breathe in that one word—*safe*—letting it soak into my trembling limbs. But I also inhale the most alluring and delicious scent. A scent rich of spice and wind and power, laced with something forbidden that has my back arching and sets a blaze to the burning throb between my legs.

I blink hard, trying to free my sight from the haze that won't leave. But through the dimness I see full, luscious lips, a handsome, sharp-angled face, firm jaw, and a perfect nose. Focusing harder, my eyes meet dark depths rimmed in gold.

Prince Kage?

His hands move against my sensitive skin to adjust, but every move, every touch, every brush of his breath against my skin sets my nerves alight. My head drops back, and I let out a breathy moan. The throbbing between my legs intensifies. I need friction. I need something to relieve the burning pain.

Prince Kage curses before darkness folds around us.

Nausea overwhelms me, but a cool hand slowly sweeping over my forehead instantly eases it.

"Get a healer," the prince orders.

Footsteps quickly scurry away. I'm laid on a bed, but my eyes are too heavy, too hazy, so I keep them closed, still clasping onto consciousness.

"Where am I?" I can barely get the words out. My tongue feels swollen.

"At the castle."

Someone enters the room and I hear murmuring before a soft hand touches my forehead and icy fingers press against my wrist. They peel one of my eyes open and then the other, but everything is a blur.

I hear whoever it is let out a deep sigh. "It appears she's been given the Lure drug."

"What the hell is that?"

"It's a highly potent drug that intensifies the user's sexual desires, highness."

"Can you give her something to counteract it?"

"I'm afraid there is no remedy except allowing it to pass through her system. She'll need to be watched tonight. The side effects of this drug can be brutal. Just this week alone, I've treated four separate cases. However, the other women weren't as... *fortunate* as she is."

"Fortunate? You call this fortunate?" he snaps.

There is a brief pause. "They abused the others, highness. One passed because of her misfortune."

"That is not a fucking misfortune!" The prince roars, making me flinch. "Someone who lives in Terr drugged and raped them. If I find out who it is, I will skin them alive."

"Yes, highness."

"Is there anything we can do to... alleviate her symptoms?"

"I can give her something for the pain, but this is a new drug. Any medication has an insignificant effect."

Yes. Give me something I want to say, but my mouth won't open.

"Give it to her," the prince replies, and I'm thankful.

My head raises slightly, and they pour a bitter liquid down my throat. I try to concentrate, to swallow, and not to let it drip down the sides of my mouth.

"This should help relieve some of the symptoms for the next few hours. Unfortunately, it is my last bottle. I was planning to make a trip to the Apothecary tomorrow. However, you will need to monitor her fever and heart rate and alert me if either of them gets too high. Also, from observing the other patients, if she does wake and cannot find relief for her symptoms..." he pauses briefly, "she will suffer."

I want to sleep. Sleep and not wake up.

"How long before the drug wears off?" the prince asks.

"A few hours," the healer replies.

"I understand."

His voice sounds like I feel. A few hours is a long time to be feeling this way.

"Tell no one she is here," the prince orders.

"I have not seen nor heard anything going on in the castle, your highness."

"Thank you, Digby."

"Of course, highness."

I hear the healer gather his things and leave the room. A few seconds pass before a new set of heavy footsteps enter the room.

"Find the captain and tell him to get his ass back here immediately. Speak to no one. Keep this secret."

"Yes, my prince."

Hot needles prick my skin, and I groan as the drug finally severs that last thread holding my self-control. I can't move. Can't think. My head is heavy and spinning, and I still can't seem to open my goddam eyes.

Desire is blazing through and ravaging every part of me, leaving me raw and vulnerable. I need relief. I need something to stop the throbbing pain. Or I need to pass the hell out.

My dress is too tight. It's rough and scratchy, making my skin raw—at least it feels that way—and as much as I yank, I'm unable to rid myself of it. Off. I need it off.

"It hurts," I groan. "Take it off."

Before I get an answer, my eyes darken.

Eighteen

PRINCE KAGE

What have I done? Why did I bring her here?

Thank the gods Elara's passed out for now.

I was enjoying the celebration, walking down a street, when a shooting pain struck my chest, followed by emotions of hopelessness and desperation. I don't know how, but I knew it was Elara, and knew she was in danger.

Ever since I touched her at the meeting, I can't stop thinking about her. She's somehow burrowed under my skin, and the haunting memories I saw of her past have constantly replayed in my mind ever since.

Without thinking, I opened a portal. I didn't even know her location, but my magic did, because it delivered me right to her. Blessed stars Vera wasn't around when I disappeared. I know she'll come looking for me, and because of her insane jealousy, if she finds Elara here...

She can never find out. I'm engaged, and being with another woman alone is not only forbidden but will have steep repercussions which Elara will bear the brunt of. Deadly consequences that I will not allow her to face because of my actions.

I opened a portal and jumped to her. *I* brought her here. But I had no other choice. No one was around, and the sight of her drugged and weakened body on the street... No, I couldn't leave her there, even if I wanted to.

Thank the gods there are no witnesses. The five bastards that surrounded her are dead. I killed them all, with no regret. They fucking drugged her and were going to rape her. I know this because I read their filthy, twisted minds, and because of what they planned to do with her, they deserved death. Those kinds of assholes are not worthy of living in my kingdom. They'll never terrorize women on the city streets of Terr again. I made sure of that.

I also found, inside their minds, that Zarah was behind it—the Chancellor's daughter—another obsessive little bitch. She must have seen Rem and Elara together and punished her because of it. My magic is itching to teach her a lesson. One she'll never forget. However, she's protected because of her father.

Gently, I sit on the edge of the bed, trying not to disturb Elara. My fingers run over the tattered hem of her gown. Even in this terrible state, I cannot take my eyes off her. She has been a continual dream, a fantasy turned into reality, and now that she's here, she is even more beautiful than I could have ever imagined. Ever since I saw her in the palace, I can't fucking think straight.

Beads of sweat are dotted across her forehead, but I dare not touch her.

Why has she come now? Is this some twisted game of fate? If it is, then *fuck* fate.

I trust the healer and my guards not to speak a word, but no one else can ever find out about tonight, which is why I've brought her here, to this very room. It's my mother's old room, and it's off-limits. It was locked up after her death. My father forbade anyone from entering, and it hasn't been touched since.

I snuck in once. I opened a portal here a few days after her funeral, just to smell her pillow and her perfume. However, those scents triggered emotions I wasn't ready to deal with. The pain was too raw, so I left and never returned. Until now.

My mother was the only person who wasn't terrified of me. She was the only one who told me I was good when the world cursed me and my gifts. But two years ago, they found her dead, in her bedchamber. The coroner said she died in her sleep, but I know that's bullshit. Someone murdered her. I don't know how, or why, but I have vowed to find out the truth.

Elara moves, a painful moan escaping her lips. Her hand is reaching for something that isn't there, so I grab hold of it.

Shit. She's burning up.

"Help me," she breathes, followed by another pained moan. I raise my palm and let my shadows surround her, cooling her body temperature.

With a snap, Rem appears, standing near the door. His eyes immediately widen when he spots her. "What the hell happened?"

I try to suppress my anger. I know it wasn't his fault, but I'm still pissed that it happened. "Why was she left unattended?"

"I—" he stutters, shaking his head. "There was an explosion. I went to find out what had happened. Maeve was on her way to her."

Fuming, I face him. "She was drugged and cornered, Rem! Five assholes were going to rape her."

"What?" Rem snaps, hands fisted at his sides. "Who?"

"It doesn't matter."

"The fuck it doesn't!" He strides over until he is a few feet from me. "Who is responsible, Kage?"

I shake my head, my eyes landing back on Elara. "It doesn't matter, because they're all dead."

"Shit." He paces the room, shoulders slouched. "What are we supposed to do with the five bodies whose deaths will need to be explained?"

I glance at him with a smirk. "That's why I have you, Captain."

"Bastard," he snarls.

Elara's passed out again, so I gently lower her hand, resting it next to her. "I need you to watch her, Rem. I must find Vera and explain why I disappeared. She's probably interrogating everyone at the celebration."

"What are you going to tell her?"

"That I was sick."

He smirks and shakes his head. "Like she'll believe that."

"She has no choice."

"What do I do with her?" Rem's saddened eyes shift toward Elara.

I know Rem. The despondent tone in his voice and aching look in his eyes are telling. He is smitten with her, and I hate that it bothers me so much.

"Nothing. Digby just left and gave her something that should help her for a few hours. Just watch her. I'll be right back." I pause right before I open a portal. "Rem. Zarah is responsible for what happened to her."

His eyes shut and head drops as he curses under his breath. He knows he should have been there or should have taken her with him. He could have avoided this situation, but I won't beat him up about it. He's already doing that himself. Besides, our magic doesn't turn back time. This was a hard lesson learned. I will gather my guards and members of the court and make sure it doesn't happen to anyone else in Terr.

Stealing one last glance at *her*, I open a portal and jump back to the city.

I finally return to Rem after convincing Vera that I'd left because I was feeling unwell. She begged me to stay with her, but I told her I needed to go over plans to get my father and the other rulers back. It's not a lie. We need to discuss their return, but for now, until our deadline, they have informed us they will be safe and well fed until we meet their demands. We have one week, which is why the team will leave in five days. The team Elara is now a part of.

After seeing her past, I don't want to put her in more danger, but I also see how strong she is. She's a fighter and I know she can, despite having no use of her gifts, help accomplish getting them back. She's been well-trained, and because the Avkans don't have power and fight with weapons like those on Earth, she might be our best hope.

When I arrive, Rem is sitting on the side of the bed, holding her hand. She's in a long nightgown.

"Who changed her?" I say with a little too much bite. No one can know she is here, and the thought of Rem changing her doesn't sit right with me.

When he sees me, he releases her hand and stands. "Maeve came and changed her but had to leave. She promised not to say anything."

Relief washes over me.

"She's in pain, Kage. She keeps moaning. What can we do to help?"

I shake my head. "It's a new string of powerful sex drugs. Digby said if she doesn't get relief, she will suffer."

"Shit. For how long?"

"Until it wears off... a few hours."

Elara moves again, her brow pinches, and she lets out another pained moan. "Help," she breathes. "It hurts." Her hands fist in the sheets, as her body twists. Fuck.

"Even if she has to suffer, no one is allowed to touch her," I order.

Rem turns to me with a look in his eye. "What if you go into her mind? Make her believe she is getting relief, but you won't be touching her."

"That's an invasion, Rem. Do you understand what that means... what I'll be doing? I can't do it. I won't."

My gift allows me to jump into someone's mind. I can read it, erase it—in part or completely—and even have the ability to trap them in an alternate reality. In the past, I've never used it except as a form of torture, to extract information.

Rem takes a defensive stance in front of me. "I think she'd rather have a sex dream than be in pain. She's asking for help." He shakes his head. "You're the only one who can do this, Kage. Help her."

Elara moans again, her face riddled with pain.

"I will do it on one condition. After it's done, I will erase her memory, and you'll take her to her room. I don't want her to remember that they drugged her, that I found her and brought her here, or what I'm about to do. Nothing, Rem. If she asks about anything, just tell her she had consumed too much at the celebration and you helped her back to her room."

"What about Zarah?"

"Do you think she wants anyone to know she was behind drugging Elara and the deaths of those assholes? If she knows what's best for her, Zarah will keep her mouth shut. We can deal with her later."

Elara groans in pain, her legs rubbing against each other, her hand dipping between her thighs, trying to find relief. "It hurts."

The sight of it gets me hard.

"Do it Kage," Rem urges.

"Fuck. Bind her arms and legs to the bed. I don't want her touching me. This has to be a total mind thing."

Rem immediately opens a portal and jumps. Within minutes, he's back with bedsheets, which he shreds into long strips. We secure her arms and legs to prevent her from moving, and then I turn to Rem.

"Make sure no one enters. I'll call you once it's done."

Rem nods. "Just make sure she's not in pain. I'll keep everyone away." With that, he walks out of the room, leaving me alone with Elara.

I sit on the bed next to her and push the wet strands of hair away from her face. Gods, she is beautiful. This girl has been invading my dreams since I was a boy. Now, I'll be entering hers. Pain or not, she'll have to give me consent before I do anything to her, even if it's in her mind.

As she groans again, I close my eyes and concentrate.

A soft light slowly illuminates a bedroom. My bedroom. It's the only place I could think of on short notice and under pressure.

I pause, my chest tightening as I watch Elara asleep on my bed, lying in a silky white bedgown... and fucking hell. *What am I doing?*

I come closer and she stirs, then slowly, her eyes slide open. Blinking a few times, she sits upright, her eyes pinned on me.

"Prince Kage?" Her eyes search the area, trying to find her bearings, but they wince shut as if she's in pain. "Where am I?"

"We're in my bedroom," I answer softly.

"Why?"

Shit. I didn't think she'd ask all these questions.

"Why am I here?" she asks again, but before I can answer she folds over in pain, and I instinctively run to her side.

Nineteen

ELARA

Pain. My body is feverish and there is a throbbing between my legs that won't relent. It grips me, and fear overcomes my mind, knowing the consequences of the drug. Zarah said whatever they blew in my face would make me want to screw everyone in Terr. *That bitch.* She'll get hers. Payback is a bigger bitch than she is.

Prince Kage moves to my side, but my mind is spinning, and so is the room.

The black sheets surrounding me feel like silk and the brush of them against my sensitive skin makes a moan of pleasure involuntarily erupt from my throat.

Glancing at him, I get lost in those dark, gold-rimmed eyes. I cannot deny that his beauty is unparalleled. From the moment I met him, even if he is an asshole and standoffish, everything about him is appealing to me. His eyes, his face, his scent, his lips... full, luscious lips I want to taste and feel against my skin.

What am I thinking?

I blink... pulling myself from the fog hazing over my eyes and clouding my mind.

"What's happening to me?" I groan, my voice thick. I try to move, but it makes the throbbing between my legs worse.

The prince curses under his breath, indecision embedded in the deep lines on his brow. "Do you want the truth or a lie?"

"Truth, of course," I hiss. Why is he asking me this?

He lets out a deep sigh, then sinks onto the edge of the bed next to me, those dark eyes pinned on mine. "All of this..." he says, addressing the room with a wave of his hand. "This is not real."

I shake my head, glancing around. It looks real. Every detail, from the cracking fire against one wall, the large king-sized bed, the dark wood and luxurious furnishings, and accessories gilded in gold. "I don't understand."

He exhales loudly, raking his fingers through his thick onyx hair. "We are in your mind. I brought us here through Dark Vision... one of my gifts."

"Why?"

He hesitates for a moment, his expression troubled.

"Someone drugged and attacked you at the Messis celebration."

My head throbs as flashes of Zarah, the men with her, and the pusher blowing something in my face, and then...

"You—you saved me," I breathe, pointing at his chest.

He nods, his eyes assessing.

"Why are you in my mind? What is this place?" My teeth grit together as another wave of pain shoots through me. And why, despite the goddam pain, do I want to jump his bones, straddle his lap, run my fingers through his thick hair, and lick his lips to know what he tastes like?

"This place is my bedchamber," he replies, snapping me from my sex driven thoughts. "We're here because it's a place familiar to me, therefore, easy to recreate. The real reason I'm here is because you are in pain, and there is no remedy for the drug they gave you, other than offering you relief."

I move and the aching grows stronger. "Why are you truly here?" There must be an ulterior motive.

"I came to help," he says simply, his expression unaltered.

"How can you help?"

"The healer said, the only way to stop your pain is for you to find relief. I won't allow anyone to touch your body without your consent, so I brought you inside your mind. Here, I technically won't be touching you. Not really, however, it will feel like I am." I swear I see a slight grin on the corner of his lips. "Your actual body is safe outside and will remain so. But I am here..." he pauses, and I swear those dark eyes grow darker, "to offer my services."

Those few words have my thighs clenching together, eliciting a moan. Gods, this must be a dream. Why would he, of all people, want to help me? Besides, he's in an arranged marriage. I saw the look in his fiancé's eyes when she saw me in his arms at the meeting. Between her and Zarah, I don't know which one is worse.

"What about your fiancé?"

A wicked grin creeps on those sinful lips. "Because this isn't real. She doesn't need to know."

"Why you? Why are you doing this?"

"Because I am one of two people who has Dark Vision in all Celestria. That, and I—I can't bear to see you in pain." I see it then, in his eyes, the honesty and sincerity. I can also feel that he's speaking the truth. He saved me from those men, so I doubt he would want to harm me. Besides, this is just a dream. This drug is making me think and do things I normally wouldn't do. Maybe it's just a twisted desire of mine playing out in my head. It must be. This can't be real.

"This is not about me, or about sex," the prince says, like those words are supposed to reassure me. "Like I said before, I'm here to help relieve your pain. Nothing more, nothing less."

My skin is sensitive to every brush of material. My legs are trembling, and all I can think of is finding that relief I desperately need. There is no way, in the condition I'm in, I can do it myself.

"I'm here, Elara," he says, leaning in. "Just say the word. Give me your consent, and I will help you."

His words intensify the throbbing between my legs, but it's the way he spoke my name. Hearing it flow from his lips like a gentle caress, I nearly come undone.

Gods, he is gorgeous. And his scent, *hell*, even if this isn't real, it's his distinct scent, a scent I crave. I cannot deny that the moment I met him, I felt something. Even more when he touched me at the meeting. I felt that jolt through my entire body, a sensation I'd never felt before, and ever since that moment, especially now, I feel dangerously drawn to him.

But this is in my mind. This must be a drug-induced dream. There is no way the Prince of Terr would want me in real life. But I'll take it, because I don't want the pain, and who wouldn't want to have a handsome prince helping to find relief? This is a once in a lifetime dream come true. Even if it is a dream, I'll take it and deal with the asshole prince in real life later.

I glance into those dark eyes, as beautiful as a starless night, and nod. I want this more than I'll ever admit.

A beautiful grin curls on the corners of his lush lips, and it makes something inside of me snap.

Without hesitation, I grab the back of his neck and pull his lips against mine. I shouldn't have, but I don't want to stop. If I'm going to do this, I'm going to do it without reservation or hesitation. This is my dream. I can do whatever the hell I want.

I'm startled when the prince's kiss matches mine with dominance and force. His hands fist in my hair, drawing me closer as he claims my mouth, and *gods above*. He tastes like darkness and power and shadows. I can't get enough.

Cradling my face in his palms, he bends my head so he can go deeper. A groan rises from inside his throat, echoing through my entire body. I know, without a doubt, that if he touches me where the ache is, I will shatter.

His kiss alone is dizzying, and I want more. Desire more. Crave more, but the growing pain in my core and between my legs has me severing the kiss.

Whimpering, my back arches and my head drops back, but he captures me and gently guides me down onto the bed. Leaning above me, dark shadows swiftly extend from his body and coil around my wrists and ankles. They are smooth and cool, sending a tingling sensation throughout my sensitive limbs.

When I look back at him, I see nothing but a gorgeous, dark prince, filled with power. So much power I can barely breathe. This is truly a dream. A dream I don't want to wake from.

The prince leans over. "Are you certain you want this?" he asks again, his eyes laden with want.

"Yes," I exhale. "I do."

Without hesitation, his mouth crashes down on mine, his kiss ravenous and hungry. Moving from my lips, he leaves a pathway of blazing kisses down my jaw, neck, collarbone, and then... his mouth reaches my left breast. His lips encase it, while his teeth nip and pull at my nipple through the thin bedgown.

I feel his hand slowly gliding up my thigh, higher and higher, until I feel him reach my center. I gasp and fist the sheets as a finger slides beneath my underwear and right inside me, stroking slowly. A moan rips from my throat and my back arches when he adds a second finger. I try to move but his shadows keep me pinned down, keep me restrained.

With his mouth and fingers moving in tandem, I cry out. Stars burst over my vision as I ride out my first wave of ecstasy with his fingers inside me.

But those fingers don't stop. Neither does his mouth.

"Kage" I breathe. Begging, pleading, demanding, fighting against the shadows that won't allow me to move. I need to touch him, to taste him. I want to run my fingers across his bare skin and through his hair.

The drug has turned me into a horny bitch, but right now, I don't care. I want him. I want Kage... the man who is here, right now. Not the asshole, engaged prince.

He pauses and pins me with a heated gaze.

"Fuck," he groans. "Say it again."

"Say what?" I pant, still fighting against his shadows.

His warm breath brushes against my ear. "My name, Elara. Say my name."

"Kage," I exhale, and his eyes grow even darker.

His mouth crashes over mine with a hunger that makes my toes curl and the entire room spin. "I need more," I beg against his lips. I want to feel him inside me.

He pauses, breaking the kiss, his face inches away, his dark eyes pinning mine while his shadows continue to hold me down, keeping me from touching him.

Lowering, he speaks into my ear, low and soft. "You want more?"

I nod, my heart hammering against my chest, that ache rebuilding between my thighs.

Serious obsidian eyes, gilded in gold, find mine, binding me with a gaze that burns like an inferno. "If I take you, it won't be in your mind, and it won't be a simple thing. If I take you, I will own you, possess you, and claim every part of you. I will brand your body, inside and out. I will memorize every curve and every line, and when I'm done, I will know what every inch of you tastes like. Before I take you, Elara, you will have to decide if you want to be with me, because once you do, there will be no turning back. Once I take you, *Min Vesmír*, everyone will know that you're mine."

His words steal the breath from my lungs. I know he can hear my heart pounding inside my chest. It's loud and erratic, and right now I'm incapable of filtering whether it's the drugs or him making me feel this way. Whatever it is, I crave it, and want anything he will give.

"Kage," I breathe, arching my back, trying to find some friction between us. "Please."

"What do you want, Min Vesmír?"

I don't know what he's calling me, but from his lips, it sounds delicious.

"I want you. I want more," I beg.

A groan rises from his throat as his mouth crashes onto mine. His tongue strokes inside, deep, gently licking and urging mine, drawing out a soft whimper. His hand dips beneath my bedgown, stroking my thigh and I gasp as he again finds my center, and slips one finger inside, then a second as his thumb circles my clit.

I nearly shatter, but he stops, and I groan in agony as he breaks our kiss, slowly sliding down my body. I watch in complete awe as the Prince of Terr kneels on the ground at the foot of the bed, those dark gold-rimmed eyes fastened to mine.

Grabbing my thighs, he pulls me down toward him, and when I'm at the edge of the bed, he offers me a devilish smile. Hooking his fingers around my underwear, he slides them off.

With one slow movement, his head dips and his tongue licks my center.

The touch of him against my sensitive flesh has my head falling back and eyes clenching shut. He lets out a moan of pleasure as his tongue delves inside me, his mouth sucking and fingers stroking. The sight of him feasting on me, and the way his mouth feels... I rapture.

A second wave of ecstasy explodes through me, and I curse, shattering around his tongue and mouth as he continues to devour me. Unable to move from his grip, I shudder under his touch, trying to catch my breath as I tumble from the high he's carried me to.

His shadows restrain me until he's finished and I'm thoroughly drained. The throbbing pain subsides, and I'm perfectly satiated.

Licking his lips, like he loves what he's tasted, the prince gets up and moves to the side of the bed. His shadows release their grip on me, and our eyes find each other. It's then I see a shift of emotion in him.

"What's wrong?" I ask, my eyes unusually heavy and nearly impossible to keep open.

"Absolutely nothing," he breathes. "And that's the problem."

I can tell he's hesitating to tell me more, but I can barely stay coherent.

Still on a high, words tumble from my lips. "I wish this moment was real. I wish *you* were real."

He pauses, his eyes narrow and brows furrow. "Who are you? A demon come to torment me?"

I smile, fighting the sleep, trying to drag me into darkness. "No. I'm just Elara."

The bed sinks as he sits next to me, pulling the sheets over my body before his fingers graze the sides of my face. "I don't think you're *just* anyone. You're the girl who has been in my dreams all my life. But now you're here. You're real, and as much as I try to fight it, I want you."

I try to focus on the words he's spoken, but those two sentences have my head whirling with so many questions and too many emotions.

"You want me?" I exhale.

Why can't my eyes focus? Why can't I stay awake?

The prince gives me a sad smile. "This is all just a dream," he breathes, his fingers tenderly stroking my forehead, making my eyelids weigh heavier. "When you wake, you won't remember any of this."

I grasp his hand, fighting to keep my eyes open. "What if I want to remember?"

"You can't," he murmurs. "It's too great a risk."

My heavy eyes finally close. "I don't want to forget."

"Sleep, Min Vesmír. Tomorrow will be a new day."

His scent wraps around me, that wonderful scent of rich spice, and wind, and power that is his alone, and I swear I feel his lips press against my forehead before I'm submerged into darkness.

TWENTY

PRINCE KAGE

Whatever the hell just happened, even if it was within my Dark Vision, has wrecked me. The girl in my dreams has somehow slipped into my reality and is wreaking havoc, not only in my heart, but in my mind.

Wanting her puts her in great danger. It is forbidden for me to go against the arranged marriage that will strengthen our realm. If I annul the engagement, the person I break it for will suffer and be severely punished.

So, what the hell am I supposed to do?

Vera is gorgeous, but she's a bitch who I barely relate to. She wants one thing... to become a princess, and eventually the queen who will produce a future heir to the throne of Terr.

I fucked her once, but that's all it was. She doesn't differ from any of the others. I got nothing out of it because I know my heart and mind don't belong to her. They will never be hers, even if we are married in the future.

It was different with Elara, though. Even though it was in my Dark Vision, I felt something. I don't know what kind of spell she holds over me, but what I do know is that because of her... I'm fucked.

I erased her memory. Everything that came after her and Rem were walking toward the Evergreen. She won't remember anything after that, which includes me coming to save her, or anything that happened in her mind.

Rem has already taken her back to her room and his cousin, Maeve, agreed to stay with her while she recovers. Knowing that, affords me some peace of mind.

Before he left, I told Rem who she was. That she is the girl in my dreams—the one I call Min Vesmír—my universe. I'm not sure how he took it. His expression was solemn. I know he likes her, but now he knows who she is to me, and how I've felt about her for most of my life. He's heard most of the countless dreams, even when he was sick of me telling them. I know he also feels my frustration.

I can't stop thinking about her. Even now, my chest aches after hearing her tell me she didn't want to forget. But she must. She can never remember what happened between us. I just wish I had the power to erase my own gods-damned mind, too.

All I can do now is focus on getting my father back and hope that Elara will survive the mission if she still is a part of it. It will be dangerous, but I have faith that Rem and the others will train the team well. Five days before they leave for Avka, and I know it will be the longest five days of my life.

Twenty-One

ELARA

Everything aches.

I feel like I've been trampled over by a hundred elephants.

Peeling my eyelids open, I squint, trying to focus on my surroundings, but can't figure out where I am. I need caffeine, or Advil. Preferably both. Anything to relieve the shooting pain in my head.

"You're up," a female chimes from a corner of the room. Turning, my head throbs with the movement. "Looks like you need a healer."

"Maeve," I groan, closing my eyes and rubbing my temples. "What happened to me?"

She heads over to my bed and sinks down on the edge next to me. "You drank too much and passed out, so Rem portal jumped you back here."

I try to think back, and the only thing I remember is having the three drinks with Maeve. Then walking with Rem to a place called the Evergreen where we were going to meet Maeve. The rest... there is nothing. A blank space that I can't fill in.

"Gods, I really am a lightweight. I must be the talk of Terr."

Maeve shakes her head. "Do you really think people were interested in you passing out? There were countless others who did the same. Believe me, no one noticed."

"Except you and Rem," I point out.

"Rem was glad to get away. He hates large crowds."

"What about the prince? Didn't he have to stay to protect him?"

She smiles at me. "Rem asked, and the prince gave him the night off."

"He did?"

She nods.

"Then he must know I'm the reason."

"I don't know." She shrugs. "I wasn't there when Rem whisked you away."

I fall back onto my pillow, and the aching in my head surges.

Maeve heads to the kitchen and returns with a glass of water and a vial. "The healer instructed me to give this to you when you woke up." She places the water down on a stand next to the bed and pulls the top off the vial. "It's medicine. Drink up."

I sit up and pour the liquid down my throat. It's bitter and burns going down. "What the hell is this?" I cough.

Maeve laughs, handing me the water. "Give it a minute. If it's bitter, it's better. Well, that's what my dad always told me."

I drain the water and lay back down, and within a minute, my head goes numb. After a few more minutes, the pain completely subsides, so I sit up and twist my body from side to side.

"Wow. This is a miracle drug."

Maeve shrugs. "Temporarily. The symptoms will return in a few hours."

There is a knock on the door, and she turns to give me a sly look. "That should be Rem."

Gods. I must look like death.

Hopping off the bed, I make a beeline toward the bathroom and hear her rolling laughter follow me down the hall. "I already put an extra change of clothes in there for you."

"Thank you," I shout, right before I shut the door.

After looking in the mirror and confirming I'd danced with death, I hop in the shower, lather up my body with sweet smelling soap, and scrub my hair.

When I'm done, I dress in black leggings with a fitted gray blouse that buttons low in the front, showing a little more chest than I'm used to, with a belt that wraps around the waist. It's not something I would normally wear, but I can't deny that it looks good.

Placing my ear against the door, I hear Maeve asking Remington a question and before he answers, I open the door and walk out.

Maeve turns and gapes at me. "Wow, I thought I looked good in that outfit, but damn, you look beautiful." She nudges Remington in the side. "Don't you think so, cousin?"

His dark eyes sweep over my body from head to toe, making me blush. "I absolutely do."

I can't help but smile and notice how handsome he looks in his captain's attire.

"How are you feeling?" he asks, concern swirling in his eyes.

"Much better after the tonic the healer gave me," I say. "And... thank you for bringing my drunk ass back here. You saved me from a lot of embarrassment."

I see a slight tick in his expression before he smiles. "Of course. It's my duty."

"So, what's the plan for today?" I ask.

"If you're still up for it, training for the mission to free our rulers starts in an hour."

I nod, assessing myself, feeling fine. "Where will it be?"

"There is a private training facility near the Central Court. Because all realms are involved, they wanted to keep the location impartial."

"I'm in, as long as the healer can provide another miracle tonic like the last one."

Remington reaches in his pocket and pulls out two vials and flashes them at me. "Your wish is my command."

"You really are a lifesaver," I laugh. "You saved me twice in a row now. I owe you big time."

"You owe me nothing," he says, tucking the vials back into his pocket. "It's my duty to keep you safe."

His duty. That's the second time he's said that. I thought I was maybe a little more than just a duty, but he warned me. He told me the bracelet he gave me during the Messis celebration was only to keep me safe, and he also said he can't get involved with anyone while working for the prince. Whatever is between us must all be in my mind. To him, I am just a girl they assigned him to protect. I'll have to keep any feelings in check and keep our relationship professional. Besides, we just met, and I'll take having the handsome captain as a friend. I just have to stay away from that bitch, Zarah, and her friends. I have a feeling, deep in my gut, that she plays dirty.

Before the training, Remington portal jumps Maeve back to her place, but she promised she'll be back this evening to check on me. It feels great to have an actual friend.

Remington suddenly appears in my living room, directly in front of me. I scream and fall backwards, but he moves forward, wrapping his arm around my back and catches me. Pulling me into his chest, he holds me there, a glimmering smile on his handsome face.

"You ready, spitfire?"

I shake my head. "Not for portal jumping."

His laughter reverberates through my chest as he lets me go and reaches for my hand. With his free hand, he opens a portal, and we step inside.

We exit the portal and land on a flat, grassy area. Ahead of us is a round stone building that looks like a castle turret, only much larger. A half dozen guards are standing at the opening in beige uniforms, and as Remington leads me toward them, they slap fists to their chests to greet him. He hasn't let my hand go as we walk through the doors, and I can see the guards eyeing me.

"If you're wondering why I'm holding your hand, it's because if they think you're with me, they won't bother you."

"So, it's part of the protection duty?"

He turns and nods, and I feel the friendship line being drawn. He's more serious today than he was yesterday. Maybe my drunken stupor and passing out totally turned him off. I don't doubt it did. I could have said or did something inappropriate, and I can't for the life of me remember.

"Will you be staying for the training?" I ask, trying to keep the conversation going.

I notice we've entered a large colosseum type setting. There is an arena in the center of the circular structure, and all around are thousands of seats for spectators that rise ten levels high. It reminds me of a football field.

"Yes, I will help with the training," he replies. He watches me scan the inside of the building. "This place is for Celestria's yearly competitions. Each realm sends their top ten contenders, both physically and magically, to compete against the other realms through a set of obstacles and tests."

"That sounds like fun. Is it dangerous?"

"It can be. There have been a few deaths since it started." My jaw slacks as he pulls me toward the right, to another set of doors. "We're this way."

Before we enter the doors, Remington drops my hand. "Follow me," he says as we enter a large white room with a long wooden table in the center. There are at least a dozen people already here, all dressed in military attire. I suddenly feel out of place and wish I had a few more buttons on the upper part of my blouse.

I also notice there is only one other female in the room. She's wearing a navy military uniform that somehow looks feminine on her. She's older, her expression stern, and blonde hair tied up into a tight bun. When we enter, her blue eyes find mine and I know she's from the western realm, the Kingdom of Asteri, like Prince Kage's fiancé, Vera, and her brother, Archer.

The others are in their realm's military colors, and I can't figure out which realm is which. A man in a brown uniform steps toward Remington and offers his hand, and I stand back while they greet each other.

The man must be in his forties, with short brown hair. Suddenly, his green eyes land on me. "So, *you're* Elara," he says with a smile.

"I am," I say, stepping to Remington's side. He extends a hand and I shake it.

"Since Remington and Prince Dargan have both vouched for you, I'm glad you're part of the team. My name is Felix, and I'm from the eastern realm, Kingdom of Doone, and designated head of this mission."

"It's a pleasure to meet you," I say, but my mind is still pinned on the fact he said the prince vouched for me.

"Felix is one of the top military trainers in Celestria," Remington says from my side, and I nod.

I'm going to have to memorize the names of the kingdoms and what they do.

"Come, have a seat," Felix says. "Elara, you can sit here with the others assigned to the mission." He points to the left side of the table. "It appears everyone is here, so we can start."

I take a seat next to the woman in the navy uniform.

The large table seats twenty and every seat is filled. Everyone looks on edge, but I guess they would be. This is supposedly a dangerous mission to save their kidnapped rulers. I noticed right away that each realm has two people representing them, except Terr. It looks like I'm the only one.

Felix begins by introducing everyone at the table and I can barely remember anyone's name, except for the female, named Freya. He continues to discuss our mission and what our aim is. Everyone is quiet until he mentions the devices the Avkans use to detect magic.

"Does everyone here not possess magic?" Freya asks. I'm glad she did because I was wondering the same thing.

"They don't," Felix said.

"How?" The word pops out of my mouth before I can stop it.

"Because we're criminals," a man sitting on the other side of Freya says. He's wearing a red uniform with gold trim and has red hair and a full beard with a scar that runs down the left side of his cheek. "They've cut us a deal. We go to Avka and retrieve the rulers, and they give us our magic back."

"I'm not a criminal," Freya says. "I was born without magic."

"How can a Celestrian not have magic?" one of the other men asks.

Freya turns to him with an annoyed glare. "My birth father was a male from Earth, and I regrettably took after him."

"What about you, girl?" The man with the red hair and beard asks me.

"She's not a criminal," Remington answers. "And her power is of no concern to you."

"Ahhh, another mutt," the red-haired man blurts, and the others laugh.

Freaking criminals. None of them deserve my time or attention, so I ignore them.

"Enough," Felix orders. "Being here today does not guarantee you a spot on this team. If you don't make the cut, you don't get the deal. For the men, you'll return to your kingdom and resume your punishment."

"How many are making the cut?" the red-haired man asks.

"Five. Four of you will be eliminated."

Murmurs erupt. They thought this was a guaranteed out-of-prison card that came with a return of their magic.

"Alright, how about we get to the training arena and see what each of you can do?" Felix says.

The men eagerly shove their chairs back and file out of the room. Freya stands and so do I, but she turns to me with a stern expression. "Look, I'm not here to make friends," she says. "I'm here as a duty to my realm and to retrieve my king and queen from Avka."

"Fair enough," I say, pushing in my chair.

I never intended to make any friends on this mission, but in dangerous circumstances, you must trust and rely on the people you're with. In life-or-death situations, if there is no comradery, the mission is doomed to fail.

Right off the bat, I can't see how this group of miscreants is going to work together to save the rulers of Celestria. I agreed because knowing the situation—that Avkans don't have magic and use weapons like the people of Earth do—I have an advantage. I've never used magic, and my skills come from years of hands-on training, which should give me an upper hand over most of the others on the team.

Felix directs us out into the expansive arena, where a dozen men wearing beige military uniforms are standing in a row. He gives them a nod and they all move to different sections where there are stations set up.

Felix stands in front of us, arms crossed over his chest. Remington, along with the rest of the men from each realm helping with the training, are standing behind him. "We will examine and assess each one of you today according to your strengths and weaknesses. Do your best, because at the end of three days, the one with the most skills will lead the team."

The men standing in front of me and Freya nod at each other with smug looks on their faces, as if they believe they will lead.

As I quickly scan the arena, I notice a firing range, a little corded area that resembles a boxing ring, and a long course with rope ladders, things to crawl beneath and over, plus three large, heavily padded guys right at the end.

Gods, I'll be needing those tonics tucked into Remington's pocket immediately after today's training.

"All of you need to head to the changing rooms where you will find new training uniforms," Felix says.

We're released, so I follow Freya into the woman's changing room, where there are two uniforms laid out on a bench, each with our names on it. At the foot of the bench are new boots and socks. Freya picks hers up and heads into one of the stalls, so I do the same.

The uniforms are beige tracksuits which are very comfortable. The black boots are also lightweight and flexible. After I exit the stall I do a few stretches, which feels amazing, and I notice Freya is watching me.

I smile at her, but she doesn't smile back, and that is awkward as hell.

"Stay away from the men. They are pricks who like to dominate and won't bat an eye to hurt you and put you in your place," she says.

I shake my head and stand in front of her. "My place is wherever the hell I want it to be, and today, it won't be beneath any man. I'm not afraid of them."

Freya scoffs. "You should be. They've been locked up and had their magic removed for a reason. I'm just warning you to be safe."

I don't care if she wants to roll over and let them piss all over her, but not me. I'm done being a punching bag.

"Thanks for the warning," I say. "I'll be fine."

Without another word Freya walks out, so I follow her and meet up with the rest of the group, who are wearing the same boots and tracksuits.

Twenty-Two

ELARA

Remington is waiting, clipboard in hand, for everyone to assemble. When all nine team members arrive, he glances at me and gives me a dashing grin that makes the butterflies in my stomach take flight.

"Follow me," Remington says, leading us over to the area that looks like a shooting range. There are five targets set up, from left to right, and instead of guns on the table, there are throwing knives.

Remington stands off to the side and clears his throat. "I will evaluate each of you on how well you can throw the knives and hit the targets. Each knife that hits the inside of the circle will get a point. If one hits the dead center, you will get three points. The maximum you can earn on this obstacle is thirty points."

During my training on Earth, I loved throwing knives. It was challenging and took a while to master, but once I learned the proper stance, grip, how to calculate distance, and maintaining momentum of the throw to hit the target, it was a lot of fun. And being ambidextrous, I was damn good at it.

Remington glances down at his clipboard and makes a check with his pen. "Red, you're up."

The red-headed jerk steps forward with a smug look on his face.

"You have five practice shots, then you'll have ten tries to hit all five targets," Remington explains.

They spread out the targets, about five feet from each other, and they are at different distances. The furthest seems to be twenty feet away.

"Let me show you all how this is done," Red says, picking up a knife. As soon as he aims, I know he doesn't know what he's doing. I shake my head and when I turn, see Remington looking at me with a smirk.

I shrug and cross my arms over my chest, wishing this could go a lot faster.

Red throws his first practice knife, and it misses the target by a foot. He curses and grabs another one, aims and throws. I'm laughing inside because I know the way he's throwing... he won't hit shit. And I'm right.

After the five terrible practice throws, the next ten shots miss every goddamn target. Three of them hit but bounced off. When he turns, his face is red with anger and likely shame, but instead of walking back to the line, he marches toward Remington, hands fisted at his side, standing a few feet away.

Remington stares at him like he's bored. "Can I help you?"

"Why the fuck do we need to throw knives?" Red barks, spittle flying from his mouth. "I doubt we'll throw one goddam knife on Avka."

Remington shrugs. "You never know. With no magic, you should learn to throw and hit something."

"I bet no one here will hit one of those goddamn targets, much less five," Red growls.

Remington's eyes sweep over to me. "Elara, please show this man how it's done."

I tilt my head and give him a pointed look. Why is he doing this to me? Does he want these men to hate me even more?

"Her?" Red laughs. "She'd be lucky not to slice her fingers off."

That remark pisses me off. He's called a challenge, and I never back down from a challenge.

Dropping my arms from my chest, I walk toward the table. One helper has already gathered Red's knives from the ground and brought them back. Five practice blades and ten for the targets.

"Good luck," Red mocks.

I glance at him and smile. "I don't need it."

He laughs and when I turn my back to him I hear him say, "Who does this bitch think she is?"

Picking up two blades, I decide I probably need a practice shot. It's been a few weeks since I'd last thrown a knife, but it's all muscle memory. It shouldn't be a problem. All I need is to have my shoulder's square, firm wrists and elbows tucked in.

I decide to throw two blades at once, so I bounce the knives in my fingers, one in my left and one in my right, assessing the weight. With a firm grip on the handles, I choose my first target and decide to start from left to right, quickly estimating the distance between each target.

Feeling confident, I take my stance and send both blades flying. I know what a successful throw feels like, and this one feels right.

Sure enough, both blades land side-by-side, directly in the center of the target.

Without hesitation, I pick up the next two knives, aim and throw. Before they hit the target, I grip the next two and send them, until I have executed all ten shots.

There are gasps and whispers behind me when all ten knives have hit all five targets, dead center.

"That's bullshit," Red roars from behind. "She had to have used magic."

I turn and face him, sick of his shit talking. "If I had magic, I wouldn't be on this team, dumbass. And *that* is *not* bullshit," I declare, pointing toward the targets, "that is what you call a *bullseye*. It's a skill, of which you've proved you have none."

"I could kill you with one hand tied behind my back," he growls.

I glare at him. "Are you threatening me?" I laugh at him and shake my head. "I'd like to see you try."

Red snaps, and I know I should have kept my mouth shut. He's a criminal with serious anger issues, and I bet no one has ever had the nerve to challenge him, especially a woman. In seconds, he charges toward me, and the bastard actually takes a swing at my face. He's slow as hell, so I duck under it and catch his wrist. In one fluid movement, I slide behind him, kicking out his right leg and twisting his wrist behind his back. Now on his knees, I yank his wrist upward and twist his thumb, incapacitating him. He yelps in pain, unable to move. "This is also another non-magic skill, asshole," I hiss into his ear. "Try to hit me again, and the next time I'll break your fucking arm."

His face is rigid, but he groans in pain when I wrench his arm up higher before I push him forward, away from me, hoping he got the message. I won't take his shit. His or anyone else's.

For some odd reason, this whole scenario feels like déjà vu. Like I've been in this position recently, but I know I haven't. The last time I performed that move was during my training on Earth.

Remington is at my side but doesn't interfere. I know that if the man tried to hurt me, he'd be right there.

The group behind us is looking at me like I'm mad, but it doesn't faze me. I've had worse looks.

Dusting myself off, I get back into the line and Freya is the only one who acknowledges me, giving a slight nod.

My eyes slide to Remington, who makes his way back to the front with a shit-eating grin on his face. I won't let him slide on this one. He could have stepped in and stopped that bastard, but I also know he wanted me to prove my worth... not only with Red, but with the others. He saw a bit of what I could do at the training center in Terr and had faith I could take care of the situation. At least, I think he did.

I take in deep breaths, trying to come down from the adrenaline high.

Suddenly, my skin is tingly, and I have an awareness that feels familiar. My eyes scan the arena and that's when I spot him... the Prince of Terr. He's standing with Felix near the obstacle course and gods... he looks sinfully gorgeous.

He's wearing black slacks and a black button-down shirt, with a long black coat trimmed in gold. For a split second, our eyes connect, and it makes my heart jackhammer against my chest.

What the hell is wrong with me?

With difficulty, I try to keep my focus on each person throwing, and it's painfully obvious none of them know what they're doing. But I guess you don't need to learn how to throw knives when you have magic.

Out of the remaining team members, six knives hit targets, and Freya hit two of them. Her first one is on the right fringe, barely hanging on for dear life, and the second is on the top of the outer ring.

Apprehension is growing in the air, and I don't know why. Well, maybe I do, but I don't want to admit it, because the prince has been an asshole to me from the start. His attitude should be a total turnoff, but his presence does things to me that turn me on.

Gods. I need a life... and to focus.

Remington leads us to the next obstacle, which looks like a boxing ring.

The trainer of this obstacle is tall and thin with blond hair and light blue eyes. He looks at his clipboard and comes to stand in front of our group while Remington stands behind him.

"We will assess each of you on your ability to fight. If you stay in the ring, you get ten points. Defeat your opponent, you get another ten points.

Throw your opponent out of the ring, and you will get thirty points, which is a perfect score for this obstacle."

I glance at Remington, and he gives me a slight nod.

The trainer motions with his hand and from behind us a man walks toward him. He's dressed in athletic shorts and a t-shirt, but this dude is huge. He's about six-foot two, with corded muscles and looks like a professional athlete.

The trainer shakes the man's hand and introduces him. "Everyone, meet Atlas. He will be your opponent in the ring, and each one of you will get five minutes to take him down or throw him out."

Atlas smiles and waves at us. He looks like a nice guy, but I can tell he can kick ass. I hope Red is first again, because I can't wait to see him up against this guy. Given the size and physique of Atlas, I'm not sure I can take him on.

"Seven, you're up," the trainer calls.

A man with long white hair tied back at the nape of his neck and silver eyes steps forward. He's around six-foot tall and built, but his muscles are smooth rather than cut. When he enters the ring, I know I need to watch Atlas's moves and figure out a game plan. Hopefully, I won't be up for a while.

A rush of adrenaline surges through my body, and that prickly, tingly feeling covers my skin. Looking to my left, I see the prince and Felix, a little closer, talking to another man. Am I the only one who feels this way? The prince doesn't seem to be affected.

I wonder if he's here to watch. Gods, that puts a lot of pressure on me, especially knowing he and Remington recommended me, and I'm the only one representing Terr. Maybe he's here to make sure I'm not a failure.

The trainer holds up a timer and shouts, "Go!"

The match starts and the two men circle each other. Atlas moves toward Seven, but Seven backs away, skirting the edge of the ring.

"Make a move," the trainer says. "Time is ticking."

"As long as I stay in the ring, I get ten points," Seven says, staying near the ropes, keeping his eyes on Atlas.

"So, you will not engage?" Atlas asks, taking large steps forward, juking him.

Seven stumbles back and I can tell he's afraid. He knows he can't beat the man, so he'd rather run and earn the ten points.

For all five minutes, he retreats, evading every advance Atlas makes, earning his ten points.

The next two men do exactly as Seven did and flee from Atlas, staying near the edges of the ring. I'm so freaking annoyed because they have done nothing to help me see how Atlas moves. I'm wondering why they selected these criminals, these pompous cowards, for such an important task—a mission to save the rulers of their world.

Hell, I'm part of the team and I'm doubting our success and worried most of these men will be more of a hindrance.

The fourth man, a burly brown-haired dude with a tribal tattoo going down the left side of his face, starts off dodging Atlas, but two minutes in, he rushes in and tries to tackle him, but Atlas is like a brick wall. The hit he receives only causes him to take a small step back.

Atlas grabs the man and puts him in a choke hold. At three minutes in, the man is tapping out. Gods, this obstacle is looking bleak.

Freya is up next, and I attempt to give her a word of encouragement, but she ignores me and heads into the ring. When her time starts, she hugs the edge, staying as far away from Atlas as she can get. I don't blame her, and she survives the round with ten points.

Red's called into the ring next, and I can't wait to see how this plays out. Experiencing his ego, he's likely to engage with Atlas. I don't think he'll run like the others.

As soon as Red steps into the ring, he lets out a shout before charging forward. Atlas steps to the side, evading him. With quick reflexes, he reaches over, grabs Red's waist, and easily lifts him over his head before pile-driving him into the floor.

Red's head hits the mat hard, and it's lights out. Atlas grabs his leg and pulls him out of the ring. He gets zero points which I find very satisfying.

A healer comes and when Red comes to, he's confused and doesn't know what happened. When the trainer tries to explain, he calls bullshit, which seems to be his M.O.

While Red is ranting, I'm called up next.

"You got this, spitfire," Remington whispers when I walk past him.

"I'm glad you have confidence in me." I grin and step into the ring, and immediately get into my zone.

All I know is that Atlas is fast and strong. I have to be smart and hope all my years of training pay off.

A sudden rush of adrenaline shoots through me and I glance outside of the ring to see Felix and the Prince of Terr heading toward the ring to watch. Gods, the pressure is high, and so is my heart rate.

"Good luck," Atlas says from his side of the ring. He gives me a smile, and I give him a nod, shutting out everyone outside the ring. Red is still trying to argue, but I can't have any distractions. Especially the tall, handsome one who makes my heart race and skin tingle whenever he's nearby. Not to mention Remington, who has more confidence in me than I do.

The trainer holds out his timer and shouts, "Go!"

Atlas moves toward me, but I'm not ready, so I take a few steps back. There is one move I mastered back on Earth, a move my trainer named after me—the Elara. I'm hoping I can get Atlas in the perfect position so I can initiate that move, but I have to catch him off guard and somehow get to his back. That'll be hard to do because he's trained and fast.

I move forward to juke Atlas, but he rushes forward and grabs my wrist, twisting me around until my back is against his chest. His arm snakes around my neck, trying to put me in a rear chokehold.

I can't panic. I have to remain calm.

I've been in this position many times during practices and know how to get out of it.

I quickly drop my chin, digging it into the fold of his elbow, then grab his wrist with one hand and elbow with the other. Stepping forward, I put a little distance between us and when I'm in a suitable position, I kick back with all my might and heel him in the groin. It's hard, and I feel it connect. Atlas folds over with a wail of pain. His left arm releases its grip, and his head drops, so I send a backward elbow into his chin. His head flies back, loosening his grip so I pull out of his hold, twist around, and grab both of his wrists.

Before he can recover, I use my entire weight to fall backward, pushing my feet against his chest. Using his momentum, I thrust his body over me. His weight has him flying about five feet, but the propulsion carries him through the ropes. He lands outside the ring, rolling to his side, grasping his balls, and groaning.

I suddenly feel bad. I know I kicked him hard, maybe too hard, but before I can go apologize, Remington hops in the ring with a sinister grin on his face and holds out a hand to me. He lifts me to my feet when I take it.

"Holy shit, you just defeated the number one Celestrian fighter," he says quietly. "He came here to see what strengths each of you had, but no one expected him to lose to any of you. You have earned my respect, spitfire."

"Thanks," I say, blushing.

I glance over to see if Atlas is okay and notice a healer is already giving him a potion which I hope will heal his groin. Standing behind them are Felix and Prince Kage. Felix smiles at me and gives me a thumbs up, while the prince gives me nothing. His muscular arms cross over his broad chest, while his stance and facial expression remains stoic. I exhale, wondering how he could be such a royal ass.

Turning away from them, I exit the ring. All the team members, except Red, acknowledge me with a nod or congratulations, which I take as a win.

Because Atlas is out, the trainer calls the last two men into the ring. The rules have changed, and now, they can't run and avoid each other to get ten points. They have to fight, and someone must win.

After five minutes, the two of them look like hell. Swollen, bloody lips, black eyes, and bloody noses. I would call it a draw, but we'll have to see how the trainer scores it.

Twenty-Three

ELARA

The obstacle course is next, and the goal is to get through the grueling route ahead of us.

Freya shakes her head with a defeated expression. "I'm not cut out for this. I signed up to help with this mission, not to be beaten down before we leave."

I feel for her. They did not make these physical tests for the faint of heart. "Just stick with me. We'll get through this together."

"No, you go ahead," she says, shaking her head. "I'll just hold you back. You can win this."

Standing in front of her, I cross my arms over my chest. "Look, this mission isn't about winning a race. It's about making sure our team makes it through this obstacle. If we work together now, we can get in and out of Avka in one piece and stay alive to rescue the rulers. I don't care about the time. I will help you get through it, no matter how long it takes."

"Thank you," she says, and I see sincerity swirling in her blue eyes.

I quickly assess the course as the trainer efficiently explains each obstacle. The first one is a low net, two feet high, and beneath it is thick mud. We'll have to crawl through it and get dirty, then run the rest of the way with heavy mud all over us.

The next one is a cargo net, about thirty feet high, that we'll have to scale. Beyond that is a long beam, about six inches wide and five feet above the floor, which runs at least fifty feet long in a zigzag. That one is all about balance. After that is a rope climb, at least twenty feet up the side of a wall, and beyond that is the finish line, which has three men in pads who are waiting for us.

Gods, this course is no joke. It's meant for trained athletes, and it's painfully obvious that none of us trying out for this team is qualified. We'd be lucky if one person crosses the line still breathing.

The trainer has us line up, side-by-side, and somehow, Red ends up right next to me. Figures. The bastard has it out for me. I watched him in a huddle with the rest of the "criminals" after the last obstacle, and I don't like the way they've been glaring at me ever since.

"Watch your back, girl," Red murmurs, his eyes focused on the course. There is a tick in his jaw that tells me he means business.

I don't answer him because the asshole doesn't deserve my breath. Now, I'll not only have to focus on the course, but watch my back.

They will choose only five members for this mission, so they are going to do whatever it takes to qualify. The cost of a get-of-out-prison card, along with gaining their magic back, is high.

Every trainer gathers off to the side, near the finish line, watching. The prince is standing about ten feet behind them, and Remington is at his side. Together, I can tell how close they are by the way they casually talk to each other. Remington says something to the prince and slaps him on the shoulder, and he laughs in return. Gods, his smile, and laughter make him even more gorgeous. How is that even possible?

Caught off guard, I hear the trainer holler, "Go!"

Everyone sprints toward the mud pit, and a few men dive headfirst, immediately slogging their way through. The competitiveness in me wants to do the same and show them all, but I hold back and stay next to Freya.

When we make it to the pit, half of the men are almost through.

"Get on your belly," I say, showing her, "and use your knees and elbows to push and pull you through." She nods, then drops into the mud, and I do the same.

We both gasp. The mud is ice cold and thick as hell. It takes a great deal of effort to slog our way through, but Freya stays with me, and we make it covered from head to toe in thick, heavy mud.

Already winded, we slow jog to the cargo net, and I know this is going to be tough.

"Just keep looking up and take one rung at a time," I say. I start, reaching as high as I can, then grab the rope and start the climb. About five rungs up, I stop, and she copies what I did. When she reaches me, we move on together and make it to the top faster than I expected, catching up to three men who look spent and out of breath.

Next is the beam, and it's all about balance. Freya mentioned her balance wasn't very good, and I can't help her with that, but I can try to stabilize her.

Up ahead, I hear a yelp and watch one man fall off the beam. The trainer blows the whistle and tells him he needs to return to the beginning of the beam obstacle. The man curses, pissed, but stomps back to the beginning.

I turn to Freya. "I'll go first, and you hold on to my shoulders. We'll go slow. Just let me know if you need to stop." She nods and we get on the beam. Sucking in a deep breath, I have to refocus, knowing I could run through this with no problem. I've never had to help anyone before, so it's an adjustment to my patience and grit.

As we move, I feel the pressure of her palms. Freya keeps up, her hands on my shoulders, helping her maintain her balance. She pushes hard a few times, but I've grounded myself to the beam, my sole focus to keep us steady and moving.

We're a little behind the others, but not by much, and are slowly edging closer.

More curses up ahead let me know someone else has fallen off, and then I hear Red let out a boisterous string of curses. He's fallen and has to start the beam over.

Inside, I gloat, but keep my focus. We're halfway through and making a good pace. I can hear Freya's loud breath at my back, but she's pushing through.

When we finally make it to the end, I jump off and help her down, then we head toward the rope climb. This one is going to hurt. My arms and legs are already exhausted, and I know the rope climb will zap the rest of my energy.

There are knots in the rope about five feet apart, but it will take a lot of upper body strength to get to each one.

"I don't think I can do this," Freya huffs, bending over.

"Yes, you can," I say.

We've caught up with the rest, who are dripping with sweat, their chests heaving. I take off my mud-covered outer long-sleeved shirt and Freya does the same. I quickly tie one of her sleeves to mine to make it longer. To her wrist, I tie one sleeve, and tie the other one around my ankle, knotting them so they won't come free. This will help keep us connected.

"Is this allowed?" she asks.

"They said we need to get through the course. They didn't say how. Follow me up the rope. We can make it if we work together."

She lets out a loud exhale, then nods in agreement.

I start my ascent up the rope and my palms are burning. Pushing through, I make it to the third rung and feel weight on my ankle. We're halfway there.

Glancing down, I see Freya struggling to get her grip. "You've got this," I say, trying to give her some encouragement, but I'm barely hanging on myself.

"Just let me go. I can't do it," she wheezes.

"Yes, you can. Just focus on putting one hand in front of the other."

I close my eyes and focus, because for us to make it, I'll have to dig deep.

"We're halfway there. Push. We can do this!" I call back.

With a grunt, I pull myself to the next rung, but hear Freya scream. My ankle is suddenly yanked hard and my hands burn as I'm pulled down the rope, so I release and freefall, hitting the ground next to Freya.

Focusing, I see Red standing above me with a wicked scowl on his face.

"You're done, girly. Just call it quits and let the men oversee this mission."

"Fuck you," I spit, getting to my feet. Glancing down at my hands, I see blood. They're raw from rope burns.

"If you don't want to get hurt, then give up now," Red threatens, with three other criminals standing behind him. The wall in front of the ropes is obstructing us from the trainers, which is why they're being so brazen.

Freya swiftly unties the knot from my ankle, setting me free.

"I suggest the four of you get moving up that rope, or you won't finish," I say.

"Oh, we'll finish," Red says, stepping forward. "We just want to make sure *you* don't. You're cheating, somehow. I know you are."

"I don't have to cheat, asshole."

"You're a fucking girl. You can't outwit all of us."

"And you're a chauvinistic pig. What makes you think a girl can't outwit you?" I know I shouldn't be egging him on, but he's pissing me off.

I watch him pull a knife from his pocket and know I need to be careful. This asshole has no boundaries.

"You realize that if you're caught with that, you'll do more time," I say, trying to distract him. It doesn't work. The look in his eyes is wild.

"I just want my magic back," he says through gritted teeth. "I need to get it back, so just drop out now, and I'll leave you be."

"I can't do that. And if you don't let me go now, you'll be the one who suffers."

The wildness in his eyes grows. "Fucking women. Do they really think they're stronger than men?"

"No," I say. "Maybe not stronger... but we are smarter."

Reaching forward, I grab his wrist and wrench it, making the knife fly out of his hand. Red charges forward, wrapping his arms around me, tackling me to the ground. The other three rush in, pinning my arms and legs so I can't move.

Red straddles me, and I try to buck him off, but the other men hold me down tight. There is no way I can overpower all of them.

"Looks like you need to be taught a lesson, bitch." Red's hands wrap around my throat and squeeze, and his face lights up when he watches me struggle. To make matters worse, the asshole leans down and licks my cheek.

What the fuck? They shouldn't have let this asshole out. He's a psycho.

Struggling to get free, I can't move, can't breathe, and darkness is slowly encroaching at the corners of my eyes.

Then, I feel a charge in the air that makes the hairs on my body rise. I sense *him.*

Tension coils and the air seems to still. I watch strings of black mist fill the area, watch them wind around Red and the other three men before they are yanked right off me.

Once Red's hands release from my neck, I choke, gasping for air. Above me, that dark mist has coiled around their chests and necks, compressing as they struggle to get free, helplessly dangling above me.

"Your highness, you can't interfere," one helper on the field says.

"This is a fucking training exercise, not a death match," the prince snaps, his voice filled with authority and power.

Pushing up on my elbows, I watch the prince move toward me, mist coiling around his arms, legs, and wrists. His face is rigid, and eyes have gone completely black. I can feel his raw and inimitable power pulsing through the air. It alone makes me breathless.

With a flick of his wrists, he propels all four men trapped by his shadows into the rope wall. The power of the thrust splinters the wall into pieces, and when the men hit the ground, two are instantly knocked out. Red and one other are groaning in pain.

Remington appears at the prince's side, assessing the damage. "What the hell happened, Kage?" he whispers loudly. "I was gone for thirty seconds."

The prince steps to the side of me, then bends down and scoops me up into his arms. Arms that are strong and sturdy. His scent wraps around me and... gods, it's alluring and intoxicating, and I want more. I want to bury my face in his neck and breathe him in.

"Kage," Remington hisses, snapping me from my wayward thoughts. "You shouldn't."

The prince's dark eyes snap to him. "They tried to fucking kill her." His head motions to the blade on the ground.

Remington curses and reaches down to pick it up.

All the trainers arrive, their eyes wide as they spot me in the prince's arms.

"I'm fine, you can let me down now," I lie. I don't want to leave his arms, or his closeness. It somehow feels... right.

I know he can feel my body trembling. His eyes scan my face and land on my bloody hands. "Get a healer. Now," he demands to a helper standing off to the side.

"Yes, your highness," he replies, bowing before running off.

"My prince," Remington addresses him now that the others are here. "Let me take her."

"I can stand on my own," I say. I don't want to be handed off. I'm not that weak and my legs are fine.

Weighing my words, the prince nods and sets me down gently on my feet, then turns to the trainers.

"I want those men seized and taken back to their realms. I will notify the counsel members of what happened today. They will not go unpunished." The trainers nod, then the prince turns his attention back to me. "You will never see them again. Not in this lifetime."

"Thank you," I breathe, right before he opens a portal and disappears. Just like that.

Remington rushes to my side. "What happened?"

"The bastards planned this," Freya says, coming up from behind me. "Red pulled us off the rope, then threatened Elara with a knife if she didn't pull out. When she said she wouldn't, they attacked her. If the prince didn't step in, the asshole would have killed her."

Remington curses. "Spitfire, I'm so sorry I wasn't here to stop it."

I shake my head, my insides still trembling. "It's okay. The prince saved me, and I really am fine."

The healer arrives and takes me off to the side where I show him my hands. They're raw and bloody, the skin is peeled off, and it burns like hell.

"I truly am sorry. I should have been there," Remington says after seeing my injuries.

"Stop apologizing." I turn to him with a grin. "You aren't my babysitter."

"I kind of am," he chuckles, elbowing me gently in the side.

I shake my head and laugh, watching the healer dig into his bag of medicine. "Here," he says, extracting a round, black container. He places it on the side, then pulls out a clean cloth and some other supplies. "I'm going to need to clean out your wounds before I can heal them," he says with a worried look on his face.

"I'm not a stranger to pain. I can take it," I say, holding my palms out in front of him.

The healer quickly and efficiently cleans the mud and debris from my wounds, then applies the salve and wraps them in clean bandages.

"By tomorrow morning, you should be good as new," he says.

"Thank you. What's your name?" I ask.

"It's Digby," he answers with a bow of his head. "And it's a pleasure, miss."

He seems familiar. I've never seen his face before, but there is something about his voice and his name... I feel like I know him, but I don't. Another déjà vu moment.

Guards have come in and bound Red and the other three men. When I look at them, Red glares at me, his expression seething. I shrug and shake my head. He had a choice, but his ego and psychotically deranged mind led him to his fate.

"Come on, spitfire. That's enough for today. Let's get out of here," Remington says.

"What about the training?" I ask.

"We've seen enough," Felix says. "I'm sorry you had to endure that, Elara, but you helped us weed out the trash."

I nod and turn to follow Remington out of the arena when Freya grabs my wrist. I pivot to face her.

"Thank you," she says, her mud covered face sincere. "I don't trust easily, but you didn't leave me behind. You helped me, pushed me, and I want you to know that I appreciate what you did."

I place my bandaged palm gently on her shoulder. "We're part of a team. I wanted to make sure we got through it together."

Freya smiles, then gives me a nod. "I'll see you tomorrow?"

"See you tomorrow," I reply, then turn to Remington and let him lead me out.

Once outside, he opens a portal, and we enter without hesitation.

Twenty-Four

PRINCE KAGE

Raking my fingers through my hair, I pace my bedroom floor.

I was going to kill those fucking cowards, but that would have brought unwanted attention and scrutiny on both me and *her*. I should have sucked their souls from their worthless corpses but held back for her sake. If so much wasn't at stake, those bastards would already be dead.

Staying away from her is vital, but also exhausting. I can't shake her from my gods-damned thoughts and it's driving me insane. My entire being aches to be near her, to make sure she's safe and out of danger, but my hands, and balls, are tied to Vera.

For the past years, I've tolerated that bitch for the betterment of Terr. I've put my own wants and needs aside to serve my kingdom, but ever since Elara showed up, my mind and emotions are in a fucking tailspin.

Yes, I got a glimpse of how fucked up her life has been when I jumped inside her head, but that only makes me want to protect her even more. To make sure she's safe from any predator... but I can't.

Fucking fate. Fucking stars.

In less than a week, she'll be traveling to Avka on a mission with a team I would never approve of. We only considered the bastards because they don't have magic and Avka has remarkable magic detection devices. As soon a Celestrian arrives in their world, they know.

We've dispatched several portal jumpers to rescue our rulers but have never had an exact location of where they were being held. Our jumpers went in blindly and were captured by the Avkans before they could reopen portals to return. Only the stars know if they're still alive.

Knowing she'll be leaving and will be unprotected, traveling to a dangerous world with no magic and a useless team is driving me insane. She just arrived and we're delivering her to the wolves. If it were anyone else, I wouldn't give a shit, but it's *her...* Min Vesmír.

At this moment, all I care about is her returning safely, rulers or not. They've been faithful to Celestria for centuries, and have successors already set up to rule should anything happen to them.

Yes, I desire for them to come back, but to me, she is of the utmost importance, and I'll ensure she returns, even if it's not to me.

TWENTY-FIVE

ELARA

We portal jump into my new living area, and the nausea is overwhelming. Plopping down on my small couch, I bend over, head between knees, taking deep breaths, trying not to vomit all over the floor.

"Can I get you anything?" Remington asks, concern lacing his voice.

"I'll take one—or both—of the vials, please," I reply, holding out my hand. My head is throbbing along with the rest of my body.

In a few seconds, I feel both vials press into my palm. "You did good today, spitfire, but I know you need to rest. Do you want me to get you anything before I leave?"

There is one thing I do need, and my stomach agrees. "Food. Please."

"What do you want? I'll try to get it for you."

"Anything. I'm not picky."

"I'll see what I can gather up. Can you give me an hour?"

I nod and glance up at him. "Of course. I'm going to rinse off all this mud and then soak in a hot tub."

"Alright, I'll see you soon," he says, opening a portal.

"Thank you," I say, watching him disappear, and find it weird that I'm getting used to it.

Out of the tub, clean and relaxed after downing one vial, I decide to head over to the bed and lay down for a bit before Remington comes back with sustenance. Laying on the small twin bed I sink down into it. I've never been on a bed so soft. The one I had growing up was lumpy and very uncomfortable. Cuddling under the covers, I roll to my side and shut my eyes.

"Elara," a voice murmurs, gently nudging my arm.

I sit up and blink, trying to get my bearings.

"I'm sorry to wake you, but I brought you food," Remington says.

Wiping the sleep from my eyes, I sit up. The aroma of spices and chicken fills the air, making my stomach growl.

Remington brings a piping hot bowl of soup over with a spoon and sets it on the nightstand next to me. It's filled with vegetables, noodles, and chunks of chicken, and smells divine.

"I put some food in your refrigerator, but I made you this," he says. "Let me know if it needs more salt."

I glance up at him and blink. "You made this?"

He gives me a sheepish grin. "I did. My mother used to make me chicken soup when I wasn't feeling well, and I loved it so much I asked her to teach me how to make it."

My heart swells, and I try to imagine him in the kitchen. "You went through all that trouble for me?"

"It was no trouble. Besides, I owe you for not being there to stop that bastard from hurting you."

"You don't have to apologize. It happened so fast. Too fast, even I wasn't prepared." Taking the bowl, I place it on my lap and dip my spoon in. After a few blows, I place it in my mouth and... holy moly... it's amazing.

"Mmm," I hum. "This is the best chicken soup I have ever tasted."

"Really?"

"Really. The chicken soup I was served when I was sick came in a can." I take another spoonful and close my eyes as it touches my tongue. The flavors, whatever spices he used, are so good. "Thank you so much."

He grins and crosses his arms over his chest. "Anytime."

"Aren't you going to eat with me?"

He shakes his head. "No, I've already eaten, and you need to rest."

Tilting my head to the side, I exhale. "I just napped for... I don't even know how long it was, but I already feel better. Besides, I could use some company."

He pulls his antique watch from his pocket and glances at it. "I can stay for a few minutes, then I have a meeting with the prince."

I take another bite. "Of course, you do. Please thank him again for coming to my rescue."

"I will." He dips his head and I see concern riddled all over his expression. "What's the matter?"

He shakes his head. "I just don't want you to get hurt. Be careful around the prince. He's engaged, and his fiancé is not someone you want to cross."

I wonder why he's telling me this. "I know he's engaged, and I would do nothing to jeopardize that. Besides, other than saving me, he's made it clear he wants nothing to do with me... a Changeling."

He is about to say something, then stops and pauses. "If you decide you don't want to be a part of the team, I'll understand and so will everyone else."

Shaking my head, I swallow another spoonful of soup. "I'm not giving up because some assholes threatened me. Besides, I promised I'd help get the rulers back, and I meant it. I want to earn a place here in Celestria, and this seems to be my chance to do it. So, tomorrow, I *will* be there."

Remington gives me a lopsided grin and opens a portal. "Sounds good. I'll come back tomorrow morning and get you."

"Wait," I say, and he pauses, turning to me. "I—I just wanted to say that you are the only person I trust, the only person I can rely on here, and I also want to say thank you for everything you've done for me."

"It's my pleasure, spitfire," he says with a glimmering smile. "It's been a whirlwind of adventure since you arrived, but I'm glad you're here."

"I'm glad you were the one who extracted me."

"I am, too."

"See you tomorrow."

He gives me another handsome smile, raises his hand, and disappears.

Arriving at the training center the next morning, the mood is somber. Felix tells us that last night, the Avkans attacked the Kingdom of Sol in the southern realm and killed twenty-two Celestrians before disappearing. The only way they could disappear that fast is with portal jumpers, and only those originating from Terr can wield that kind of magic. So, who are they?

We can only think they are Changelings, but if that's true... who trained them? Only someone trained in portal jumping can open a portal or teach others to do the same.

Five of us remain after the guards took Red and the three others who aided him back to their prisons. Five who will travel to Avka and attempt the retrieval of the rulers. That team includes me and Freya, along with three men—Seven, Callas, and Roman.

Seven is from the Central Realm, the Kingdom of Nahla, known for water magic. Callas and Freya are from the Western Realm, the Kingdom of Asteri, known for air magic. And Roman is from the Eastern Realm, the Kingdom of Doone, known for terra magic.

The remaining four days of training will consist of hand-to-hand and weapons combat, along with learning the map of Avka and the route their intel found that would lead us to the rulers.

Apparently, they are not in a prison, but in a secure building in a remote location that is heavily guarded. They riddled the surrounding facility with cameras and alarms, along with their magic detection devices.

It won't be easy to get to the rulers because they are all that is keeping Celestria from attacking Avka. The new Avkan ruler has issued a warning that if Celestria attempts to attack them, the rulers will die. Time is of the essence. It's critical we retrieve them soon because the moment we do, Celestria will send their militaries from all five realms to attack Avka.

War is coming. It's imminent, but until we rescue the rulers, Celestria's hands are tied.

During training, each one of us has our own personal trainer to go through combat steps, and thankfully, I am paired with Remington. On the mats, we square off.

"Come on, spitfire. Pin me three times and we can call it a day."

I slowly circle him, remembering how I broke his nose the first time I saw him. "Three times? Really?"

He nods with a sly grin. "Three, and I'll treat you to lunch."

"Deal." A wide smile curls on my lips.

Remington is almost a foot taller than me, and for the first time, is not in his captain's uniform. Instead, he is wearing black sweatpants and a matching t-shirt that somehow makes him look devilishly handsome.

When a whistle blows, he charges toward me, so I quickly dive under his attack and kick out both of his legs. Remington falls onto his stomach, so I quickly hop up with feet on either side of his hips, grab hold of the waistband of his sweatpants, and tug upward. When his midsection pops up, off the ground, I throw my body to the side, hooking my legs from the back, around his front, and lock them in while slipping my arms under his armpits, wrapping one arm around the back of his head.

"Shit," he huffs, trying to get out of my hold, but I have him completely immobilized.

I chuckle and start my next move, dropping my bottom foot hook and climbing over his side to mount him. Once I have him on his back, with me mounted on his front, I slide my arm and lock it around his neck, then squeeze. His eyes widen as he quickly taps my shoulder, making me release.

Suddenly, I feel that pricking of my skin and an awareness that *he* is here. I turn and see the prince staring at me while I'm still straddling Remington–his personal guard. The man looks like a god, gorgeous and majestic. He is flawless, and my stupid body wants to move closer to him.

Remington coughs and sits up on his elbows. "Gods be damned, you're fast. I didn't even see that one coming."

I break the connection with the prince. "That's one," I say, sliding off him, hopping to my feet, and holding out a hand to help him up. He takes my hand and stands, then I quickly get back into position and hold up two fingers. "Two more," I say with a challenging smile.

Remington laughs and shakes his head, taking his stance.

"Whoa, that was freaking hot," Callas, from the western realm, says. "Why can't we train with her? I wouldn't mind having her straddle me like that."

"How about you shut your fucking mouth and learn something useful," the prince snaps and everyone turns to him. He looks furious but turns his attention to Cyrus, who is standing right next to him. Cyrus glances at me and waves, so I wave back, wondering why he's here.

Did he find out any information on how to release my powers, or who my birth parents are? He strokes his long gray beard, nodding, as Prince Kage continues to speak to him.

"Why does she only get three pins? Isn't that special treatment?" Seven complains from the mat next to us, his brow dripping with sweat and palms resting on his knees.

His trainer grabs his arm and flings him down on the mat, then jumps on him, quickly putting him in a choke hold. "She gets three pins because she is highly trained and you aren't," he says, releasing Seven, whose face has turned beet red and is now coughing and gasping for air.

Remington turns and faces the other team members. "The Avkans fight fiercely without magic, so hand-to-hand combat will be your greatest asset. What you are learning now just might save your life, so don't take these training exercises lightly."

He's right. You must undergo rigorous and repetitive training until the movements become ingrained in you and come naturally when engaging in combat. I know, as well as the trainers, that five days is not enough. All they need is to learn a few moves that can keep them alive.

Remington takes a stance on the mat, but I notice his demeanor has changed a bit. He's a little more serious, and I know it's because the prince is here. Hell, even I feel a little more guarded, a little more... tense. I can also feel the weight of those dark eyes on me, and it makes my stomach twist. I'm not sure why, but it does.

The whistle blows and Remington moves forward. We circle each other, and that's when he lunges toward me. I grip the left chest area of his sweatshirt with my right hand, and the sleeve above his right elbow, then break his balance by moving toward him before sweeping out the back of his leg with mine. This quickly puts him on his back with me standing above him. I give him a wide smile and hold up two fingers.

"I'm feeling hungry, captain."

He lets out a boisterous laugh, rolls to his side, and hops up to his feet. "You'll have to earn this last one, spitfire."

I tilt my head to the side. "Have I not earned the last two?"

He gives me a dashing grin. "You have," he says, rubbing his palms together, "but I am just warming up."

TWENTY-SIX

ELARA

There is no doubt the captain can kick ass and I wonder if he's been going easy on me. Everyone else stops and creates a circle around us, wanting to see if I can get the third pin.

But I can still feel *him*—the Prince of Terr. I feel that pulsing power that follows him. It tingles under my skin and is thrumming through my veins, and the feeling confuses the hell out of me. Why does it only happen when he is close?

A quick glance to my left and my eyes connect with his—dark and endless. He's standing off to the side with Cyrus and Felix and my heart picks up pace at the sight of him.

The whistle blows and I'm caught off guard. Before I can refocus, Remington runs at me, grabs my waist, and forces me onto my back. This time, he's on top of me, straddling my abdomen, pinning my wrists above my head, to the mat.

"Gotcha, spitfire," he declares with a grin.

I've been in this position countless times and return a mischievous smirk.

"Do you really?"

I move quickly, thrusting my midsection upward while sweeping my arms downward, which causes him to fall forward, flat on his face. I don't have time to see if he fell on his nose. He curses and struggles to sit up, so I wrap my arms around his waistline and press my head against his chest. Gods, even sweaty, he smells good.

As he tries to pull me off, I elbow his thigh—which causes him to groan—then lock my left elbow around his right and flip him over. It happens fast. His eyes are wide and mouth agape as I peer down at him, seated between his thighs.

"That's three..." I say, tapping his abdominal muscles, which are solid as a rock.

Everybody claps, and Felix steps next to me. "You have proven yourself worthy, and with your skills, we have appointed you to lead the team to Avka."

I swallow hard and point at my chest. "Me?"

Felix nods. "If anyone can get the team through this, it's you." He turns to the others. "Does anyone have an issue with our decision?" There is tension on Seven's face, but he and the others shake their heads. "Good then. The rest of you will continue training and master the basics, which will help keep you alive."

I suddenly feel the hairs on my body stand erect.

"Maybe I should employ her as my personal guard," a rich, husky voice speaks from behind me.

The prince scoffs at Remington, then reaches down to me, and I pause, staring up into his mysterious, mesmerizing eyes. As soon as my fingers touch his, there is a surge of energy between us. I yank my hand back and flex it, wondering what the hell that was.

"Elara," Cyrus says coming up beside me. "I need to speak with you privately."

"Of course," I reply, my pulse still racing as I peek up at the prince, who pins me with an expression I cannot read.

"Please, follow me," Cyrus says, beginning to walk away. "You too, Prince Dargan."

I turn to Remington, who gives me a nod of understanding along with a smile. "I'll be here when you're finished."

"Okay," I reply, then follow Cyrus.

There are so many concerns percolating inside of me. All the *whys* and *what ifs* racing through my mind.

Cyrus leads us over to the doors that take us back into the rooms and we walk into the one with the white walls and the long table.

"Have a seat," he says, and I do.

Prince Kage grabs the chair across from me while Cyrus remains standing in front of us.

"Elara, I am troubled by the power seeping from the spell placed on you. It's a trace amount, but it could place you in jeopardy on Avka," Cyrus says.

"So, what are my options?" I ask. "Do I have to leave the team?"

"If that is what you prefer." The prince says as he leans forward, awaiting my answer.

I shake my head. "I can't leave. The team is inexperienced and without me, I'm afraid they will fail. I'd rather go alone than with four others who will only be liabilities."

The prince gives me a knowing nod. "Why do you think they chose those criminals? They've been stripped of their power, but it was removed because they murdered others wielding that power. They are doing this hoping to regain their magic, but we have no intention of giving it back to them. We are sending them, ultimately, as a diversion for you," he explains.

"You mean they'll be collateral damage?" Gods, if that's true, then they predict they will not return from Avka.

"If that's how you prefer to see it, then yes."

I shake my head. "If that's the case, I want Freya off the team. She is an innocent who genuinely wants to help."

The prince leans forward. "Freya is well-versed in Avkan technology. She can hack into any system, deactivate it, and switch it back on while no one suspects a thing. She's on the team for a reason. You need her."

I relax back in my chair. "So, what about the trace of magic trickling out of me? Is there a remedy?"

"There is," Cyrus replies. "Someone will have to siphon that residual power from you."

"Siphon it out?" That sounds simple enough. "I'm fine with that. I've never had access to my magic, anyway, so I don't feel like I'll be giving anything up. But I have one question."

"Go ahead," Cyrus says.

"Will it hurt?"

"No, it won't hurt, but power sharing is... how do I put this? Not something Celestrians do often or easily. It's a very intimate procedure, and only someone powerful enough can perform it."

I glance at the prince. "Powerful... like a royal?"

"Precisely," Cyrus acknowledges with a smile.

So, the prince will be the one to perform it. "What will happen with that extra power?"

"When the practitioner consumes it, it becomes a part of them. It adds to their power."

"Can I get it back when I return?"

Cyrus frowns. "Sadly, it cannot be returned. There has been only one Celestrian who could return power to others, but she is no longer with us."

"So, how much residual energy will he be consuming?" I point to the prince but keep my eyes on Cyrus.

"If you are going to Avka, all the residual power will need to be siphoned. The Avkan detectors are superior at exposing magic, even the slightest trace," Cyrus returns. "Your safety is our priority."

"You mean the safety of the rulers," I correct. They can't mean me. I'm no more important than their rulers.

"You have the option to step down from the mission and keep your magic," the prince says, his eyes serious. "It's up to you. You have been in Celestria for less than a week. You don't have to risk your life for any of us."

I'm shocked he's saying this. Until now, he's been so standoffish, and didn't even think he cared, but the mystifying look in his eyes makes me think otherwise. When he is near, I feel wildly attracted to him, and that frightens me. I've never felt that way about anyone. Even Remington, who I feel I'm growing closer to each day.

I shake my head, knowing I can't give in. "I arrived in Celestria with nothing and know no one. I've trained for years, and I'm thinking fate had a hand in it... for this moment. If I can help, I will, because maybe this will help me find my place here." I lay my palms down on the table and stare directly into the prince's eyes. "Once you consume my power, will I be undetected by their magic devices?"

"You will," he responds with a dip of his head. I turn to Cyrus, and he nods in agreement.

"Okay, I'll do it." Crossing my arms over my chest, I smile at the prince. "You're the imminent ruler of Terr, which is now my country. So, how about we call the giving of my power to you as an early coronation gift?"

His brow rises and lips turn up into a wide smile, which is as bright as the sun. Seeing him this way makes my insides twist and my heart flutter. Gods, how can one man be so attractive? It's not fair.

"I accept," he says.

Leaning in on my elbows, I ask, "Have you ever performed this procedure before?"

He shakes his head. "No."

"Then how do you know it will work?"

He remains composed. "It will work."

I have no other option than to trust him. It's that, or quit the team, leaving three criminals and a tech specialist to save Celestria. I just arrived here and refuse to let a power-hungry egomaniac ruin my new home, my *true* home. There is so much I want to explore, experience, and learn about, and I won't be able to do that if it's destroyed. That's why I am going. That's why I want to help.

"I think we should go somewhere private," Cyrus says. "My office should suffice. It's safe and secluded, and no one will bother us there."

A wave of anxiety hits me. "When are we going?"

"Now," the price says.

"Yes. Yes," Cyrus agrees. "We should do it promptly so you can continue to train, and we can be sure you will draw no trouble in Avka."

I stand and nervously twist my hands together. "I'm ready."

The prince also stands and opens a portal. Cyrus immediately steps through and disappears, but the prince waits, glancing at me. "After you," he says, his hand gesturing to the portal he's created.

It's then I realize I've always had Remington's hand before entering a portal, and I don't know if I can manage going in one by myself. He did save me from Red and the others who tried to kill me, so he can't be all that bad.

Stepping up to the prince, I hold out my hand to him. He peers down at it but doesn't move.

Clearing my throat, I glance up at him. "I'm still new to portal jumping," I admit. "I'm still a bit wobbly on my feet and might need your hand to keep me steady."

His eyes soften, and he accepts my outstretched hand. As soon as we touch, a flood of energy shoots through me, causing me to gasp. I pull my hand back and look at him.

"What was that?" I ask, breathless.

The prince pauses, his expression addled. "I don't know, but I think it's something we both aren't ready for," he replies, before grabbing hold of my hand again and stepping through the portal, pulling me with him.

TWENTY-SEVEN

ELARA

On the other side of the portal, I double over, feeling nauseous, but a coolness suddenly coils around me, eliminating that sick feeling. I straighten my back and turn to the prince, who is still holding my hand.

"Was that you?"

He shrugs his broad shoulders, a lopsided grin gracing those sinful lips. "It's nothing."

"Well, thank you."

"You're welcome."

"Follow me," Cyrus calls from down a hallway.

The prince releases my hand, and a coldness replaces it. Then he moves, and I slowly follow after him.

The corridor we've landed in is long and dark with sporadic sconces lit on the walls. It smells musty and I don't see any windows, but there is a chill in the air that makes me shiver.

"Where are we?" I mutter.

The prince answers me over his shoulder. "We are up past the northern realm, in a place where Cyrus retired. He prefers isolation, and with magic, he made this place inaccessible to anyone. We're only here because he invited us." He hesitates before stopping and facing me. "He came out of solitude for you. You really confounded the director of assessments, so he summoned Cyrus for guidance."

I suddenly feel awful that I caused Cyrus to leave his home and wonder if he is okay returning to civilization.

"Don't feel bad," he says, taking a step toward me. "Everyone has been wondering what he's been up to, and now he has a purpose to come out of reclusion."

"How do you know him?"

"Cyrus ran the Central Court for three centuries. He's maintained peace and gained recognition in all five realms. He retired five years ago, and no one has seen him until now."

"Are you two coming?" Cyrus huffs, standing in the only lit doorway down the hall.

"We should go," the prince says, but I reach out and grasp his wrist.

"Is he really over three hundred years old?" I whisper, having trouble wrapping my mind around that number.

He laughs at my shocked expression. "I suspect he is over six hundred years old, but..." he leans in closer, "he could be older."

My eyes widen even more because, holy shit, I've met no one over a hundred. Cyrus does *not* look centuries old. Hell, the man is in better shape than most fifty-year-olds I've met on Earth.

He laughs and seizes my hand, and this time, there is no shock, just a flow of warmth throughout my entire body. I close my eyes and welcome the heat that's now replacing the icy cold that was seeping down into my bones. I know he feels it too, because his hand tightens around mine as he leads me down the corridor.

We enter a wide, dim room with a few candle-lit sconces along the walls. It's occupied with countless books, parchment, and scrolls, with a solitary wooden desk in the center with more volumes piled on and around it. I'm in awe as my eyes sweep over the long bookshelves lining the walls, laden with even more ancient tomes and scrolls.

"Welcome to my world," Cyrus says with arms spread wide. "It may look like a mess, but I know where everything is." He taps his temple with his finger, which makes me giggle.

"It's wonderful," I say. When I was in middle grade, I would spend hours at the library, strolling down the rows of books, searching for my next escape. Those memories were some of my happiest.

On his desk, I spot a large black leather-bound book that says Royal Registration—Vital Birth Records, and it makes me wonder —

"Have you found out anything about my birth parents?"

Cyrus glances at the book, then at me. "No, not yet, but I have hope I will uncover them soon."

"I guess I'm not listed in the royal registry," I murmur. I had hoped that maybe I was someone important.

He shakes his head and picks up the book. "No. I thought you might have been a royal. This book accounts for every royal pregnancy and birth, including miscarriages, stillbirths, and any missing royals." A sad smile turns down the corners of his lips. "That just means I was looking in the wrong place. I've already requested the Celestrian Birth Registry from Terr since we know your heritage stems from there. At least a part of it."

"What do you mean, *part*?"

"Although you have the features of someone from Terr, I believe one of your birth parents is from another realm. But because they have blocked your power, it's almost impossible to tell." He ambles toward me and places a gentle hand on my shoulder. "We'll find them, Elara. Don't you worry."

Prince Kage nods. "If there is anyone in all of Celestria who can find them, it's Cyrus."

Cyrus smiles at the acknowledgement. "I'm still searching for a way to release your power, too. Hopefully, when you return from Avka, I'll have some answers for you." He pats my shoulder, then claps his hands together. "Alright, let's focus on the matter at hand."

Cyrus heads to the back of the room and disappears behind some shelves. Moments later, he returns with a bunch of white candles cradled in his arms. Striding over to a small bare space on the floor, he sets the candles in a large circle. Once he's finished, he heads back to his desk and rummages through the drawers until he withdraws a piece of chalk.

Entering the ring of candles, he draws a pentacle, and around it, five smaller circles with symbols inside them.

"They represent the elements of the realms—terra, fire, water, air, and ether," Prince Kage explains.

I nod, my eyes focused on Cyrus as he draws more symbols around the outer ring.

"What are those?" I inquire.

"Runes of protection," the prince answers, his hand still clutching mine.

"Prince Dargan," Cyrus speaks, rising and inspecting his work. He gives a nod of self-approval, then turns toward us, his eyes moving down to our linked hands.

Instead of letting go, the prince's grasp tightens, and tingles shoot through my palm.

Cyrus's gaze shifts to Prince Kage's face. "Would you like me to assist you, or would you like this to remain... private?"

I glance between them, wondering what the big deal is. He's just going to draw my residual power out and absorb it into himself. It shouldn't be complicated, right?

"I'd like you to stay, Cyrus," he responds. "I need you to be certain she is safe."

Cyrus nods. "Of course." He holds out a hand to the ring of candles and his drawings inside. "Come, then. Both of you will need to step inside the center of the star."

The prince moves, our hands still joined. When we step into the middle of the star, he releases my hand and wraps his arm around my waist, drawing me around until we are facing each other. The air grows heavy, and my heart is hammering. His presence alone is intimidating and being face to face with him somehow makes me feel exposed.

"Are you sure you're okay with this?" he asks, those dark, gold-rimmed eyes narrowing on mine.

I nod because I can't find my voice standing so close to him.

Cyrus remains just outside of the ring. "Elara, like I stated before, this is a very intimate exchange. It's quite rare."

"Why is it rare?" I question.

"Because *no one* wants to give up power. This is *not* a spell to remove the power of a criminal. I know of only one usage of this spell, a few millennia ago when Celestria was still new. A queen gave up her power to her husband so he could defeat an opposing army."

"Did he win?"

Cyrus smiles and glances at Prince Kage. "He did."

My eyes also shift to the prince. "Was he from Terr?"

He nods. "Yes, he was my great, great grandfather, and ruler during that time."

"He was one of the greatest rulers in Celestrian history," Cyrus adds. "But that is a story for another day." Facing me, his expression turns serious. "Prince Dargan will be absorbing your power, and once he does, it will create a connection between the two of you. It's inevitable, because part of you will live inside of him... and your power will become his. However, the ritual itself is," he pauses, and I swear I see his cheeks blush, "sensual."

I swallow hard. "How sensual? Are we talking about sex?"

"No. No," Cyrus wheezes, waving a hand in front of him. "From what I've read, physical contact is necessary, but the sensual part is more of a feeling shared between the two involved. Sharing power is supposedly a very intimate act."

My eyes move to Prince Kage's. "Are you sure this is what *you* want? If it is as intimate as he says and there is a connection, I know your fiancé won't agree with it. You saw what happened when she saw you touching me. Besides, you are engaged with an entire kingdom that will be under your care. If this is going to cause you trouble, then I'll pull out."

The prince scoffs. "I don't give a shit what anyone thinks, especially Vera. Nor do I care," he replies with a stern look. "This has nothing to do with them."

"Elara," Cyrus adds, "Prince Dargan is the only one powerful enough to perform this transfer. There is no one else."

Towering more than a foot over me, the prince lowers his head a few inches, his stern expression softening. "I'm in, but we can leave right now if you decide you don't want to do this."

There is no way I can walk away now. The fate of the rulers, and possibly the planet of Celestria, lies in my feeble, non-magical hands. I feel the weight of it growing heavier with each passing day.

Taking in a heavy breath, I straighten my back. "I'm in, too, and nothing will change my mind."

A smile creeps on the corners of the prince's lips.

"What do I have to do?" I ask.

Cyrus walks over to his desk and unrolls an old scroll, squinting as he reads. "Each of you must maintain three points of contact with the other at all times, skin-on-skin, and that connection must be kept unbroken until the transfer is complete."

Prince Kage nods, then takes a step forward. His left hand grasps my right, interlocking his fingers with mine—the first point of contact.

Next, his right hand slips behind my neck, gently cupping it. I follow his lead and do the same, sliding my left palm to the back of his neck. This already feels intimate, and it's only the second point of contact. With both hands occupied, my heart thrums wildly, wondering what the third will be.

Closing his eyes, the prince speaks words in a foreign tongue that sounds ancient. The candles in the sconces on the wall flicker, while a heaviness fills the air. His melodious voice reverberates through the room, through my soul, and I feel every word inciting and awakening something inside of me.

For the first time, I feel that residual power stir. It feels like a warm hug from a friend I've never met but has been with me my entire life.

When the prince opens his eyes, they are completely black, and the change makes my breath catch. Tendrils of shadow emerge from his being and slowly curl around us, enveloping us in darkness while binding us together.

I gasp, feeling his raw and unmitigated power vibrating through the surrounding air. It's dominant and commanding, but also gentle and careful as it coils around us.

As soon as Kage stops speaking, every candle around the circle ignites in flame. Cyrus steps back so I focus on the dark prince, whose eyes are now fastened on mine. Devastatingly beautiful, I peer deep into those onyx depths, as haunting as a starless night sky. Every fear and every concern I have dissolves beneath the warmth of his gaze and touch.

Need swells within me and I don't know where it stems, but with every breath, it grows stronger and stronger.

As the prince's shadows completely encompass us, my body feels wired and hypersensitive to every sound and every movement. His shadows gently feathering against my skin are like haunting caresses and the pressure of his fingertips causes heat to surge through my body, straight to my core. I also feel a tingling energy radiating from where his hands are touching me.

My breath quickens and heart races as I breathe in his delicious scent. Everything happening between us is arousing a sexual desire I've never experienced before. It's overwhelming, causing my eyes to close and back to arch.

Without warning, the prince tugs the back of my neck toward him, claiming my mouth with a kiss so passionate, a moan escapes my lips.

Three points of contact that cannot be broken. I am now at his mercy.

His kiss is alluring, his tongue is rapture, and his touch consumes me like fire. A groan rises from deep inside his throat, reverberating throughout my body while his shadows coil tighter around us.

Shifting our joined hands behind my back, he presses me tighter against his muscular frame. I feel the solid length of him between us and *gods*. He is incredibly blessed.

Then I feel it—my power ebbing away. It's a tug from the depths of me that moves toward our points of contact. It's not painful, but erotic. Warmth radiating wherever our flesh is touching.

Groaning into my mouth, the prince's kiss turns dominant and hungry. His tongue, soft but demanding, ravages my mouth with deep, fervid strokes. I'm dizzy, but my need for him surges until it's overwhelming. I want him. I need him. I'm thirsty and he is that satiating drink.

His hands caress my body, satisfying the cravings that have been deprived for too long as he draws power from me. Our breaths are heavy, hands clenched, mouths moving in unison. My heart is pounding against my chest, and his is answering with the same pulsing fervor. His touch, his taste, his scent... it's complete ecstasy.

His knee slides between my legs, putting pressure on my highly sensitive center. I move against his thigh as he pushes closer, grinding into me, nearly causing me to climax.

Then, I hear a voice breaking my trance and calling his name.

"Prince Dargan!" It's Cyrus, but his voice is muffled. "It's complete. The transfer is complete," he calls from outside our shadowy cocoon.

No. Not now. I don't want this to end. Whatever *this* is.

I moan, feeling the bitter separation between us as the prince breaks our kiss. Just when I think he's going to step away, his arms fold around me, pulling me against him. Wrapping my arms around him, I melt into the warmth of his embrace—a precious, stolen moment shared without words. His lips, soft and wet, press against my forehead and I hear him whisper two words, so soft, I can barely hear them. "Min Vesmír."

I've never heard the words before, but they make me feel something... an intimate familiarity, and it confuses me.

As his shadows recede, the prince takes a step back, letting a coldness sweep between us, instantly seeping into my bones. My limbs feel weighted, and my legs are trembling.

As soon as he releases his arms from around me, my knees buckle, but he shoots forward and catches me before I hit the ground, lifting me into his sturdy arms.

"She's weak from the power drain," Cyrus says. "She needs to rest."

"How long will it take for her to recover?"

"That depends. She no longer has that residual power to assist her, so you will need to call a healer for an anodyne."

I try to speak, but the words die in my throat. My arms won't lift, and legs won't move. The power transfer has depleted *all* my energy. Exhaustion sinks its claws deep into me, and as much as I try to fight it, I'm losing and quickly descending into a state of unconsciousness.

"You did well," the prince whispers in my ear. "Now, sleep well and recover."

Knowing I'm safe in his arms, I close my eyes and unwillingly slip into darkness.

Twenty-Eight

PRINCE KAGE

I'm fucked. There is no way I can be with anyone other than Elara. Especially after she transferred her residual power to me. I can feel it inside me, even now, brushing against my power like a soft caress. Her power is lusty and vigorous and filled with light energy. It's the total opposite of my dark and violent magic.

Elara is also a Death Dealer... which I clearly saw when I was in her mind. Until she arrived, I've been the only Death Dealer in all Celestria. We will need to train her once her power is restored because she will hold the power of life-or-death in her hands.

From the moment we touched, I knew she was mine. The connection between us is undeniable. But being a prince, I don't have a say. I cannot be with her unless she is a royal. Elara is a Changeling, left on Earth for a reason. Cyrus researched and determined that Elara cannot be a royal because they log every royal pregnancy and birth in Celestria, whether it's miscarried or full-term. They have accounted for every single one.

Cyrus also assumed that because of the remnant of considerable power seeping through her barrier, she might have been the daughter of the

Empress. But the child the Empress carried in her womb is dead and buried with her. The infant bears the six-sided star on her forehead—the enchanted insignia only passed down through the line of the Empress. The healers also said she carries the same DNA as her mother. This alone proves that the infant buried with the Empress was the one in her womb, and undoubtedly her offspring... not a Changeling, which rules Elara out.

A knock on my door snaps me from my thoughts. "Enter."

Rem ambles in, a harsh expression on his face. "I know what happened between you two."

He's talking about the power transfer, and he looks pissed.

"It had to be done. Her safety and her life are on the line. If the Avkans detect even the slightest amount of magic in her, she's as good as dead."

Sighing, he rakes his fingers through his hair and drops down on the foot of my bed.

"I know. It's just... she's special to me too, Kage. The moment I collected her, I felt a strong connection with her. She's like no one I've ever met." He shakes his head and leans over on his elbows. "Why did she, of all the people in the gods-damned universe, have to be the one in your dreams?"

"Don't think I haven't been asking myself the same damn question every single day since she arrived." I exhale and stand in front of him. "Rem, you know me. You know I can't control my feelings, especially when it comes to her."

"Yes, *but* you're engaged. You know how obsessively jealous Vera is."

"Speak for yourself," I growl. "Zarah is just as obsessed with you."

"Yes, Zarah is deranged and a bit psychotic, but at least her parents are not as insane as Vera's. There is no way in hell they will let you cancel the marriage arrangement. They've always wanted a piece of Terr," he says, a desperate look in his eyes. "I fear the day they find out about Elara and the power transfer between you. The royals of Asteri have a reputation, Kage. You know this. They aren't people you mess with. If they think there is *any* threat against Vera becoming Princess of Terr, they'll make that threat disappear. They'll make *Elara* disappear."

I shake my head, but I know he's right. The rulers of the western realm have gone through lengths to make those who have gone against them disappear. Unfortunately, we didn't find this out until after the marriage arrangement was made. The citizens of both kingdoms expect us to unite, and now that both kings have agreed upon and signed off on the union, we cannot stop it.

"I won't let them hurt her, Rem. I'm stronger than their entire royal line, and I swear to the stars that I'll kill them if they try."

"Yes, *you* are stronger, but Elara isn't. She has *no* power to defend herself. You already saw what happened during Messis, and again during the obstacles. She's danced with death several times since she's been here. Yes, you were there to save her, but you can't and won't always be there for her in the future. Against Celestrian magic, *she is helpless.*"

I hate that he's right and despise how frustrated and helpless his words make me feel.

"Then what am I supposed to do, Rem?" I protest. "Tell me, because I am going out of my fucking mind."

"You do nothing," he says with a deep sigh. "Right now, she's training to go to Avka. You need to stay away and let her concentrate on the mission."

"I can't. You don't understand. *She's real*, Rem, and every gods-damned cell in my body wants to be with her, to protect her, and make sure no one fucking messes with her."

"If you want to keep her safe, you have to, Kage. There is no other option. You can't let anyone know or see your feelings for her, especially Vera. Until we figure out a plan, you have to be smart, even if that means showing indifference to Elara when anyone else is around." He presses his thumb and finger against the bridge of his nose. "Everyone at the obstacles saw you not only save her but sweep her into your arms. Your concern and the way you act around her *will* put her in danger."

I slam my fist on the dresser and pace the floor in front of him, my head and heart pounding. "You have to protect her, Rem." I stop and pin him with a serious gaze. "Be there for her when I can't. Train her to put up mental shields. There isn't much time, but if the Avkans catch her, we can't have them digging around in her mind." I close my eyes and exhale.

I know he has feelings for her and leaving her in his hands is shredding my fucking heart to pieces, but Rem is the only one I trust with my life.

"I trust you, Rem," I say. "Until we sort this out, I want you to stay with her."

No, I don't want this, but also know it's the only option I have.

Rem stands and places his hands on my shoulders. "You're doing the right thing, Kage. I cannot promise my feelings for her will go away, but I promise you I will train her well and protect her."

I've never felt more helpless in all my life. I am the strongest royal in Celestria, yet I am powerless when it comes to her. I've never wanted to protect anyone like I want to protect her. I want to make her happy, to fill in the void that was missing all her life. But most of all, I want to claim her as mine, because yes, I am a jealous bastard.

However, Rem is right. Right now, I can't let my feelings for her cloud my judgment. I'm the Prince of Terr. I have to play this smart, or my life will be ruined and hers will be in danger.

Until I work this shit out, she'll have to rely on my best friend to keep her safe and make her happy. She already trusts him. I see how easy they are together and watch the way they interact, and I'd be lying to say I wasn't jealous.

"Go." I hold out a vial of medicine I retrieved from the healer. "She's sleeping but will need this when she wakes up."

Rem nods and takes the vial from my hand. "I'll let you know when she leaves for Avka and will keep you updated. I pray the stars are on our side, brother."

I turn my back on him and move to the window, knowing that after he's gone, I'll have to harden my cold, aching heart.

"So do I."

Twenty-Nine

ELARA

It's nighttime. Two moons and countless shimmering stars hang in the vast sky above, illuminating my surroundings. I'm standing in a field of green surrounded by lush, flowering trees in pinks, lavenders, and blues. In front of me is a small creek that flows toward a larger pool of water, glistening with celestial light.

This magical place is foreign to me, but somehow, it feels familiar.

"Elara," a silvery voice calls from behind.

I turn to see a girl with long golden hair and gold eyes standing in a white gown that shimmers in the gentle breeze. She's beautiful, no older than I am, with a brilliant glow radiating from her being. Her face lights with a smile as she regards me.

"Elara, do you know who I am?" she asks.

"I don't think so," I reply, watching her bare feet slide through the feathery grass. Fireflies take to flight and circle around her, and I shake my head, entranced at how spellbinding she is. I know I've never met her. I'd remember meeting someone like her.

"*Are you sure you don't know me?*" Her brows rise, while a grin curls on her lips. "*I've been with you your entire life.*"

It's then I recognize her voice. The voice that's been in my head since I was a child.

"*Are you—*" Emotions brew inside me. "*Are you the voice in my head?*"

"*I am,*" she replies.

Tears brim in my eyes and spill down my cheeks. Her voice has been my only friend, my guardian and constant salvation. Since the beginning, she brought me comfort and peace, and during a time when I wanted to end it all, she offered me hope and assurance that the dark days would eventually pass.

"*Where have you been?*" I weep. "*I haven't heard from you since the meeting at the Central Court.*"

She moves to stand directly in front of me and takes my hands in hers. They're soft and warm and fill me with that same soothing embrace her voice had for all those years.

"*You're home now, Elara. You no longer need me.*"

"*That's not true. I need you,*" I sob. "*You're the only one who has ever been there for me. I can't do this without you.*"

"*You already have been,*" she says softly, raising her hand to brush away my tears. "*You're fulfilling your destiny here without me.*"

Tears continue to flow down my face. "*Who are you? What's your name?*"

"*My name is Elwyn, and I'm part of you, Elara. Half of a whole.*"

I shake my head, confused by her words. "*I don't understand.*"

"For now, you don't need to understand. But when the time is right, fate will bring everything that has been hidden in darkness to light."

She's speaking in riddles, and I can't seem to put them together. "Do you know who my parents are?"

She nods but doesn't answer. "I'm so proud of you, Elara, of who you have become, and who you will become once your power is released."

"You know about my power?"

Again, she nods.

"Why didn't you tell me?"

"I was a mere voice in your head. You wouldn't have believed me."

She's right. But — "If you're leaving, where are you going?"

"I am finally going to where I belong, but I will always watch over you."

"Why? Why have you been with me all these years?"

"It was my duty, but also my pleasure."

I'm so utterly confused. I need answers and she's skirting around all of them.. "How are we connected?"

She smiles as if she can read my thoughts. I know she can. "Your answers will come in time," she sighs, her brow furrowing. "Soon, there will be arduous and deadly trials you must endure. Always remember, you're never alone. Your true mate will protect you, but you must also protect him. You are much stronger than you think you are, Elara, and just when you think the end is near, don't fret, because it is only the beginning."

More riddles that are making my head spin.

"Who is my true mate?"

Elwyn gently lays her hand against my chest. "Your heart knows."

Leaning forward, she presses her soft lips against my forehead, leaving a tingling warmth in the wake of her kiss. "Be safe and be strong, Elara, because the fate of Celestria does indeed lie in your feeble, non-magical hands."

I grin and can't help but laugh. "I guess you do still hear my thoughts."

She chuckles, and it makes my heart swell. "I do."

Wrapping my arms around her, I feel her do the same.. "I've only just met you but have known you my entire life. I feel like I'm losing a sister." New tears burn my eyes and fall down my face. "Thank you for being with me, Elwyn. You have been that light, guiding me through my darkest days. I know it's because of you I am still alive and still breathing."

"That's not true," she replies. "I was just a voice, something you could have easily ignored. But you continued, you fought, and you conquered all the obstacles placed in front of you. I had nothing to do with that."

Elwyn takes a step back, and it feels like a part of me is being torn in two. When I see a tear escape her eye and roll down her cheek, my heart cracks. She's leaving and I'm already feeling alone.

Deep sobs rip from my chest. "Please don't leave me."

Elwyn tries to smile, but her lips are trembling. "I must. You're home now, and I know you will find your place. Now, I must leave and find mine."

I let out a pained wail as her body starts to dissipate.

"I love you, Elara."

My heart is shattering, and I don't know if I will ever recover from this loss. I'm losing her, my only faithful friend, and the pain is unbearable.

"I love you too, Elwyn."

She folds her hands over her heart, closes her eyes, and completely fades away.

I shoot up as a painful sob escapes from my chest. My face is soaked with tears, and I feel ice cold. Every limb feels weighted, and I could literally sleep a few more days.

Glancing around, I find myself back in my room and wonder how I got here.

The prince must have brought me back.

Emotions brim as I recall my dream. A dream that felt so real. Did I truly meet the voice in my head? Celestria is a place filled with magic, so it must have been.

"Elwyn," I whisper her name, tucking it safely into my heart.

My thoughts shift back to the power transfer and my heart picks up pace. The prince, the feeling of his touch, his lips, his taste, his scent... it's seared into my memory.

Is Prince Kage my true mate?

I truly don't know. People have damaged and misled my heart too many times. Yet, there is one question that has me second guessing. How can the prince be my true mate when he has an arranged marriage with a princess?

That is something you cannot easily break, especially when it involves the joining of two realms.

I sigh, wiping the tears from my face, when I hear a knock at my bedroom door. I yank my blanket up to my chest and call out, "Come in."

The door opens and Remington walks in with a dashing smile on his face. "Hey spitfire, how are you feeling?"

I instantly feel a little lighter. He has a way of doing that, which makes me wonder if perhaps he is my true mate.

No. I shake my head. What am I doing? I can't think about mates, nor do I need one. My life is complicated enough.

Remington clears his throat and hitches a thumb out the door. "Um... if you don't want visitors, I'll jump right out of here."

"No!" I yell, throwing a hand up, startling him. He laughs and takes a step into the room.

He's dressed in his captain's uniform and looks as handsome as ever.

"I'm sorry," I sigh. "I was inside my head for a bit. I had a terrible dream that I lost someone especially important to me."

His expression saddens. "Is there anything I can do to make you feel better?"

I nod and grin. "I believe you owe me lunch."

His dimpled smile makes my tummy flutter. "I did, but you skipped out on me yesterday. However, they ordered me to give you this." He ambles over to my bedside and holds out a vial. "It'll help you recover from the power transfer."

Heat rushes to my face as I think back to what happened between me and the prince. "You know about that?"

"I'm the prince's personal guard and best friend. I know everything that involves him."

I swallow hard, wondering how much he knows.

"Take this, and if you feel up to it, I'll take you to the Evergreen for lunch."

I snatch the vial from his hand, pop the top, and down its contents. My face scrunches as the bitter liquid touches my tongue. "Gods, that stuff is horrible."

He laughs again and takes the empty vial from my hand. "How long should I give you to get ready?"

"What time is it?"

He pulls the antique watch from his pocket. "It's almost noon."

"Give me thirty minutes and I'll be ready."

His lips curl up into a smile. "I'll be back in thirty."

I nod and watch him leave, and as soon as I hear the front door snap shut, I hop out of bed. My weak legs buckle under me, and before I can catch myself, I end up on my ass. I roll onto my back and laugh. Thank the gods no one was around to see that.

Turning onto my knees, I use the bed to lift myself back up. My legs are quivering and feel like they want to collapse, but I slowly drag myself to the closet, snatch up the only clothes I have—a uniform—and head to the bathroom.

Nearly an hour later, clean and dressed, my legs feel stronger. I step out of the bathroom to find Remington laying on the couch with one arm tucked behind his head and eyes closed. As my bare feet pad closer to him, he slides one eye open and gives me a lopsided grin.

"I was going to give you another minute before I broke down the door to see if you were still alive," he chuckles.

"I'm sorry. My legs were weak. When I got out of bed I was like a new baby fawn taking its first steps, but the tonic worked. I'm much steadier now."

"A new baby fawn, huh?" he smirks.

"Yes. A new baby fawn," I retort. "They were weak and jittery, and I..." I stop, not wanting to embarrass myself further.

He sits up and leans forward, elbows on knees, head tilted to the side. "You what?"

"Nothing. I'm starving," I say. "What does the Evergreen serve, anyway?"

"You're evading my question, spitfire."

"I am not." I hurry to my room and slip on socks and boots because that's all I have. The heels Maeve gave me for Messis never made it back here, and I'll have to remember to ask her why.

"You're totally evading... and the Evergreen serves all kinds of things. My personal favorite is their astral puff." He stands and stretches his long limbs before he opens a portal.

"What's an astral puff?"

"It's a pastry of sorts, but savory, stuffed with meat, vegetables, and gravy."

"Oh, that sounds delightful. I want that."

He offers his hand to me, and with a smile, I accept it as we enter the portal.

We exit just outside of the Evergreen, and I double over, taking in deep breaths, trying not to retch on the street and mortify myself.

"You alright?" he inquires.

I nod after a few more breaths, feeling a little better. "I don't know if I'll ever get used to that."

"Just give it time. You'll be a pro once you can open your own portal."

"Gods, I hope so."

The sun is shining, so I tilt my head back, close my eyes, and bask in its warmth.

I'm suddenly yanked, and when my eyes snap open, Remington holds a finger to his lips while pulling me to the side of the building.

"*What?*" I mouth the word.

He holds up a hand, and we both glance around the corner of the building. Princess Vera exits with a trainer for the upcoming mission, and she looks livid. He's from the Kingdom of Asteri—the same realm as she is.

We both stay silent and listen.

"I'll fucking kill her," Princess Vera snaps. "And why the hell was Kage there, anyway? He's not a trainer."

"I don't know, highness," the trainer says, bowing his head. "I know he saved her from those men, and when we arrived, I saw him embracing her tightly in his arms. He looked... deeply concerned."

Shit. They're talking about me.

The man pauses, his eyes avoiding Vera, like he's afraid to speak. "There is also one other thing I overheard. However, I'm uncertain if it's the truth."

"Well, tell me!" she screams, her voice sending jolts along my spine.

I hold my breath, waiting for his answer, knowing he'll damn us both.

"Cyrus arrived with the prince, and not long after, they exited with the girl. The talk is, there was a transfer of power between them."

"What?!" Vera's face contorts, burning bright red. "I'll siphon the air from that bitch's lungs when I find her!" She slams her fist down and a wall of powerful air strikes a chair and shatters it in two.

I gasp and Remington pulls me further to the side of the building, his body flush against mine. His eyes are wide, head shaking at me, but I shrug and furrow my brow. Maybe he thinks I'll do or say something to rile her. I'm not that foolish. I don't want to die today.

He told me about the Kingdom of Asteri's air magic and wild natures, and I just witnessed it firsthand. Vera is freaking crazy and immensely jealous. Then again, who wouldn't be? Prince Kage is not only gorgeous, but he is the most powerful male in all Celestria. Even I would be protective if he were mine.

"Kehr, take me to the prince," Vera barks.

Kehr is not the trainer, but someone from Terr.

Gods, her outburst has me concerned. What will she tell the prince when she confronts him? I know I'm already screwed and have a suspicion she'll accuse me of seducing him. Then she'll have me locked up, or worse.

A snap in the air causes Remington to move away from me. "Fuck," he curses, pacing back and forth, raking his fingers through his hair. He looks even more distressed than I am. Of course, he would be. His mission is to defend his prince.

"What can we do?" I ask, my breath quickening and heart pounding against my chest.

His anxiety is making mine surge and I wonder how bad this situation could really get.

Remington finally stops in front of me and clutches my shoulders. "Elara, please help me. Vera knows what transpired between you and Kage, and that not only puts you in grave danger, but the rulers of Asteri will not let Kage go free. His reputation and his throne are at stake."

Gods.

I nod, hearing the thump of my heart in my ears. Remington has not used my real name since I arrived, so I know he means business. I've never seen him so unhinged, and it worries me.

"I'll do my part. Just tell me what I need to do."

"Just follow my lead. We have to convince Vera that there is nothing between you and Kage, and that whatever transpired was just a mistake."

I nod again, not really understanding where he is heading with this, but I'll do whatever is necessary to save the prince, his reputation... and my life.

"I'll do whatever you need me to."

He nods, but his gaze is distant. "Alright, we have to leave immediately and fix this before it gets out of control and escalates beyond repair."

"Hey, I'm with you," I say, trying to assure him. I hope my compliance buys him some peace.

He nods, then holds out his hand and I take it as he opens a portal, and we step through.

I guess the astral puff will have to wait.

Thirty

PRINCE KAGE

"Kage!" Vera's piercing voice sends a shiver up my spine.

I let out a breathy exhale. *What the hell does she want now?*

Both of my guard's eyes go wide after hearing her tantrum, so I dismiss them from the room. "Be thorough with this matter and keep me informed."

"Yes, my prince," they reply, slapping their fists against their chests before hastily exiting.

I've sent them to investigate the Lure drug and to uncover who is producing and distributing it within Terr. I also ordered them to locate the men who used the drug to seduce and rape those women, and to use whatever methods necessary to capture them. When I find the bastards, I will make them suffer by my hands before giving them an excruciating death.

The door to my study explodes off its hinges, skids across the floor, and collides into my desk, sending paperwork scattering in all directions.

What the fuck?

Vera walks in with a crazed look in her eyes. They've gone completely white, and a cyclone of wind is encircling her.

"You bastard!" she hollers, stomping toward me. Raising a hand, she sends a blast of air aimed at my face, but I extend my arm, my shadows shooting out to keep it from reaching me.

"What the hell is wrong with you?" I growl.

She stops and thrusts a finger at me. "That bitch!" she curses. "Are you having an affair with her?"

"What the hell are you talking about?"

Another portal opens and the head chancellors of Terr and Asteri step out. I don't need this shit right now. She must have summoned them as witnesses.

"The Changeling!" Vera shouts. "Did you power share with her?"

All eyes pin on me, so I hesitate, wondering who the hell told her. It couldn't have been Cyrus or Elara, and I know Rem wouldn't say anything.

"Son of a bitch!" she rages. "When my parents return and hear about this, they will strip you of your title and your throne. Even your father won't be able to help you."

"You're taking this too far, Vera." Her freaking temper is reckless and unruly. "You don't know the entire story."

"Taking it too far? You're my future husband, and you've been caught multiple times with that bitch in your arms. Trainers said you saved her, and now I find out you power shared with her?" She is panting heavily, her eyes are wide with a crazed look. "The arranged contract gives me grounds to request that your power be removed if you breach it. You've committed an unforgivable offense, Kage, and Cyrus, too, for allowing it to happen."

I try to remain calm, but this bitch is out for blood. "Like I said, you don't know the whole story."

"Then why don't you tell us, Prince Dargan," Damien Faust, Asteri's chancellor, says. "We were told to come here to investigate an affair and possible power transfer."

Faust is a pompous prick. I can see in his eyes that he's already judged me.

Everyone knows there has always been a rift between Asteri and Terr. The land, the resources, and the magic are superior here, and the other rulers would give anything to get a piece of it.

The king and queen of the western realm jumped at the chance to have their daughter marry into Terr. They said that a marriage alliance between the two kingdoms would solidify Terr as the dominant realm. But I know that with this marriage, Asteri would have a foothold here. My mother was against the arranged marriage, but after her death, my father was too distraught and naïve enough to not see what they were planning. I know they're snakes, ready to slither in and consume whatever they can.

"We can't make a judgment off of hearsay," Edson Wessex exaggerates. He's a stout old man with dark gray hair and a long beard, and also the chancellor of Terr *and* Zarah's father.

Wessex gives me a tight smile and a bow of his head. "The sooner you prove your innocence, my prince, the better."

He looks bored, and I know he hates petty disputes. Especially with my father gone, the rulership of Terr doesn't need to be under any scrutiny.

But how can I prove my innocence when there were witnesses who saw me save Elara? I admit it was reckless to gather her in my arms, knowing there were trainers from other realms there. Rem was right, but there was no way I could stand back and do nothing to help her.

As for transferring power, we did it in secret with no one knowing, because we knew if anyone found out, it would lead to this. Power-hungry leaders looking for any way to take down the royals of Terr.

"Prince Dargan," Faust says. "If you cannot prove your innocence, I'm afraid I will have to bring you in for questioning."

"Come on, Faust. There is no concrete proof," Wessex says, coming to my defense.

"There is proof," Vera interjects, her eyes on Faust. "All the trainers saw them together during the coaching for the Avkan mission, and the trainer from Asteri overheard them talking about the power sharing between them."

I fist my hands, my power stirring inside, wanting to lash out and hurt someone.

The Asteri rat. He must have snuck into the rooms while we were discussing our private matters. When this is over, I'll rip out his tongue and make sure he never speaks again.

Faust turns to Vera. "Don't worry, princess. We will interrogate the trainers, and have the prince taken in for examination to prove the power sharing."

"You can't take him now. With our king missing, Prince Dargan is the standing ruler of Terr."

"Rulers are not above the law, Wessex," Faust counters. "He is not only engaged, but we did not give him permission to perform such a spell. If found guilty, the Central Court will decide his punishment."

A buzzing energy rushes through me right before another portal opens. When Elara steps out, my body goes tense. I can feel her power, the power I extracted from her, brushing under my skin as if it recognizes her.

Rem steps beside her, his hand grasping hers. I suddenly feel apprehension and fear, and my pulse is racing. I wonder what the hell is wrong with me, then it hits me. Those aren't my emotions I'm feeling... they're hers. It must be a side-effect of the power transfer.

"What is she doing here?" Vera snaps. In a flash, she throws her arms forward, sending a slicing wind toward Elara. My shadows thrust outward, coiling around Elara and Rem, yanking them away as Vera's wind collides with my desk, cleaving it in two.

"That's enough!" I roar, the walls in the room rattling. "If you use your power one more time, I'll have my guards escort you out."

"See!" Vera aims an accusing finger at me. "He just proved he chooses her over me."

"It proves nothing," Rem says, stepping forward. "I don't know what you heard, but there is nothing going on between Prince Kage and Elara."

"Of course, you'd say that," Vera snips. "You're his best friend."

"Can you prove this, captain?" Wessex asks calmly. "We need evidence."

Rem steps closer to Elara, gazing lovingly into her eyes. "Because she is with me," he breathes. He then leans toward her, his free hand cupping her face as he presses his lips against hers.

The room goes silent.

My entire body tenses, and I try to hold my composure, but this... this is shattering me.

Elara stiffens, her eyes wide for a moment before I feel a surge of confusion and another wave of anxiety followed by... enlightenment. She closes her eyes and sinks into his kiss.

Gods, I want to grab her, open a portal, and whisk her away from all this bullshit. But it will not go away. I must deal with this.

Thirty-One

ELARA

Remington's kiss takes me by surprise. I'm not expecting it, especially in front of the prince, his fiancé, and the chancellors, but quickly understand what he's attempting to do. The chancellor asked for proof, and he's giving it to them. I told him I'd do whatever he asked and would follow his lead, so... shutting my eyes, I let Remington take the reins.

He keeps the kiss chaste, no tongue, but it's still intoxicating and has my heart racing. When we part, I'm left out of breath and slightly embarrassed as he faces the chancellors.

The chancellors, Remington quickly explained when we arrived, were Faust, from Asteri, and Wessex, from Terr. Wessex happens to be Zarah's father.

"Elara is traveling to Avka in a few days and has been selected to lead the team that will attempt to rescue the rulers," he explains, still gripping my hand. "She is a Changeling, and as an infant, someone cast a powerful incantation which sealed her power before they sent her to Earth. She is our greatest hope, but Cyrus said there was residual energy leaking through that seal. If she travels to Avka and they detect even a trace of her power, the mission will fail."

He faces me again, his expression filled with affection. "She's important to me, so I begged the prince to take the residual power from her." Remington then shifts to face Prince Kage, and with his back turned toward the others, he gives him a wink.

"The prince initially refused," Remington continues, swiveling back to the others, "but I reminded him of our friendship and that he owed me for being his personal guard and captain of his army. After practically begging on my knees, he finally gave in. So, if there is someone to blame for this, it's me. And if there is any penalty given, I am the one who will accept it."

Vera's eyes were totally white when we appeared but have shifted back to their icy blue, and she's staring at me with contempt. "What about him protecting her at the training center? Why was he embracing her?"

"Captain, I have a few questions for you first," Faust interjects.

Remington halts and motions to him. "Go ahead, ask me anything."

"You said there is a seal constraining her power?"

"Yes, allegedly it was done when she was a newborn, before they transported her to Earth."

Wessex and Faust exchange bewildered glances.

"Who would do such a thing? Do you have any idea?" Wessex queries, worry etched in his expression as he looks at me.

"We have no leads," Remington replies. "But Cyrus is investigating it."

I hate that this discussion is about me, and I'm literally here not uttering a word. There is a reason I prefer isolation. My life isn't an open book for everyone to scrutinize, and I don't want or desire anyone's pity. I just want to get the hell out of here and eat a freaking astral puff.

"You still haven't given me an answer," Vera snaps, arms crossed over her voluptuous chest, icy eyes shooting daggers at me. "Why did he have her in his arms at the training center?"

The chancellors look from Vera to Remington for his answer.

Remington nods. "The reason is simple," he explains. "The team contains criminals who had their power stripped from them. During training, Elara excelled, and they felt threatened by her."

I was about to speak when Remington continues.

"I had to leave the training for a moment and made the prince promise to watch over and protect her while I was away. I'd suspected the men would try to prevent Elara from being on the team, and I was right. One of them attacked her with a weapon, but the prince kept his word and rescued her on my behalf. I'm indebted to him for that." Remington wraps an arm around my waist, drawing me to his side, and doing my part, I lean my head against his shoulder.

Vera's face sours, but both chancellors nod, like they are accepting his story.

"It seems someone misled you, your highness," Wessex says to Princess Vera. "It's evident that Captain Ward and Elara are the couple here."

Wessex bought it.

But... Ward? Is that Remington's surname?

"I think it's odd that *she* isn't voicing her opinion," Vera says, sneering at me.

I've seriously had enough of her. She may have the title of princess, but she's just another mean girl who thinks she's better than everyone else.

"Why should I?" I say, stepping away from Remington. "So, you can manipulate my words and accuse me?" When I'm pissed, my mouth runs on its own, and I usually regret it afterwards. But I'm not afraid of her. Someone needs to put her in her place.

"What you did is unbefitting of a princess and a future queen. You're in a position of authority, yet you easily took false information and spread it, which shows how naïve and immature you are." She looks like she wants my blood, but the anger inside me grows as I direct a finger at the prince, keeping my eyes fastened on her. "You almost destroyed your fiancé's reputation with a lie before trying to find out the actual truth. That proves to me that you have no loyalty to him and makes it evident this arranged marriage is not rooted in love or trust, but of obligation." I turn my attention to Remington. "I don't want to be here. I'd like to leave."

"You bitch," Vera snaps, and the air in the room grows ice cold. "You have no right to speak to me that way. Are you aware of who I am?"

I confront her again, a smirk on my face. "I don't care who you are, but I believe that if you are a royal, you should never demand respect... you earn it. Right now, I have zero for you."

Remington coughs and covers his mouth to stifle a smile.

The wind picks up, and although her eyes go completely white, she does nothing. "Is anyone going to do something about that? Did you hear what she said to me?"

"Why?" Wessex asks. "She did nothing but express the truth. You called us here to witness something you thought was from a reliable source that turned out to be false information." He sighs and shakes his head. "This was an utter waste of my time." He then turns and bows his head to the prince. "Prince Dargan, I must leave, but you have my deepest admiration for being a devoted friend. I'm sorry you have to tolerate this."

Vera gasps, stunned at his words.

I don't like Zarah, but her dad is literally one of my new favorite people.

"Thank you, chancellor," the prince utters. Wessex grins, opens a portal, and steps through.

"Wait!" Faust calls, hurrying toward him, but the portal closes. "Stars be damned! I traveled with him. How am I going to return to the Central Court now?"

"One of my guards can transport you," the prince replies.

Wanting to leave, I take hold of Remington's hand, and he creates a portal. Right before we step through, I face the prince and incline my head and see a slight glimmer of amusement rise on those beautiful lips.

We arrive back in my room in Terr's training center. I don't feel as sick as I usually do and wonder if it's from all the heightened emotions I'm feeling.

Remington releases my hand and plops onto the couch, letting out an exasperated breath.

"We did it." I say with enthusiasm, holding my hand up to him. He stares at it but doesn't move. "On Earth, if someone does a good job, you slap their hand." I use my other hand to demonstrate.

"Why?" His nose crumples.

"I don't know," I shrug. "It's just what they do. It's called a high-five."

"High-five?" He chuckles before he leans forward and slaps my hand.

"What you did..." I exhale. "I know the prince is grateful."

He pins me with a heated look. "I kissed you."

I nod, feeling my face heat. "You did. I mean, I was shocked at first, but..." I give him a wide smile, "I liked it."

"You liked it," he says, contemplating the words, stroking his jaw. "It would have been a lot better if we didn't have an audience. Especially the prince. I felt... convicted."

My brows tighten together. "Why would you feel that way?"

"It's complicated," he says, shaking his head, pressing a thumb and finger to the bridge of his nose.

I stand in front of him, crossing my arms over my chest. "Nope. No way. You can't leave me with an *'it's complicated'* answer to that question."

He leans back on the couch with his dimpled grin. "I can't tell you why. It's the prince's story, not mine."

The prince's story? There is no way he is leaving now without telling me what it is.

"Captain Ward, you are digging yourself deeper and deeper into a hole."

Remington bursts with laughter. "Come on, spitfire. If I tell you, he's likely never to forgive me."

"I don't care. Our friendship ends here if you keep me in the dark."

He leans forward, rubbing his face in his palms. "Fine, but you have to promise me not to say a word."

I roll my eyes at him. "I've been in Celestria less than a week, and you're my only friend. Who do you think I'm going to talk to?"

He exhales, then gives me a nod and pats the couch next to him. I move over and sit facing him.

"First, I want you to answer one question." His expression turns serious, and it makes my gut twist.

"Ask away," I say.

"How do you honestly feel about Kage?"

Oh, he's going with a sucker punch question. I stare into those dark, gold-flecked eyes, and really think about it. I never really took time to contemplate exactly how I feel about him because there are so many emotions that rush through me when he's nearby.

"Well?" he asks.

"I—" I let out a heavy breath. "I really don't know. I mean, I barely know him, but whenever he walks into a room I—" I don't enjoy discussing my feelings. I've never been open about them to anyone, except Elwyn—the voice in my head who knew every one of my deepest secrets.

Remington reaches over and takes my hand in his. "If I'm going to tell you the truth about him, you need to be truthful with me."

"Just give me a minute," I breathe. "It's difficult for me to talk about my feelings openly with anyone."

"Do you have feelings for him?" he asks directly, making my heartbeat quicken.

"I don't know exactly what I'm feeling," I say, honestly. "When we first met, I didn't like him. I thought he was a pompous prick who hated me."

"And now?"

I shake my head and lean back, letting my head drop back onto the couch. "I feel a lot of things. Before he enters a room, I can feel him. I don't understand how, but it's like there is a charge in the air, and... I just know it's him." Closing my eyes, I think about the prince and my mind automatically travels to the transfer of power and how intimate it felt. "I don't know why, but after Messis, I feel like he's changed." I try to pull myself back into reality because I could easily get lost in that moment. "I don't feel that contempt from him like I first did, but I do feel a pent-up frustration."

"But... how do you feel about him?"

I roll my head on the back of the couch to face him. "It's complicated."

He laughs and gets up, pulling a chair from the table and setting it down in front of me before he sits on it. I sit up straight, anticipating whatever he's about to tell me. Instead, he asks another question.

"What happened when he touched you, not only at the Central Court, but during training?"

Thinking about those times, my breath quickens along with my pulse. "I honestly don't know. Whenever I touch him, there is a surge of energy that happens between us. It feels like I'm being electrocuted."

His expression drops.

"What? What does that mean?"

He shakes his head, and I know he knows.

"Captain, tell me what that means."

Those dark eyes fix on me, his expression melancholy. "When I was younger, I asked my father why he loved my mother. He said he knew she was his from the moment he laid eyes on her. He also said he felt something inside he never felt with anyone else, and when he introduced himself to her, and took her hand in his for the first time, it felt like a bolt of lightning struck him."

The air is heavy and I'm finding it hard to breathe. "Is there something that explains those feelings?"

He nods, and my heart thumps loudly against my chest. "It happens when you find your true mate."

I freeze, hearing Elwyn's words in my head. *Your true mate will protect you, but you must also protect him.* Did that happen already? Prince Kage saved my life at the Training Center, and I saved him by helping Remington clear his name, but somehow, I don't feel like this is what Elwyn was talking about.

"He can't be my true mate. He's a prince and I'm... nothing. Besides, he's engaged to that crazy bitch who would kill me in an instant if she ever found out I had any feelings for him."

"We have to keep up our act, for the time being."

"Act?" I ask, and Remington nods. "Okay, if we are being open, how do *you* feel about me?"

I want to know because I feel like there is something between us.

"I can't compete with him," he says, his gaze dropping to his folded hands. "He's my best friend, and he's been in love with you for his entire life."

I shake my head, completely baffled by his words. "How could he be? I just met him."

He gets up and starts slowly pacing in front of me. "Ever since he was a child, Kage had dreams of a girl. She visited him often, especially when he was feeling sad or troubled. Every time my father brought me to the palace, he talked about her like she was someone real. Like she was the most important person in his life.

"In his dreams, she never spoke to him, but he said he knew exactly what she was thinking. He loved her smile and said it was brighter than the sun. When she smiled, he knew everything bad he was going through was going to get better.

"I asked him once to describe her to me. I'll never forget the look on his face, and I've never seen it since. He looked... happy. Truly happy. And when he described her, he had a sparkle in his eyes." Rem's gaze fixes on mine. "He said she was beautiful, the most beautiful girl in the entire universe, with long black hair and hazel eyes rimmed in gold."

The room suddenly feels like it's spinning, and I can't breathe in enough air.

"He even gave her a name," Remington murmurs. "Min Vesmír. He said it meant *my universe.*"

My heart stops and I feel faint. I heard those words, heard the prince whisper them to me after the transfer of power. This can't be right. I can't be the girl he dreams about.

"There is a reason his emotions go haywire around you. He told me the other night that *you* are Min Vesmír. You are the girl in his dreams, and he's confused, because you've suddenly materialized in his world. You're real, and he doesn't know how to deal with it."

"He shouldn't," I sigh. "He's engaged."

"Vera?" Remington scoffs. "He doesn't love her. He never has. What you said today hit the nail on the head. There is no love or loyalty between them. This marriage is one of obligation and duty between the two realms. That's it."

I shake my head. "Still, they are going to be married and I won't get involved."

"I think it's already too late for that. If you are his true mate, there is no way he will let you go. I know, Kage. I grew up with him and knew the only girl he ever loved was the girl in his dreams. But now that you're real and there is a genuine connection between you?" He rakes his fingers through his hair. "He's trying to do the right thing, but he can't hide his feelings for you."

"What about you?" I ask. "How do you feel about all of this?"

"I care about you, spitfire. Ever since we met, and you broke my nose, I knew you were someone special."

We both laugh and the tension in the room dissipates.

"There is no question I could easily fall in love with you," he continues, making my heart swell, "but realizing what is happening between you and Kage, I know that if I take our friendship any further, it will ruin him. I've never seen him so affected by anyone else as much as he is with you, and as much as it kills me not to pursue you, I cannot betray our friendship."

"I guess I'm doomed by the stars, never to be loved by anyone."

"Two men are smitten with you and will protect you at all costs. I don't see that as a terrible thing."

I shrug and sigh. "One is engaged, and loyalty shackles the other. I guess it could be worse."

He laughs and shakes his head. "If the stars had given you to me alone, I would have already locked you down."

"Hmmm," I hum, tilting my head. "That sounds a little barbaric."

He shrugs. "Call it what you want."

"Well, captain, since you've obviously friend-listed me, I have to be truthful. I'm kind of upset with you right now."

His smile drops. "Why?"

I frown at him. "Because I'm starving, and you didn't get me an astral puff."

"Shit," he curses, chuckling and immediately opening a portal while extending his hand to me. "To the Evergreen," he says, standing and pulling me to my feet.

I'm glad nothing has or will change between us. In fact, I feel our friendship has grown stronger because of this.

"Thanks, *Rem*. You are the best," I say.

He gives me his signature dimpled grin and elbows me on the side. "Anytime, spitfire."

THIRTY-TWO

ELARA

It's our last day of training and Rem has me memorizing the map of Avka and the area they suspect the rulers are being kept, while the others are continuing their part of the training. We go over the steps of the mission until I ingrain them in my mind.

Being the leader, I have to be sure we know exactly where we're going. We get one shot to do this right and can't afford to take one misstep.

The pressure is on. Again, just last night, the Avkans attacked the eastern and western realms, targeting their military officers and their regiments. Two officials from Asteri and three from Doone were assassinated, as well as over two hundred soldiers.

Remington looks exhausted. They sent portal jumpers from the Central Court to summon each realm's military officials in the middle of the night. I know he's been up since, tightening Terr's military and guards.

This has to stop. We have to bring back the rulers, or the Avkans will continue to destroy Celestria.

"Hey, I know this is a lot to shoulder, but I wouldn't trust anyone else to lead this mission. I know you're ready," Rem says, breaking my stressful thoughts.

"Thanks, Rem. You don't know how much I appreciate your support." His dimpled smile makes my chest thump a little louder. "What about the rest of the team? Do you think they're ready?"

"As ready as they can be," he sighs. "Don't worry about them. I want you to focus on the mission. When you get there, it will be a little after midnight. Freya will temporarily deactivate the entire electrical system around the location, which should give you a few minutes to get into the facility undetected. Once you're in and find the dining hall, one of our men on the inside should meet you there and will escort you to the area where they are keeping our rulers. When you confirm they're there, press this button. We'll have our jumpers ready for extraction." He hands me a small round device with a red button in the center.

"How have you been in communication with them?"

"We have a secret location outside of the facility where our jumpers send all messages written on a special type of paper that is undetected by the Avkans. Only someone with Celestrian blood can read it. One drop, and the paper will reveal any correspondence. Another drop, and it disappears. We give them three days to reply before our jumpers return, grab their response, and jump back."

I nod. "And this device will give you our location?"

"Yes, once you press and activate the button, it will tell us your exact coordinates. However, you'll have to stay in that area until they get to you."

"How long will it take?"

"To lock down your position and send the jumpers... it should take no more than five minutes."

Five minutes can feel like a lifetime when you're in danger, but I keep the thought to myself. I know Rem will make sure they get to us as soon as possible.

"One more question," I say, and he nods. "What will happen—gods forbid—if they capture us? We can't let them have the devices or they will capture our jumpers."

"That, too, has been considered. Like the communication, each device can only be activated by someone from the team. There is a small needle under the button that will prick your finger when it is pressed. Once it verifies your blood, it will become active." He lets out a deep sigh. "If they take you—gods forbid—try to conceal it. If you have no alternative, crush it."

This is so overwhelming. It doesn't even feel like it's real... everything I've done in the past week. I feel like I could wake up in my home tree back on Earth and count this all up to one crazy dream.

Rem gently elbows me on the side. "How about I treat you to dinner and drinks and then head back early? Tomorrow is going to be a big day."

"Sounds like a plan," I say, grinning at him.

As we exit the room, I spot Vera leaving the training center. An uneasiness swirls in my gut and I can't help but wonder why she's here.

"Did you see her?" I elbow Rem.

"Who?"

"Vera. I just saw her leave."

His brow furrows as he scans the exit, but she's gone. "Maybe she came to see if Kage was here."

I sigh, letting my growing anxiety deflate. "You're probably right. I wouldn't doubt she tightened the leash, making sure he isn't anywhere near me."

"Don't worry about her. She can't do anything, knowing me and Kage are protecting you."

I glance over to Seven, Callas, and Roman, who are finishing on the mats. They're shirtless, their muscular forms covered with tattoos and sweat.

Seven takes a towel and wipes his face, then drapes it over his shoulder. His silvery eyes lock with mine, hesitating, before he nods his head to me. I do the same. Walking away, the other two follow him, murmuring amongst themselves. Nothing seems different with them.

"Elara," Felix calls, heading over to us. "Remington here assures me you are ready for tomorrow."

I nod and give him a tight smile. "I am."

"That's great," he answers with a smile of his own. Tonight, we will deliver your uniform for the mission, and tomorrow morning at ten we will all gather in the conference room in the Central Court. He turns to Remington. "We'll run and monitor the mission from there."

Rem nods, folding his hands behind his back. "We'll be there."

"Thank you, Captain," he says, tucking a clipboard under his arm. "I'm on my way to see Freya to give her some last-minute instructions, so I wish you both well." He pivots and moves away. "Tonight, I will beg the stars for help, and tomorrow will look forward to a successful mission and the return of our rulers."

"As will I," Rem replies, then holds out his hand to me. "Are you craving anything?"

I shake my head but am feeling hungry. "How about you?"

His eyes narrow. "I'm feeling like a brew and some pizza."

"That actually sounds perfect," I say, taking his hand as he opens a portal.

Lying in bed, my head is wired and I'm wide awake. My stomach is twisting, and I can't sleep knowing that in the morning I'll be traveling to another world, into enemy territory, with Freya and three criminals.

No one I trust will be there to save me if anything should go wrong, and with Elwyn gone, all the words of encouragement will be on me. I'm not feeling optimistic, especially with an inexperienced team thrown together and trained in five days. There are so many variables to this mission, and countless reasons why it should fail.

Flipping to my side, I release a heavy breath. The pressure is mounting. I feel it on my back, shoulders, and in my chest. If all proceeds as planned, tomorrow I'll be meeting every ruler in Celestria... even the King of Terr. If we succeed, I'll be a hero. If it fails...

Failing isn't an option. We have to succeed.

I desperately try, but sleep eludes me. My head throbs as I watch the sun gradually rise on the horizon, stretching its rays and welcoming a new day. I didn't want to begin this day sleep deprived and feeling exhausted, but I can't change that now.

Slipping out of bed, I zombie shuffle to the bathroom to prepare. After a quick shower, I tie my hair up into a ponytail, brush my teeth, and get dressed.

The positive—the uniform they sent is kick ass. We were measured two days ago, and I'm impressed by the quality and how fast they created it. It's black leather and fits like a glove, but the chest, molded to fit my breasts and waist snugly, is solid and almost feels like Kevlar. It's also lithe, allowing me to move freely.

The new combat boots are knee high and lightweight, and they also supplied me with a belt equipped with throwing knives.

As ready as I'll ever be, I head to the kitchen. On the counter is a small white vial and a large cup with a note attached to it.

I dropped in and saw the bathing room door closed and heard the shower going, so I'm leaving your coffee here. It's extra-large with an added kick. Also, I was ordered to give you the vial. Take it or someone will have my head. Be back in thirty minutes. — Rem.

Rem is a godsend.

Snatching the cup of coffee, I remove the lid and take a gulp. It's still hot and feels wonderful going down my throat. Next, I pick up the vial and pop the top. I have a feeling the prince was connected to this, so I part my lips and dump the liquid into my mouth, immediately coughing as the bitterness hits.

With eyes watering, I hear a snap and turn to see Rem, handsome as ever, dressed in his captain's uniform.

"You're not looking too good, spitfire," he says, a look of worry furrowing on his brow. But his eyes sweep down, taking in my new uniform. "I take that back. You look... incredible."

I quickly chase the bitter aftertaste in my mouth with more coffee. "What was in that vial? Is someone trying to kill me?"

Chuckling, he stalks toward me, his boots thumping across the floor. "It's a tonic that will keep you awake and alert for at least six hours," he says.

Thank the gods. It's just what I need. "Who gave it to you?"

He leans against the counter, arms crossed over his broad chest. "Who do you think gave it to me?"

I bat my eyes at him. "Is he tall, dark, handsome, and unavailable?"

He presses a finger to my forehead and laughs. "Possibly. He also gave me another order. I have an hour to train you to put up a mental shield."

"Mental shield? Why would I need that?" The tonic is working. My brain is buzzing, and alert and my body went from being drained to feeling energetic.

"You need it because the Avkans have a way to break into minds," he says. "If they catch you, they could find out everything about the mission, the prince, and you being a Death Dealer. We can't let that happen."

"Okay, then. Teach me."

Leading me over to the couch, I sit down, and Rem sits across from me.

"Close your eyes," he says, and I do. "I don't possess Dark Vision, like Kage, but I can enter your mind."

"What's Dark Vision?" I ask.

"Kage can visibly enter anyone's mind. He can see their memories, and he also has the ability to alter what a person sees."

"So, what he did at the Central Court, when he jumped into my mind, he used Dark Vision?"

"Yes."

"And you aren't able to do that?"

"No, but I can access your mind and hear your thoughts and can also communicate with you through telepathy. What I want you to do is put up a shield to keep me out."

"Is it easy?"

"It takes a lot of concentration and a great deal of practice, so don't worry about not getting it on the first few tries. No one ever does."

"Well, let's try it," I say.

He nods, and I close my eyes.

My head suddenly feels heavy, and then I hear Rem's voice. *"Put a shield up, spitfire. Block me out."* He's speaking, but his voice isn't coming from where he's sitting. It's inside my head.

"How?" I say out loud.

"I want you to envision a strong and impenetrable wall encompassing you. There must be no cracks and no voids within that wall. It will have to survive me pushing against it, trying to get in."

"Okay," I breathe, focusing on the task.

I know a diamond is the strongest natural material on Earth, and because it's also a girl's best friend, I decide to use it to construct my wall. Focusing, I start to build, observing the diamonds form, creating the shape of a dome with no opening around me. When it is done, I beam, proud of what I achieved. It looks powerful *and* it dazzles. That's a double win.

I spot movement outside of my newly constructed dome. A dark shadowy mist is rebounding off the outside face, trying to get in.

"Now what?" I ask Rem aloud.

"What did you do?" he inquires, this time verbally.

"Why? What's the matter?" Opening my eyes, I see him gazing at me with a confounded expression. Maybe I messed up.

"Hey, it's my first attempt, so give a girl a break." I sigh. "You told me to build a wall, so I did."

Rem shakes his head and expels a breathy laugh. "I'm not criticizing you, spitfire, I just want to know how you did it."

"You mean put up the wall?"

He nods. "You blocked me out completely. I couldn't reach you."

I angle my head. "So, that's a good thing?"

"That's an outstanding thing." A grin spreads across his handsome face. "No one has ever constructed an invincible barrier on their first attempt."

I shrug. "It wasn't difficult. Actually, it was easy."

He chuckles and runs his fingers through his hair. "You truly are something special." He smacks his palms on his knees. "All right, let's give it another go. I just want to confirm it wasn't..."

"A freak thing?"

He smiles. "I have confidence in you, but to put my mind at ease, let's try it again."

I agree, giving him a grin as I close my eyes and repeat the same process, building my dazzling diamond wall and keeping him out of my mind.

As an extra precaution, and because three is a charm, I do it again, this time even faster and easier than before.

Maybe it's the tonic. Maybe it's not. All I know is that I did it, and now I feel that much more confident going to Avka.

Thirty-Three

PRINCE KAGE

Glancing out the window, I watch the sun stretch over Terr, gently nudging its inhabitants from their slumber. On any other morning this sight would be tranquil, but knowing what the day will bring, I'm filled with an uneasiness.

Last night, I couldn't sleep.

Today, Elara will travel to Avka on a dangerous mission to recover not only my father but the rest of the Celestrian rulers.

From what I've observed about her, knowing how she holds everything inside, I have a gut feeling she didn't get any sleep either. So earlier, I requested our healer, Digby, and asked him to bring me a tonic that would assist her during the mission. He pulled through. When Rem arrived, not long after, I ordered him to give it to her, and make sure she took it.

When I asked if he had instructed her how to put up a mental shield, he apologized and said he hadn't. Grasping it usually takes days of practice, but he'll be lucky to get an hour of training in. That alone sends my anxiety through the roof.

The Avkans have abducted countless Changelings like Elara and brainwashed them. The only advantage is that Elara is highly trained in combat and hopefully should be able to avoid them. I've seen and experienced her strength and am certain she can lead this mission to success.

Rem assured he'd keep me informed and would notify me if something, good or bad, should arise. Until then, I'll remain here, in my study, expectantly awaiting her return.

Thirty-Four

ELARA

The moment we show up at the Central Court, Rem is called away.

There was another attack early this morning. This time, the Avkans struck the central realm—the Kingdom of Nahla—and slaughtered one official and fifty-three guards before vanishing without a trace. It's clear Terr will be next.

It looks like their attacks are calculated. They're testing the strength of each realm before they launch their final attack.

The Central Court Training Center is teeming with old and new faces. The atmosphere is chaotic, and the stress levels are high, but I suppose I expected nothing less. Today, they will send us out on a make-or-break mission.

The rest of the team arrives, and they lead us into a small sitting room. Mine and Freya's uniforms are similar, fitted, and sleek. I notice she doesn't have a belt, but has a bag thrown over her shoulder. Whatever's inside must be what she needs to get us into the facility.

The men's uniforms are also leather and remind me of that superhero from the Marvel Universe—The Black Panther. Only their pants aren't as form-fitting.

"You ladies are looking fine," Seven blurts in a smug tone. His white hair is tied back at the nape of his neck, his silvery eyes shifting between me and Freya. He's leaning back in his chair, arms folded over his chest, with one leg crossed over the other.

He suddenly leans forward, his eyes on my belt. "Why do you get knives and we get nothing?" he growls.

"Because she's the only one who knows how to use them, asshole," Freya replies.

He shakes his head. "That's bullshit."

"Says the criminal," Freya murmurs, egging him on.

The tension in this room is palpable. Thank the gods Callas and Roman are quiet and more on the mellow side. I can tell they're here to get their magic back.

I don't want to say something to piss Seven off more because I need this team to be on good terms when we leave here. So, I keep my mouth shut and offer him a smirk. It's the best I can do.

Being team leader, I decide to change the subject and lessen the growing tension.

"I heard about the attack on your kingdom this morning," I say to Seven.

"*My* kingdom?" He huffs, eyes rolling. "*My* kingdom threw me in prison for defending myself against a military bastard who thought he could threaten me."

"You killed him," Freya says flatly. "You used your water magic and drowned him."

Seven nods, no remorse in his expression. "I did, and the bastard deserved it."

"It's illegal to use your magic to kill another Celestrian," she rebuts. "You could have restrained him and told the authorities."

"The authorities?" he lets out a boisterous laugh. "His father is a court official, and he was in the military. He would have gotten off with a verbal warning."

"Why did he threaten you?" I ask and immediately want to take the question back. I don't want to pry.

He glares at me, and just when I think he's going to tell me to go to hell, he speaks.

"Like I said, his father is a wealthy official in the Kingdom of Nahla and my mother was a servant in his family home. He was a fucking pervert and would make lewd remarks to her.

"One day she came home with bruises on her face and on her arms. She told me she fell, but I knew better. After pushing her for the truth, she told me the bastard told her to suck him off. When she refused, he grabbed her and tried to force himself on her.

"She fought and got away, but I was pissed and went to confront him. He told me my mother was sewer trash and not worthy to suck his cock, and then used his magic to taunt me. He broke my arm and threatened to break the rest of my limbs.

"I didn't snap until he said the next time he saw my mother, he would teach her a lesson... using his cock. That fucker didn't deserve to breathe, so I killed him. As long as my mother is safe from the fucking predator, I am fine being put away."

The room goes silent, and I somehow can't fault him for what he did. He was protecting his mother.

"I'm sorry," I say, but before he can reply, the door opens, and Felix walks in, clapping his hands together.

He must be loaded with caffeine because he's perky, with wide, bloodshot eyes.

"How is our royal rescue team?" Felix asks.

Seven, Callas, and Roman have deadpan expressions and don't answer.

"We're ready," I say, speaking for everyone.

"Good. Good. Do any of you have questions about the mission before you depart?"

Again, the other members stay quiet.

Felix's gaze turns to me. "Elara, we are counting on you to lead this team to success."

Gods, the pressure.

"In a few moments, I'll escort you to the jumper who will transport you to Avka. He'll deliver you and return immediately because if he lingers for over five seconds, he will be detected. To be safe, you'll need to move swiftly from the area to avert any drones they might send," Felix instructs.

"How far will the facility be from the drop off point?" I ask.

"It will be two miles out," he replies. "We decided on that area because there is a forest nearby you will be able to utilize should you run into trouble."

Two miles is nothing. I ran five miles almost every morning for the past four years. However, I have four other people to account for who I can't leave behind.

There are two quick raps on the door and then it opens. A man dressed in a navy uniform walks in. "Commander," he says, referring to Felix. "They are ready."

Felix nods and the man exits the room.

"Alright. Looks like it's *go time*," he says with a half-smile and wide, anxious eyes. "Follow me."

Standing, we follow him out the door. My heart is hammering against my chest, and my gut is twisting in knots. This is it. There is no turning back now.

As we make our way down a corridor, people stop and tip their heads to us.

"Good luck," most of them say. I nod back and smile, collecting all the good luck I can get.

We are led into a large room teeming with people.

In one area there is a circular table with officials from each realm seated around it, dressed impeccably in the uniform of their kingdoms. I quickly spot the chancellors, Wessex and Faust, amongst them.

In another area is a lengthy desk with at least two dozen others seated and glancing over at one large display on the wall ahead of them. On the screen is a map of Avka with a red circle around the area their rulers are being detained.

As soon as we all enter, the room goes silent, and all eyes fix on us. Felix leads our team to the front of the room, and I suddenly feel anxious, palms sweating, my body weighted under heavy, scrutinizing eyes.

Everyone of importance is here, awaiting their rulers to return, and we're their only hope. We cannot fail.

Felix explains the mission to everyone in attendance as my eyes scan the room for Rem. I find him standing at the back, in a corner with a few others dressed in Terr's military attire. When he turns, spotting me, a familiar dimpled grin appears, and I relax a bit.

He nods at the man standing next to him and they both make their way toward us. He must be the jumper.

"Let's pray to the gods and the stars that they return to Celestria with our rulers!" Felix says with a raised fist. The room claps and heads nod as I try to focus and get my head in the right space.

Remington reaches us, and it's only then I recognize the jumper's face. He's the one from the training center in Terr. The smartass I put on his back when I first arrived.

Rem steps in front of me. "You remember Talon?"

I nod at the man whose dark eyes are fixed on me. He looks different, attractive, with well-defined features, and charcoal hair combed and tied at the nape of his neck.

"I didn't recognize you with your shirt on," I remark to Talon.

A broad smile curls on his lips as his eyes glide down my body. "We could rectify that when you return."

"Only on the mats," I say.

He flashes me a smirk. "I'll be expecting it."

Remington shakes his head and introduces Talon to the others on the team. "Talon will take all of you to the drop-off zone. When you arrive, you must head to the forest and conceal yourselves. I'd wait at least ten minutes before continuing, to make sure they haven't detected you."

"He's going to jump all five of us?" Seven questions, his smug expression on Talon.

"I can jump everyone in this room at once," Talon retorts, matching Seven's attitude.

They're both over six feet and built, and I can't tell who would win if they ever got into a fistfight.

Rem puts a hand on Talon's shoulder. "Talon is one of Terr's strongest jumpers. We chose him because it decreases the risk of detection than it would if we send multiple jumpers."

Callas, Roman, and Freya nod, but Seven seems to bristle, like something's up his ass. Fingers crossed, he won't be a problem.

Felix steps back, but Rem steps up to me, grabbing my hands. "You've got this. Just please be safe. Watch your back and come back to us safely."

I smile and squeeze his hands. "I will."

When Rem steps back, Talon holds out his hand to me, but I hesitate.

"The captain said you're a little wobbly on your feet going through portals and could use a hand."

My eyes shift to a grinning Rem, who crosses his arms over his broad chest and shrugs.

I take Talon's hand as he opens a portal. Sucking in a deep breath, adrenaline rushes through my veins as the five of us step through.

Thirty-Five

ELARA

The sky is dark when we land in Avka. I squeeze Talon's hand, steadying myself.

"You okay?" he asks. I nod and he quickly pulls me to the side, discreetly placing something into my palm, folding it shut. "It's from the prince," he whispers. "Keep it on you. Be safe."

He opens another portal and jumps through before I can question him.

"The forest," Callas says, pointing to our right.

"Let's go," I say, tightly clutching whatever Talon put in my palm, as we quickly head toward the mass of trees.

The ground is rocky, and the air on Avka is humid and has a musty odor with hints of sulfur. It's different from the pleasant smell of Celestria.

As we make our way, I scan the sky, and in the distance spot five small lights that don't look like stars. I pause and watch them closely, realizing they're moving toward us.

"Drones," I exclaim, pulse racing as my finger aims at the sky.

"Shit," Roman curses.

"Move!" Seven orders, charging forward.

We sprint for the cover of trees, and I push through, grabbing hold of Freya's wrist as we head for the center. It's pitch-black, but the trees aren't as tightly knit together as I thought. I'm not sure what kinds of trees they are, but they remind me of the giant sequoias in California, ones I've only seen pictures of and read about in books.

As my eyes adjust to the darkness, I spot a tree with a hollowed-out center and head for it. "Over here," I urge.

We all cram inside, shoulder to shoulder. It's a tight fit, but at least we're hidden and not out in the open.

"I don't think being together is a good thing," Callas whispers. "We should have split up. If they find us, we're all done for."

"They're drones," I respond. "They send them in first, so I doubt there will be anyone in the vicinity, and it'll be almost impossible for them to maneuver through the forest."

My sweaty palm tingles with whatever Talon placed inside it, and I'm even more curious to know what it is. Clutching it, I keep it hidden, not wanting the others to see.

He said it was from the prince, but is it really? For all I know, it could be something that could jeopardize our mission. The tingling in my palm tells me otherwise. I just hope it will be undetected by the Avkan devices. If it is truly from the prince, I know it will be safe.

A high-pitched sound fills the air, and everyone goes still. The atmosphere is so thick with apprehension, I could slice it with one of my knives.

The drones are here.

Every one of us stands still and silent, hearing them move above the treeline. The tension is harsh, and so is the heat of our bodies being pressed together. We wait, breaths heavy, hearts thumping, sweat dripping down our brows. The only positive thing is that Celestrians don't smell bad when they sweat.

Throughout the forest, shafts of fluorescent green light filter down through the foliage above, reaching the forest floor. They're scanning the area.

I hold my breath as a beam of light approaches us. Instinct wants me to bolt, but if we do, I know they'll catch us. When the beam reaches the trunk, Freya moves closer to me, squeezing my arm, but it vanishes, reappearing on the opposite side of the tree, and moves away.

When it's almost out of sight, we all exhale at once.

"Shit that was close," Callas breathes.

Seven glares at him, shaking his head. Because we're not out of the woods yet. I'm feeling a little queasy, but we stay silent, fixed in place for what appears like an eternity, until we can no longer hear the humming of the drones. When I believe it's clear, I nod to the rest of the team, and we exit our hiding spot.

"I wonder what would have happened if they found us," Roman says, wiping the sweat from his brow.

"Shoot us down," Seven replies. "I heard they equip Avkan drones with guns."

Callas shakes his head. "What happens if they find us out in the open with no place to hide?"

"We spread out and run," I say. "But we shouldn't have any problem now that they're gone. They inspected the area and felt secure enough to call the drones back. We just have to move quickly once we get out."

Out of the forest, Freya searches through her bag and pulls out a pair of small binoculars.

With the three men discussing the drones, and Freya conducting a full sweep of the area, I turn away and open my palm. In it sits a white stone, the size of a quarter, in the shape of a circle, which is secured to a black leather cord. It's a necklace, so I quickly fasten it around my neck.

Freya stops and points west of us. "There is an artificial glow in that direction."

After having studied the map for hours, I agree that's the way to the facility.

Quietly, we traverse the rocky terrain and I'm thankful the boots are lightweight, protecting my ankles from twisting on the uneven ground.

Above us, the night sky is splashed with dark clouds, but I see glimmers of stars peeking through. I feel like the stars are observing us, judging us, watching fate play out. I can't help but believe that fate favors the bold and the brave.

We've stopped a quarter mile from the facility and are lying in a shallow cavity in the ground. Seven is now in possession of the binoculars and is sharing what he observes while I'm taking mental notes.

Knowing we were each given a locator before we left Celestria, I crawl over to Freya. Leaning in close to her, I speak softly in her ear. "I want you to stay here. As soon as we take out the guards, depress your locator."

Her eyes widen. "What about Felix and the others?" she whispers. "They wanted us to stick together. They won't agree with it."

"They will," I whisper with confidence. "I'm leading, and they know I'll be making decisions for the betterment of the team."

Freya exhales, then nods and I see relief wash over her. It is a win-win for me. Freya will be secure, and I won't have to keep looking over my shoulder for the rest of the mission to make sure she's safe.

Seven reports there are six guards around the visible perimeter, and likely more at the back. At the front gate, there are two stationary guards, while the other four are actively moving along their boundaries. At the center of the facility, a large floodlight is sweeping the interior, and so far, I've spotted at least three cameras.

The plan is for Freya to shut down the entire electric system and before it reboots, we will have a few minutes to take out the guards and slip inside. However, I'm the only one of us fitted with weapons. I know there will be fatalities. Rem primed me for this. He warned me that it was inevitable lives would be taken and reminded me they would have no problem killing any of us.

Freya has her computer open and has been steadily inputting code or whatever it is she needs to do on her end. I glance at Seven, Callas, and Roman and nod at them. They nod back, showing me they're ready.

"Give me one of your knives," Seven whispers loudly, holding out a hand. "If we have to defend ourselves, we should all have a weapon."

I hesitate, my gut twisting, knowing they weren't given weapons for a reason. Nevertheless, this is my team. We're on a foreign planet and about to take out guards. I need them to trust me, and I should show them I trust them as well.

Slipping three knives from my belt, I hold them out. "The guards will also have weapons. Take what you can but get inside fast. We'll have to find the dining hall."

They agree and the four of us crawl out of our hiding place, each heading toward the guards we'll have to subdue.

As soon as Freya links to the facility's system, she will shut it down. When all the lights go out, that will be our signal to move in. There is no turning back now.

I'm going to take out the two at the front gate. Seven is heading toward the guards on the right, and Callas and Roman will take out the ones on the left.

Crawling on my belly, I stay in the shadows, inching closer as the guards seem to be preoccupied with their discussion.

Stopping behind a boulder about thirty feet away, I slip two knives from my belt, which leaves me with five. I glance to see the other three in position. My heart is hammering inside my chest and my breath is heavy as I focus on our task.

The rulers of Celestria are inside the facility. To stop the ruthless attacks and murders of the Avkans, we have to find them and return them safely. Whatever happens is necessary, even if that means killing someone.

Gods. This feels like a twisted nightmare, only there is no waking from this one.

I slow my breath. Waiting.

And then...

The lights shut down.

Guards are hollering and when they turn their backs to me, I'm up and sprinting toward them. One turns around and before he sees me, I send my first blade. It lands in the middle of his chest.

The second guard watches the man drop and draws a gun. Twisting toward me, I send the second dagger and it lodges between his eyes. His death is instant.

The first guard is still alive, gasping, fear embedded in his wide eyes while he holds the hilt of the dagger in his chest. He's dying.

"I'm sorry," I breathe, body trembling, gut churning, tears burning my eyes.

Seven arrives and, without hesitation, swipes his blade across the man's throat.

I gasp and look at him, but he gives me a pointed look.

"Snap out of it," he growls as sirens blare.

Reaching down, I take both guard's handguns, sliding one into my belt as Seven extracts the knives from the two bodies, wiping the blood on his pants as Roman and Callas arrive. Blood is splattered all over them and they are winded.

Without a word, the four of us slip through the front gate and sprint toward the buildings.

We make it to the first building and hear shouting. I don't know how many guards there are, but I know we don't have enough knives or ammunition.

The dining hall is three buildings away, but for now, we're ducking behind a wall of pallets as heavy footsteps race past us and toward the front gate.

"Move," I urge as soon as the way is clear.

We haul ass, making it two more buildings undetected. Before we're about to move again, the lights power back on. This changes things. It makes us vulnerable.

"Fuck," Seven hisses.

The dining hall is the next building over, but there are thirty yards of open ground we have to cover to get there. Guards are shouting and whistles are blowing. They must have found the dead bodies.

"We have to move," I urge, knowing they'll want to get to the rulers.

The floodlight is back on and as soon as it moves away from us, I sprint toward the hall, the men following close behind.

We make it and I push the doors open, coming to a screeching halt.

A gun is aimed at my face.

"Hands up," a deep voice orders, while Seven and Callas curse behind me.

Thirty-Six

ELARA

Panting, I throw my hands up in the air. My right hand is still gripping the gun, so I slide my finger off the trigger, showing I'm not a threat.

The man, dressed in a guard uniform, has the advantage, and I know there is no way I can lower my weapon and get a shot off before he can press his trigger.

There is a click followed by a light shining in my face. I squint, temporarily blinded to anything in front of me.

"We will not hurt you," I say calmly, though my heart and pulse are racing.

"You're Elara?" the man asks.

I pause, hearing my name, then nod, waiting a few long seconds before he lowers the flashlight and his weapon. "Name's Titus. Follow me." He turns and strides away.

Letting out a deep sigh of relief, I realize he must be our contact, the one who will take us to the rulers. But... how does he know my name?

I glance back to the others, who also appear relieved, and follow Titus as he moves swiftly toward a large kitchen. He marches for the back wall where there are lines of cabinets filled with canned goods and halts at one close to the middle. Clutching the sides of the cabinet, he slides it away from the wall, then leans forward and pushes against the backing behind it. Part of the wall opens into a dark space.

"Inside," he orders, his eyes sweeping the room. The sirens outside are still blaring and men are shouting.

It's a narrow tunnel, so I proceed first, then Seven, Callas and Roman. Titus enters last, dragging the cabinet back in place, closing us inside and submerging us into darkness. With his small flashlight, he shoves past us until he reaches the front and continues, guiding us down a set of steep dirt steps.

He doesn't speak, so I assume it's for a reason. We also keep quiet, not wanting to give away our location.

It's hot, the air in the narrow tunnel is stagnant and thick, making it hard to breathe. My heart rate is through the roof and I'm panicking, feeling a little claustrophobic, especially being pinned in by men behind and in front of me.

We finally make it to the bottom and Titus stops and holds up his hand before he pushes against the wall, and it opens. I suck in cool air as we enter a small concrete room.

He turns and faces me. "They know you've come. They'll take them to another location."

"Where are the rulers?" I ask.

"In the next room. The door is supposed to be locked, but the one watching it is one of us. Don't kill him. I have to head back up to the hall."

I nod. "Thank you, Titus."

"May the gods be with you." He points to the door we need to exit through and leaves.

I turn to Seven, Callas, and Roman. "You ready?" I breathe and they nod, holding weapons in their hands. Seven has two knives, Callas has a gun, and Roman has one of each.

Inhaling, I push open the door and rush in with both guns aimed forward. I move quickly down a dark hallway when I hear men shouting.

"Shit, they're taking them," I hiss.

Sprinting forward, I see one guard standing at the end of the hall with his back to me. He must be Titus's friend. When he hears me coming, he turns around. Instead of shooting, I jump kick him in the chest, sending him flying into the next room. I know the kick wasn't hard enough to knock him out, but he plays dead. Smart man.

I quickly count four guards who are cuffing a group of people. Are they the rulers?

They must be, but they're not dressed in finery. They're wearing matching gray sweatpants and T-shirts and look like normal citizens.

"Stop!" I yell, guns aimed at the guards.

One guard raises his firearm, but I shoot first. He bellows and drops his weapon, cradling his hand, which is now missing a finger. The second guard takes aim at me, but I also aim at his hand and shoot off one of his digits. His gun drops as he wails in pain.

"You bitch!" the first one cries out through gritted teeth. Blood is gushing from his severed appendage.

"Be thankful you lost a limb. It could have been your life," I snap, my eyes focused on the remaining guards.

The other two guards panic, each grabbing a ruler, one male and one female, holding them hostage with guns aimed at their heads.

"Put your guns down," the one holding the male hollers. "Put them down, or we'll kill them!"

I hear weapons from my team being dropped behind me, and I slowly place my guns on the ground and hold my hands out in front of me at waist level.

"You don't want to kill them," I say. "All of Celestria will attack Avka and everyone here, along with your families on this planet, will die." I'm not sure if that's true, but I know it'll make him think.

The male he's holding hostage seems familiar. He's tall and handsome with strong dark features, onyx hair, and a full beard. But it's his eyes that give him away. Familiar dark eyes rimmed in gold. I know he is the King of Terr, the ruler of my realm, and Prince Kage's father. I have to make sure he survives.

"Let them go," I urge. "You don't want to die today."

The guard laughs. "You're the one who will die."

I look at the king and hope he can read my mind. *Don't move. Please don't move.*

A door opens at the top of the stairs and a voice calls down. Both guards holding the rulers turn, their attention wavering for a split second. I move, slipping two knives from my belt and send them flying.

The first one hits the guard holding the King of Terr, sinking into his temple, killing him instantly. The second guard turns, and the blade sinks deep into his right eye. It pop's, spraying the queen with eye juice and blood.

The queen lets out a high-pitched scream as the guard holding her drops to the ground with a thud, his body lifeless. She runs into a male's arms, who I assume is her husband, and wails. When I see she's in safe hands, I move toward the King of Terr.

"Your highness, are you okay?" I ask, bowing my head.

"I am," he says, looking down at the dead guard. "You're skilled. Are you from Terr?"

"Yes, but only recently. They retrieved me from Earth."

His brow furrows and eyes narrow as they fix on my chest. "That necklace," he says, reaching out and brushing his fingers over it. "Where did you get it?" His face looks serious, like he knows exactly where it came from.

I quickly tuck it into the collar of my suit, securing it to my chest. "It was a gift from a friend," I reply, not wanting to speak his name. I know

Vera's parents are here, and I'm almost certain her mom was the one who got popped with eye fluid.

A door opens at the top of the stairwell and the fingerless guard's holler. "They're here! Help us! They're down here!"

I quickly pull the locator out of my pocket and depress the button, then place it in the king's hand. "Stay here. Jumpers will come for you."

Reaching down, I grab the two guns off the dead guards and face the King of Terr.

"Where are you going?" the king asks.

"I'm going to hold them off as long as I can."

I turn back to Seven, Callas, and Roman, who are standing with the other royals.

"We have to buy them time. Let's go."

Seven shakes his head. "We'll protect them. You're on your own, leader."

Bastard. His voice is condescending, and the look in his eyes tells me he's been persuaded. My stomach tightens in knots, and I have a gut feeling I know who it was.

Behind me is the unmistakable sound of a bullet being chambered. I turn as a guard steps into view, his gun aimed at the King of Terr.

Running, I dive forward as he fires the shot. I feel a thud on my shoulder, and I hit the ground, but twist my body around, aiming at the bastard, squeezing my trigger. The bullet hits the guard in the chest. As soon as he drops, two more arrive, guns drawn. I empty an entire magazine, taking both of them out before they reach the bottom.

Tossing the empty gun, I struggle to get to my feet, but the King of Terr reaches down, grabs my arms, and helps me to my feet.

"You're injured," he notes, brow furrowed as he examines the blood pouring from the wound.

"I'll be fine. It went straight through—in and out. Nothing vital," I say.

The king pulls his shirt off, takes one knife from my belt, and makes a slit in it, ripping off the entire bottom part. I don't know how old he is, but holy hell, Kage's daddy is ripped. I try not to gape at the man, but the Celestrians have been blessed with more than immortality.

"Let me," the king says. "It's the least I can do for saving my life." He wraps the torn shirt under my arm, then around my shoulder, twice, binding it tightly, creating a tourniquet.

I incline my head. "It's my duty and my pleasure, your highness."

Thank the gods I have a high tolerance for pain. I'm only coherent because of adrenaline, but once it wears off, I know I'll be in a world of hurt. I glance at Seven, Callas, and Roman, and they avoid my stare. Fucking cowards.

The door opens from above and I hear the heavy footsteps of countless guards heading down toward us. Pushing the king back out of the line of fire, I aim and drop at least seven guards before they make it down. The second magazine is empty, and more are coming.

A snap in the air fills me with another shot of adrenaline. The jumpers are here.

As another round of guards comes down the stairs, I take two blades from my belt.

"Elara!" Talon yells.

I glance at him, into his wide eyes, and shake my head. "Take them and go!"

Caught off guard, I'm grabbed from behind, but I twist and slice a guard's arm with my blade. He punches me in the gut, and I double over. Dropping to my knees, I swing around, slicing thighs and kneecaps of the guards who circle me.

"Elara, hurry! I can't leave without you," Talon bellows.

I know the order was from Rem and the prince, but it's too late. I'm surrounded. Emotion overwhelms me as I realize there is no way I can return with them to Celestria.

I'm grabbed by my arms and jerked to my feet. They cuff me after yanking my wrists behind my back. I wail as the pain in my shoulder radiates through my chest and arm.

I look at Talon, who has the King of Terr and another male ruler with white hair and silver eyes. He must be the King of Nahla. All three look at me with wide, concern filled eyes.

I see a guard raise his gun at them, and with every bit of energy I have left, I pull away and jump, kicking him in the neck. There is a snapping sound before the man falls, his limp body hitting the ground. I don't know if he's knocked out or dead, but I'm pretty sure it's the latter.

"Talon, take them! Leave now!" I bellow as I'm pushed to the ground.

A guard drops a knee on my back and shoves my head to the ground. Pain radiates through my spine.

"Please, leave!" I beg, with tears streaming down my face.

With distraught filling his eyes, Talon opens a portal and I smile as I watch them vanish.

The mission was successful. The rulers have returned to Celestria and now they can send their armies to attack Avka and save their world.

After all the Avkan guards I killed, I doubt I'll live to see it.

"Get the fuck off of me," I growl, struggling against them as they raise me to my feet.

A soldier moves toward me with a rifle and raises it. "Bitch," he says before he slams it down on the top of my head.

Thirty-Seven

REMINGTON

The jumpers arrive with the team and the rulers.

Freya returned earlier, and after questioning her, said Elara ordered her to leave Avka as soon as she was finished with her task. She saw the team slip into the gates, but nothing after that. The atmosphere here at the Central Court has remained hopeful, but everyone was on edge.

Everyone rushes toward them, welcoming them home, along with their healers, who are there to examine each one medically before they leave to their respective kingdoms. It's mayhem, but I scan the room, spotting the three men on the team but — "Talon!" I call, rushing over to him. "Where's Elara?"

He shakes his head, his expression anguished. "She didn't make it."

"What?" Fear and anger rise inside me. "What do you mean, she didn't make it?"

"There were too many guards, Rem. She held them back so we could jump the rulers to safety. She was surrounded, and they overpowered her."

No, no, no. I snap and charge toward Seven, grabbing him by his neck. "What the fuck happened? Why the fuck are you here and she isn't?"

The haughty bastard smirks. "Our mission was to bring the rulers back, and that's what we did. She's the one who wanted to play hero."

"She saved us," King Dargan says from behind me. "She saved my life, and we wouldn't be here had it not been for her. These men are nothing but cowards."

Bastards! In my rage, shadows pour out of me, grabbing Seven by the neck.

"Is she still alive?"

He nods, frantically clawing at his neck. A neck I could easily snap.

King Dargan comes to my side and places a hand on my shoulder, reining in my murderous thoughts. "She's injured, but she fought bravely."

"How bad is her injury?" I've never felt so unhinged in all my life. She's hurt and in Avka alone. There is no way to know what they'll do to her, but I know it won't be good.

"They shot her in the shoulder, but she's strong," the king says. "There was nothing we could do. They forced us to take a potion that prevented us from using our power." The king grabs my arm. "I saw her strength. She's a survivor."

Unless they kill her first.

I want to open a fucking portal and jump to save her, but I don't know where the hell she is. They could have taken her anywhere in Avka, and without the locator, it would be a dangerous and blind jump.

Kage needs to know. I promised I'd tell him as soon as they returned, but I'm afraid of what he'll do, of what he'll risk... for her.

"Captain," King Dargan says. "Can I speak to you for a moment?"

"Of course, my king," I say, finally releasing Seven. Fucking bastard drops and gasps for air. I'll make sure he and the others never see the light of day.

Digby ambles toward us, flagging me down. "I must tend to the king before he leaves."

The king sighs, knowing he has to be examined before he's allowed to leave, and allows Digby to let him examine him.

"I'm thankful you're back, your highness," Digby says, bowing his head.

"It's good to be back," King Dargan replies. "Especially knowing I won't have to put up with the rest of the royals and their bullshit anymore," he murmurs.

Digby chuckles but keeps at his work.

The king sighs. "Digby, I need something to recover my power."

The healer nods, but I can't focus on anything. I feel sick inside knowing every second that passes is a second Elara is in danger. But Digby is thorough and the king's medical assessment is taking too gods-damned long.

Talon strides over with an anguished look on his face and pulls me to the side.

"You couldn't do anything?" I growl through gritted teeth.

He shakes his head, visibly shaken. "I couldn't. I fucking wanted to. The other jumpers left, but I still had two rulers in my care to jump to safety in a room filling with guards. This entire mission was to retrieve the royals.

They were our priority, and I know if I went after her, our king might not have made it back." He pinches his eyes shut. "They had her pinned to the ground when we left. She begged me, Rem. Begged me to leave, with tears in her eyes. I've never felt so fucking terrible in all my life."

I exhale, trying to keep my shit together and not say anything I would regret.

Digby finally finishes his medical assessment of the king. "You're in great health, your highness," he says, handing the king a tonic. "This is a mixture of herbs for vitality. Now that you're back in Celestria, your power should return within a few days." He bows his head. "I'll see you back at the palace."

"Thank you, Digby," the king says, standing to his feet.

He turns and nods at me, so I dismiss Talon and follow the king out of the room. Walking down the hall, the king enters another empty meeting room where he shuts the door behind him.

My freaking heart is hammering against my chest as he faces me with a look of concern.

"What is it, my king?" I ask.

"Who is she, Remington? The girl who saved us?" he asks. He uses my real name when there are no others around.

I don't know why he's asking me this in private, but there must be a reason.

"Her name is Elara. She's a Changeling I retrieved a week ago."

"How is she connected to my son?"

My heart stops and so does my breath. "What do you mean, your highness?"

"When she arrived, she was wearing a bone marker. Did you know anything about that?"

"A bone marker?" I shake my head, completely baffled. "When she left here, she wasn't wearing anything."

The king folds his arms over his chest. "I saw it around her neck. It was undoubtedly a bone marker. And my son created it."

What the fuck?

I bow my head. "Your highness, I truly don't know."

He pauses, reading my expression as I raise my head. He would know if I was telling a lie. *What the hell has Kage done?*

Bone markers are rare and extremely painful to make. Only those with great power can create one. With magic, a piece of the conjurer's bone is severed and taken from them, and then, through more magic, they transform it into an amulet. It's called a bone marker because the conjurer can trace it no matter where it is because it's a part of them. It also carries no magic, which is probably why Kage must have performed the spell and gave it to Elara.

The asshole didn't even let me know.

The king moves toward me. "I need to see my son immediately. Where is he?"

"He's in his study, waiting for me to brief him on the mission."

"I know he'll be expecting you, but please allow us a few minutes alone before you advise him."

"Of course, your highness." Bowing my head, I slap a fist to my chest. "I have to see Felix before I leave. I'll also need a statement from you about what happened in Avka."

"You'll have it soon," the king replies, then opens a portal.

Thirty-Eight

ELARA

My entire body is aching, and my head is throbbing... especially my shoulder.

It hurts to open my eyes, but when I do reality slams me, like the freaking butt of a rifle to my head. I hope I see the asshole who knocked me out because I'd like to return the favor.

My head is fuzzy, but I remember I was shot and I'm no longer in Celestria. A wave of panic overcomes me, but I slow my breathing and focus.

Someone cut away part of my uniform on my right arm and shoulder and properly bound the bullet wound. I guess there is some decency here.

Pressing my fingers to the top of my head, I hiss, touching a tender lump. My left eye is swollen, and there is blood caked on that side of my face.

I move a little, noting I'm lying on a cot in a small room. There are two doors, one in front of me, and one to the left, and I pray one is a bathroom.

The door to the room opens and a guard peeks in. Closing it again, I hear him holler, "She's awake!"

338

I sigh, slowly struggling to sit upright, sliding my legs off the cot. I need a shower and some caffeine.

A few moments later, a woman walks in. She's older, maybe in her seventies, with pale, weathered skin and white hair that is braided down her back. It's her eyes that have me taken aback. One is pale gray, and the other is completely white.

She makes her way over to me, carrying a small pouch. "I'm Andromeda. Avkan healer," she says with an accent. It sounds familiar, almost like the Native Americans back on Earth.

I nod and slide over so she can sit next to me. If she's anything like the healers on Celestria, with their quick working magic potions, I'll take whatever I can get.

Though her hands are weathered, she gently grazes my swollen cheek with soft fingers.

"Looks like they beat you pretty bad." She shakes her head, brow furrowing as she rummages through her pouch and pulls out a small, round container. She sets it to the side, then goes to the washroom and returns with a damp washcloth.

Standing in front of me, she holds my chin steady with one hand, while the other cleans my face with long, smooth strokes. Once she's done, she places the rag, red with my blood, on a nearby table. I've never had a grandmother, but I imagine she would be a good one.

I smile at her and the kindness she's showing me, and she smiles back.

She then examines my shoulder and nods. "It will heal. The medicine will prevent infection."

"That's good," I say, but it still hurts like hell.

Retrieving the container she placed to the side, she opens it and applies the lotion to the swollen skin around my eye and cheek. It feels cool, and soothing. She extracts another small container from her bag, shaking two pills into her hand, then heads over to the table near the door and pours me a glass of water.

"This will help with the swelling and the pain." She holds both out to me, and I take them.

"Thank you." I swallow the pills and drain the water. I know it won't work as fast as the Celestrian potions, but I'm thankful.

She grabs hold of my hand and squeezes. "Don't fight them. You'll only end up injured or possibly dead."

"I won't. I don't have a death wish today." Her words fill me with a sense of dread and has my stomach in knots. She knows who these people are. She knows that the possibility of me getting injured or killed is there.

Smiling, she gently pats my hand. "Good. Good. Be smart. Be safe."

"I will," I say, before she gathers her things and walks out the door.

As soon as she exits, a brawny, chocolate-haired, brown-eyed guard with a long scar down the left side of his face enters and heads toward me with a set of handcuffs. He's around six feet tall and looks intimidating. I hold out my wrists, not wanting to piss him off. I'm in no position to fight him.

My head is still throbbing and there isn't a place on my body that doesn't ache.

"Follow me," he grumbles with a scowl on his face.

"Where are we going?" I ask nicely, my gut churning, knowing wherever it is, it won't be good.

The grumpy guard doesn't even look at me, he just keeps walking, then replies, "You'll find out when you get there."

I can tell he hates his job.

We walk down a long, stark-white hallway and exit through a door that leads outside. The heat is sweltering and then I hear... "That's the bitch who took Fred's finger!"

I turn toward the voices and see a gaggle of guards standing in the shade of a building and shudder. They look nothing like Celestrian men who have an otherworldly beauty. These men look like they've been inbred. Some have long scraggly hair and beards, most have blackened teeth and tanned, weathered faces.

"We should take her fingers," another shouts, and the others agree, heckling.

I step closer to the grumpy guard and I'm not sure why. I doubt he'll keep them away from me. However, the assholes are staying put and not making a move toward me.

"She's fine. I'd fuck that," a guard says, hocking a loogie and spitting it on the ground.

"Maybe we should take turns," another laughs, and they all hoot and holler in agreement.

I want to vomit. Perverted pricks.

Instead of minding my own business, like I should, I raise both cuffed hands and flip them off. That makes them laugh and curse even more, continuing to make lewd remarks, which I completely ignore.

The grouchy guard leads me toward another building at the back of the grounds and opens the door. As soon as I step inside, cold air hits my heated skin. They have an air conditioner in here, and it feels wonderful. The room is a living space, with a king-sized bed in one area, a large living room, and even a small kitchen that's elegantly decorated. It's luxurious for a facility in the middle of nowhere.

"Wait here. He'll arrive shortly," Guard Grump says in his deep voice.

"Who?" I ask, but he doesn't answer, just walks out.

I can't believe they left me alone, but then again, there is probably a guard at every exit. Despite the danger I know is lurking outside, I quickly search for a bathroom and spot a door near the bedroom area. I make a beeline for it. Opening it, I let out a breath of relief.

Thank the gods.

I quickly relieve myself and wash my hands, thankful the guard cuffed me in the front and not behind my back. As I exit the room, the front door opens and a potent scent of spicy cologne wafts in. A man strides toward me, average stature, with sun-kissed skin and deep brown eyes. Shoulder length russet hair frames his chiseled jaw. He's attractive, wearing black slacks and a navy button-down shirt, but still nothing compared to the alluring Celestrian men.

Abruptly halting, his head tilts slightly to the side and a broad grin rises on his full lips as he appraises me. "So, you are the one who stirred up my guards and helped rescue the Celestrian rulers?"

My guards. He must be a big shot, someone in a powerful position. I'm going to have to play this game well and try to win him over so I can leave here alive.

Striding over to a small wet bar, he takes out two glasses and places them on the marbled top. Those dark brown eyes meet mine, and I can't help but sense a tremble of fear shoot up my spine. There is something about this man that isn't quite right. He plucks a decanter filled with amber liquid from under the counter and pours some into each glass. Grasping the glasses, he slowly strolls over to me.

"Care for a drink?" he asks, holding one out.

I decide to take it from him, not wanting to seem unappreciative. Besides, I watched him closely and didn't see him place anything suspicious into either of the glasses.

"Thanks."

"Have a seat," he says, leading me over to the couches. I sit on the smaller loveseat, while he sits directly across from me on the larger one.

Wanting to get right to the point, I take a sip and ask, "Who are you?" The liquid burns going down my throat.

The man also takes a sip, reclining back and casually crossing one leg over the other. A sinister grin curls on the corners of his lips. "I think the bigger question here is, *who* are *you*?"

Shaking my head, I place my glass on the cocktail table in front of me. "I'm nothing special," I say with confidence. "Just a simple girl they selected to lead a team and save our world from the psychopath who wants to take it over."

He hums, taking another sip. "You think our king is a psychopath?"

I shrug and lean back. "If he goes around killing innocent people because he wants to take over their planet, then yes. I believe he is."

He tilts his head to the side and holds out his glass to me with a grin. "Fair enough."

"It's your turn," I say, matching his grin. "Tell me who you are?"

"I am—" he pauses and takes another sip, then leans forward, a darkness in his eyes. "I am Adhan Merak. The psychopathic king."

Thirty-Nine

ELARA

Shit.

King Adhan Merak's eyes shift, acknowledging somebody behind me. I twist and my entire body stiffens, seeing eight men enter the room. Six are guards, but there are two others clothed in long white robes. One man in white is carrying a large box, and my intuition tells me that whatever's inside is not good.

One guard drags a lounge chair toward us, and I immediately notice straps attached to the arms and legs. The air is suddenly thick and harder to breathe. My heart is hammering inside my chest and the hairs on my body rise with a sense of doom.

Another guard steps behind the king and aims a gun at my chest. I'm helpless. My hands are bound, my body is injured, and I have no power or anything else to fight back with.

King Adhan leans forward, elbows on knees, a triumphant smile along with a dark and evil expression shadows his face. The kind of evil that makes your skin crawl and has no conscience or remorse.

"You cannot win this fight, Changeling," Merak says, his tone deadly. "Soon, you will become our greatest weapon."

"You're wrong." I shake my head, trying to hold my trembling limbs steady. "I'll never serve you."

A wicked grin forms on his lips. "You won't have a choice." He motions with his head and two of the guards move forward, grasping my arms and pulling me to my feet. I wail as the wound from the gunshot radiates pain throughout my arm and chest.

"Bastards!" I curse.

Steadying myself, I grit my teeth and glare at the king. "You'll all die. Celestria will send their armies and wipe you out."

King Adhan laughs, then gets up from the couch and strides to me, squeezing my chin in his fingers. "Perhaps," he says, leaning down and sliding his tongue over my lips. "Or perhaps I'll keep you for myself."

I spit on his face, and it drips down his mouth. Instead of wiping it off, he licks it with his tongue and moans like he likes it.

Sick bastard. "You *are* a freaking psycho."

He rubs his forehead against mine. "You have no idea."

I struggle against the men, my shoulder screaming with pain. "Get away from me!"

"Now that we have you, you will never escape. You're mine now," he says.

The men pull me away. "You can't do this!"

"I won't." He motions to the men in white. "They will."

"You asshole!"

I struggle, uncaring that the guard still has a gun pointed to my chest, but they're strong and I'm injured. They drag me to the chair, forcing me into it, and strap me in so tightly I can't move. The circulation in my limbs is limited. My breath quickens as the white-robed men take the box and extract a large device from it and place it on a tall table with wheels. The device looks terrifying, filled with buttons and wires and other gizmos I've never seen. It looks like a science fiction nightmare.

They wheel the table next to me. One of them steps right beside me and starts placing small metal discs attached to thin wires on my forehead and temples.

It must be a form of neurotechnology.

"You can't do this," I wail, desperately trying to loosen the straps. "It's unethical!"

The man laughs and continues pressing the discs to my head. "There are no neurorights here on Avka. Mental privacy, your identity and free will... it's all an illusion. On Avka, the king owns everything and everyone."

The white-robed man turns to the king for approval, and the king gives him a nod.

Ass kisser.

My entire body is trembling, not only with fear, but with anger. "Do you all agree with this bullshit? Letting one narcissistic, mentally unstable man rule all of you?" I laugh when none of them answer. "You're all just as sick and twisted as he is."

I know what they're going to do. They're going to crack into my mind and then brainwash me like they did to the other Changelings they kidnapped. I won't let that happen. I can't. I'll have to focus and put up a shield like Rem taught me.

My hands are sweating, but the pain pill the healer gave me is finally kicking in and relieving some of the pain. Other than that, I'm helpless and there is nothing I can do but focus and keep these assholes out of my gods-damned mind.

"Why do you take Celestria's Changelings and brainwash them?" I ask, trying to buy me some time.

I pray to the stars that Rem and the prince find a way to rescue me. It's the only glimmer of hope I have to hold on to.

King Adhan Merak answers, standing behind the men. "The Changeling minds are the easiest to indoctrinate. They are powerful beings abandoned on Earth, who know nothing about their origins or how to use their power. Their minds are fragile and pliable, and with a little persuasion, they become our greatest weapons."

I shake my head. "I have no power, so no matter what you do to me, I'll be worthless against Celestrian magic."

"That may be so," the king says, stepping forward with a shrug. "You may not become a weapon, but I will use you for your greatest assets." His hand sweeps down my chest and grasps my breast, squeezing while a smile slithers on those vile lips.

"You sick bastard," I growl, straining against the restraints. My wrists are stinging, the straps so tight they've broken skin.

Adhan Merak leans forward, his smile lethal.

"Soon, you'll see otherwise," he breathes, before he turns and addresses the men in white robes. "Break into her mind. I want to know who she is, why she was chosen, and who sent her. When you have the answers, I want you to wipe her mind clean and input the Changeling behavioral modification."

"No!" I scream, bucking, trying to free myself from the chair.

My body stiffens as the second man in white moves to the opposite side of the chair. In his hand is a needled syringe filled with a clear liquid. "Hold her down," he orders.

Two guards appear in front of me. One presses my shoulders onto the chair while the other grabs my head and twists it to the side. I scream as I feel the prick of the needle entering my neck, followed by the rush of fluid being pressed into it.

Almost instantly, my world spins, and my brain goes numb. My eyelids are heavy, and limbs feel like they're lead, so weighted I could sink and fall right through the chair and then the floor beneath.

"She's loaded and docile," the king says, his words muffled.

The faces surrounding me are pulsing, going in and out of focus. I'm suddenly released, but I'm sapped. All the fight has gone out of me, and I don't know where it went. I need to find it. I can't let them have my brain and everything in it.

The king grabs my head, making me look at him. "I'll return when you're compliant, love," he says into my ear. "I admire your fire and fight. It's a total turn on for me." He leans forward and places a kiss on my lips. "You're *mine* now."

"Never!" I turn away from him, not wanting any part of him to touch me.

"Let me know when it's finished," the king says before walking out.

"Fire it up. Let's see what's in her mind," one of the white-robed men says, pressing buttons on the mind device that makes it come to life.

My mind is heavy. It feels like I'm slogging through thick mud just to think clearly. I need to stop them. I can't let them see inside my mind, but... but I can't remember how to stop it.

Why can't I remember?

There is a jolt through my body, starting at my head. My body goes stiff, and my eyes slam shut.

Behind my lids, my entire life plays out like a video, from the beginning, like how it did when Kage touched me. I'm reliving it all... all the memories housed in the recesses of my mind. Memories I had buried deep and wanted to forget.

My heart aches as I'm taken through my lonely childhood years. Then the bullying, the training, followed by the moment Cole takes his last breath. Each memory more grueling and heart wrenching than the last.

The memories advance to when Rem arrives. When he finally reveals his face in the holding room, I smile inside, but also feel horrible for breaking his nose.

Those memories continue in Celestria, from the holding room, the assessment, then Rem taking me to Terr and the Ebony Palace where I met the prince.

So many emotions run through me. Emotions I can't grasp as it all fast forwards to a scene I'm not familiar with. A scene I don't remember.

It's during Messis. Zarah is there with her friends and a few men who are surrounding me, like predators circling their prey. One man blows a fine dust into my face, and I cough, my eyes burning as I realize what he's done. He drugged me.

I fight back, kicking one guy's ass, but then... the drug kicks in. Next, I'm stumbling, and after a conversation with Zarah, confirm she was behind it all. She set the men up to drug and then rape me because she claims Remington is hers.

Why don't I recall any of this?

When Zarah exits with her bitches, and I'm left alone with the wolves, chaos ensues. The drug is grasping me, but I continue to fight for my life. The man whose ass I kicked earlier overpowers me, throwing me over his shoulder. I fight, but I'm weakened, helpless to free myself from his hold.

My mind whirls, and my stomach roils, making me feel nauseous as I watch myself being kidnapped, knowing what is coming next.

Suddenly, the entire memory goes dark. A loud roar makes the hairs on my skin raise, followed by a familiar, powerful voice.

The man carrying me drops me on the ground. I'm curled in a heap, a drugged-up mess, but I'm scooped up into another set of arms. Muscular arms that hold me against a broad chest.

My heart constricts as the face of my savior comes into focus. The man I thought hated me, who shunned me, who seemed like he wanted nothing to do with me, was the one who came and rescued me. He is my hero... my dark knight with obsidian, gold-rimmed eyes.

"You're safe now, Elara," he says, and my chest fills with warmth.

He saved me. The prince saved me, but I don't remember any of it.

The healer had explained to the prince that I needed relief against the Lure drug and after Rem's encouragement, the prince came to my rescue... again, relieving me of the pain the drug would have caused.

The memories continue, and what happens next between me and the prince, inside his Dark Vision, has my core heating and back arching.

Gods, he not only relieved the pain, but actually looked like he was enjoying it, and then... the words he spoke to me, saying what he would do if I ever wanted him, has my heart hammering inside my chest and my toes curling.

Did this really happen?

I hear voices outside of my head and reality slams me in the face. I'm not alone. There are men out there watching everything in my mind. Men who saw what happened between me and the prince, and heard what Cyrus said to the director about me being a Death Dealer.

No!

Shield. I need to put up a shield, although it's probably too late. They heard too much, and now know too much. Intimate things that could easily end not only me, but Kage.

Concentrating, I construct a dome of diamond around the area of my mind that is projecting my memories. With significant effort and focus, and with sweat coating every inch of my skin, I make sure the shield is solid and there are no gaps. When it's completed, I hear loud voices on the outside.

"What happened? It's not working."

My head is spinning, brain cumbersome, but I keep focusing and keep the dome tightly secured around my memories. *I can't let them in.*

The voices outside are getting louder, angrier.

Sharp pains shoot through my head, growing fiercer as I hold the shield tightly around me. These are my thoughts. My life. My memories. I don't want them seeing any more of it.

Sweat drips down my brow and my limbs are trembling. I don't know how long I can hold it, because the drug is overpowering me and I'm growing weaker.

"It's her," a voice growls. "She's keeping us out of her mind."

"Impossible," another snaps. "She's a Changeling. There is no way she could master a shield, especially being doped up."

"Then what is it? It's not the machine."

"Give her half a dose more. If she is doing it, her mind will fold."

"No," I groan, the stabbing pain in my head nearly unbearable. I clench my teeth and fists together, my head throbbing.

If they shoot me up again, I won't be able to keep them out of my mind. They'll erase it all. As much as I despised my life, I want to keep every memory, good and bad. Every single memory is one that has molded me into who I am.

Strong hands grip the sides of my head, twisting it to the side.

"No!" I wail. "Don't touch me."

A deep sob erupts as fear surges through me, anticipating the next shot of drugs to be pressed into my neck. But it doesn't come.

The air in the room suddenly goes icy. There is a recognizable snap followed by a surge of power that explodes in the room. Sliding my eyes open, I witness shadows pour from an open portal, spreading through the space, along with a familiar scent that fills me with warmth. Tingles surge over my skin, along with an unmistakable awareness, one that makes my chest heave and tears pour down my face.

He is here. *He* came.

Guards scream and guns fire at the powerful being stepping out of the portal. Alarms blare and I know time is ticking.

He shouldn't have come. They'll capture him.

His eyes, completely black, snap to me. A loud growl rattles the entire room when he sees that I've been bound and drugged, and somehow his eyes grow even darker. Shadows twist and coil around him, around his waist and limbs, then they shoot out. One-by-one, men drop, their lifeless bodies hitting the floor.

It's then I realize what's happening. He is a Death Dealer, and I am witnessing his power firsthand. Prince Kage is not only dark and beautiful, but he is death incarnate—ripping souls from their bodies, leaving empty husks strewn across the ground.

His shadows seem to move of their own volition, snatching guards off their feet, coiling around and crushing them. The snapping of bones and ear-piercing screams of agony are resounding in my ears.

More guards rush in, but they're no match for the dark prince. His rage seems to fuel his power.

In the recesses of my mind, I hear Rem's voice...

There is a reason they fear our prince within the five kingdoms.

In the chaos, one of the white-robed men extracts something from the mind device and sprints toward the door.

"Kage!" I scream, but his eyes and mind are focused on one thing... death.

The white-robed man escapes the madness, and I know whatever he had in his hand is something that could destroy me. The King of Avka will know I'm a Death Dealer. He'll know that someone blocked my power and that the Prince of Terr and I are connected. When he does, I know he'll use it against us. I have a sinking feeling in my gut that he'll come for me, especially with his dark and twisted mind. Especially when his last words to me were... You're *mine* now.

Through the shadow, I see countless bodies strewn on the floor, blood seeping from their orifices... eyes, ears, mouths, noses. The harrowing screams continue, along with the shouting of more guards arriving, followed by gunfire.

I feel a tug on my limbs and realize I'm freed from the straps. A powerful arm wraps around my waist and pulls me up and into a firm chest.

"I'm here, Min Vesmír," Kage breathes, his dark eyes softening as he scans my face. "You're safe now."

His voice... gods, his voice is the most beautiful sound in the entire universe.

I'm safe. With him, I know I'm safe.

Wrapping my arms around his neck, I lean my heavy head against his chest and breathe in his enticing scent.

He came for me.

More voices and gunshots fill the room, but he covers me with his body, shielding me as he opens another portal, and we jump through.

FORTY

PRINCE KAGE

Before the portal jump to Avka.

I stand as a portal opens in my study and my father exits. Letting out a deep sigh of relief, I know the mission was successful.

"Father," I say, walking over and wrapping him in a hug. "How are you?"

He hugs me back, then slaps his palms on my shoulders. "Much better now that I've returned."

"I'm glad. Terr isn't the same without you." I scan his body and spot a bloodstain on his shirt. I also notice the bottom part is torn off.

"It's not mine," he says, noting my concern. "I'm fine."

He walks over and sits in one of my chairs and I can see how tired and pale he's become in the week he was gone.

"How have they treated you?" I ask.

"Like criminals would," he sighs. "They forced us to drink a potion when we arrived that stripped us of our power. They forced all eight rulers of Celestria into one room and held us there the entire time. The real punishment? There was one fucking washroom. That alone was a gods-damned nightmare."

"Did they feed you well?" I ask.

"They fed us porridge and water, but we were helpless. For the first time in all my life, I felt powerless and defenseless. I've taken for granted how much our power is a part of me. How it aids me in everything I do." He looks down at his hands, fisting them, then he looks up at me with a blank expression. "During that time, I've also come to learn how much I love solitude."

I can't help but chuckle. "How was it spending quality time with your future in-laws?" I smirk.

He shakes his head. "I don't know how they rule an entire realm. Every other ruler was sick of them and their antics. The queen of Asteri is the most annoying woman in all Celestria. The entire time, she whined about everything. I swear, my fucking ears would have bled, and my head would have exploded if they didn't save us. Her husband is just as bad, catering to her every whim. She's an entitled bitch who actually thought she deserved better than all of us. Can you believe she asked the Avkan guards to remove her and her husband and place them in a private room? The woman is delusional."

I shake my head and murmur, "The apple doesn't fall far from the tree."

My father's expression drops. "Look, son. I know this marriage isn't what you wanted, but it will strengthen Terr."

I turn to him, eyes narrowed. "Terr doesn't need strengthening, father. It's already the strongest realm in all Celestria."

"I know, but it will keep the Asteri at bay. The last thing I need is for them to attack Terr on a breach of marriage. I'm sorry, Kage."

A portal opens and Rem steps out. I'm expecting to hear good news, but when my eyes slide to him, he appears tense and unsettled.

"What's wrong?" I say, moving toward him, my gut knotting.

Rem looks to my father, but I stride up to him, grasping his arms. "What's wrong, Rem?"

He swallows, his brow furrowed. "It's Elara."

Hearing her name causes my pulse to spike. "What about her?"

My father steps beside me. "Kage, I saw the bone marker around her neck," he says. I turn my attention to him. "What compelled you to give it to her?"

"Where is she?" I ask, pinning my attention back to Rem with a serious look, trying to rein in my emotions and keep them in check.

"What made you give her a bone marker?" My father asks, his voice rising.

My heart rate is through the roof, and I'm trying to steady my quickened breath, but I keep my eyes fastened to Rem. "Tell me now. Where is she?"

"Avka," he replies.

"Why?" My body is trembling. I can feel my power—and Elara's—brushing under my skin.

"She saved us," my father replies with a calm sternness. "I am here because of her. But who is she, Kage? Why have you given her a bone marker?"

My father wouldn't understand. He doesn't know about my dreams. I never once told him about her. Rem is the only one who knows my secret.

My blood pressure rises. She's on Avka. She saved the rulers, but what happened? Did she escape and run away, or do they have her?

"She risked her life to save every ruler in Celestria. You don't think that deserves a bone marker?" I say through gritted teeth, my anger seeping through.

"You are engaged, son, a signed contract between two realms. Giving someone a bone marker is not a simple matter, especially another female."

I see Rem fidgeting. His expression is a mixture of worry and anguish. My fists clench, and it takes everything in me to restrain my power.

"Tell me, Rem," I order him.

"She's injured," Rem exhales. "According to Talon, she was shot and then bound by the guards who surrounded her."

The fine thread tethering my self-control snaps.

Closing my eyes, my shadows coil around me. I release the power inside that has been itching to be set free. Then, I focus on the bone marker, and speak the enchanted words that will lead me to it.

"Kage!" my father hollers, but I no longer care what he thinks. "Kage, stop! I order you!"

Elara is injured and alone in Avka. Who the fuck knows what they'll do... or have already done to her? I'll kill whoever injured her. I'll kill anyone who touches her.

I can feel my father trying to calm me, but without his power, he cannot stop me.

Closing my eyes, I let my shadows fold around me and let my rage fuel my power.

I open a portal—knowing my magic will lead me to the bone marker, lead me to her—and without hesitation, I step through.

Forty-One

ELARA

We land in the middle of a forest. The air is tepid but there is a sweet smell to it, unlike that of Avka. There are trees surrounding us on all sides, as far as my eyes can see, and I don't see a way out.

"Where are we?" I ask.

Kage's eyes sweep the area and soften. "A place Rem and I used to come and play as children."

He sets me on my feet, but his hands stay on me, his eyes sweeping over me from head to toe before landing on my shoulder. His brow furrows as he spots the bandage.

"You're safe now," he says, his voice soft, melodic.

Safe. I'm safe.

I nod as tears fill and spill down my cheeks. Gazing into his dark, gold-rimmed eyes, my heart thrums loudly and my chest fills with warmth. I not only see a gorgeous immortal—a prince of Celestria—but I see hope. I see a hero. A champion who rescued me, despite his position and the danger involved.

"You came for me," I breathe.

The prince smiles, his thumbs gently wiping away my tears.

"No matter where you are, Min Vesmír, I will always come for you."

My chest heaves with a sob as I fall into his chest, his arms folding around me. His shirt is wet, so I pull back and scan his black tunic. It's then I notice a hole in it.

A wave of panic punches through my gut as I realize he's been shot. I wipe my damp cheek and gasp, seeing my hand covered in crimson.

His eyes look heavy, and I see him waver.

"You're injured," I breathe.

He glances down at his chest, then nods. "I suppose I am."

His eyes suddenly roll back, and his legs buckle, so I throw my arms around his waist, trying to hold him up. His weight carries us both to our knees.

"Kage!" I cry, but his body goes limp in my arms.

No, no, no. This can't be happening.

Panic overwhelms me as I gently lay him back and bend over him, putting my ear directly above his mouth and nose. I exhale when I feel his breath, slow but steady.

He's alive. Thank the gods he's alive. He jumped us to this place, and I have no idea where it is. I don't know if there is anyone here who can jump us back to the palace.

"Please wake up. Please," I beg, but he isn't moving.

Blood is flowing from the wound in his chest. I need to stop it. I'm not sure if the injury will kill him, but he's immortal. He can't die, right?

I swiftly unwrap the bandage from my shoulder, but there is nothing on my suit I can use to press over his wound. Leaning over him, I find the hole in his tunic where the bullet went through and stick my fingers in it. I pull, ripping it from top to bottom.

My heart shudders seeing his entire torso covered in blood. The hole, dark and oozing, is near the center of his chest, so close to his heart. Trembling, I pull him toward me, on his side, and check his back. There is no exit wound. The bullet is still lodged somewhere inside him, and I don't know if that's a good or a bad thing.

My body is weak, the drug still heavy and coursing through my veins, but I focus and can hear Elwyn's words repeating in the recesses of my mind.

Your true mate will protect you, but you must also protect him. You are much stronger than you think you are, Elara, and just when you think the end is near, don't fret, because it is only the beginning.

Stripping his blood-soaked shirt off him, I tear it into shreds and use it to press down over his injury, but I need to keep pressure on it to stop the bleeding.

With effort, and despite the pain radiating in my shoulder, I get the bandage around his back and bind it around his chest, compressing the material over the wound. I know this won't work for long. He needs a healer.

Scanning the entire area, I spot a large rock formation through the trees, about fifty yards away. On one side, I see an opening.

"I'll be right back," I whisper, getting up and hurrying over.

My head is still spinning, and my legs are unsteady, but I make it and duck inside the gap in the rock. Inside is a small space, but it will fit Kage and keep him out of the elements until I can find help.

Quickly making my way back over to him, I realize there is no way I am going to carry him that distance. There is nothing around me to construct a stretcher, so I'll have to drag him.

Moving back toward the cave, I find the straightest path and remove any large or sharp debris that could injure him. When it's cleared, I rush back.

Fastening both of my arms under his armpits, I tug him to a sitting position.

I don't want to drag him by his wrists or ankles, because doing so would rip the bandage off. So, sucking in a deep breath, I steady myself and yank. His body barely moves an inch, but I yank harder, again and again, and keep yanking. Inch by inch, exhausted and suffering, I am determined to reach the cave. I have to save him. I have to protect him.

By the time we make it, I'm drenched with sweat and my muscles are spent. The pain in my shoulder is excruciating. It's throbbing down my chest and arm, but I push through and get his large frame inside the cave entrance. Safely inside, I slide down the back wall, pulling my knees tight against my chest.

Kage moans, his sweat coated brow furrows. Reaching over him, I grab hold of his hand. I feel him squeeze my fingers, then watch his eyes flutter open, but immediately shut again.

"Kage, how do we get out of here? How can I help you?" I don't know if he hears me, but his hand squeezes mine again.

There is a cave down the river.

It's his voice, but I'm watching his lips and they're not moving.

Inside are magical flowers, black lotus, but a witch guards them.

I realize he's speaking to me in my mind. Rem did it while we were training and told me it's part of their gift.

"Can the flowers heal you?" I ask aloud.

Yes.

"How do I get there? How do I find the cave?"

You must be careful. His voice is weak. He lets out another groan of pain and my heart shatters.

"Tell me, Kage. Tell me how I can find her," I urge, knowing he's fading.

Head to the river. Follow the sun.

When his hand goes limp, I know he's passed out.

I brush the wet strands sticking to his forehead away, and then stand on trembling, weary legs. Carefully stepping over him, I make my way to the cave exit.

I hope what he said is true. That there is a magical flower that can save him. The witch I'll deal with when I get there, but right now, my greatest fear is him dying.

Glancing back at his handsome face, I know that he's safe here, for now. His chest is still rising and falling, but I'll have to hurry. I must find that magical flower.

He risked everything to come and save me, and now I'll do whatever it takes to save him.

"I'll be back." I say, sending the promise not only to him, but to the universe. "Wait for me."

Gathering every ounce of strength left within me, I leave the cave in search of a river, a witch, and a magical black lotus flower.

End *of* Book 1

The story will continue in Book 2...

Those Forbidden Shadows!

A NOTE FROM THE AUTHOR

First, I want to say, thank you so much for reading Those Savage Stars. I really hope you enjoyed reading it as much as I loved writing it.

I was nervous, because after 11 years of writing YA, this is my first New Adult book. The readers asked for something grittier, so this is my attempt to deliver something new. In the meantime, because I left you with a cliffhanger, I'll be working hard to finish the next part of the story.

I can't wait for you to continue the adventure!

Happy Reading,

ALSO BY CAMEO RENAE

If you liked Those Savage Stars, check out Cameo's other award winning, complete series.

Heir of Blood and Fire Series

Hidden Wings Series

Midway Trilogy

In My DreamsDuology

Misteria (Middle-Grade Fantasy)

All are available on Amazon and free to read in Kindle Unlimited.

ACKNOWLEDGMENTS

My heart is full knowing I have an amazing team behind me, who helped shaped this book.

Karla Bostic, Ewelina Rutyna, Halee Harris, Cheree Castellanos, Bernice Brown, Shawanda Davis, Kimberly Belden, and Amber Garcia... Thank you for being the best Alpha/Beta team and providing me with wonderful feedback. I'm lucky to have you all and your eagle eyes. You are my dream team!

My husband, Vance, for being my greatest support and my best friend. I love you!

Lastly, I appreciate you, dear reader, for taking the time to enter my world, read my stories, and breathe life into these characters. You are amazing and I can't wait to share more adventures with you!

ABOUT THE AUTHOR

Cameo was born in San Francisco, raised in Maui, Hawaii, and now resides with her husband in Las Vegas. She is a dreamer and caffeine addict who loves to laugh and loves to read to escape reality.

One of her greatest satisfactions is creating fantasy worlds filled with adventure and romance. It is the love and incredible support of her family and fans that keeps her going. One day she hopes to uncover a magic wardrobe and ride away on a unicorn. Until then . . . she'll keep writing!

www.cameorenae.com

Printed in the USA
CPSIA information can be obtained
at www.ICGtesting.com
LVHW050849220224
772193LV00011B/130/J